Praise for *The Last Four Days of Paddy Buckley*

"[Jeremy] Massey has an eye for black humor and the details of a life fully inhabited. . . . He's got the natural voice of a storyteller."

—NPR

"Refreshing. . . . It takes the subject of death and turns it into an adventure that is both funny and thought-provoking. . . . A mix of black comedy, adventure, and hilarious love story, *The Last Four Days of Paddy Buckley* is smart storytelling from a writer whose knowledge of the undertaking business shines through."

—*The Irish Times*

"Jeremy Massey does for Ireland what Carl Hiaasen does for Florida."

—*The Charlotte Observer*

"This is what we call 'a nightstand book' at our house: It will joyfully make its way from my nightstand to my husband's. The gifted Jeremy Massey has created a complex, fascinating, and hilarious Irishman in Paddy Buckley, the delightful center of a novel brimming with passion, humor, poetry, and wisdom that only comes from the Emerald Isle, where the best stories are born."

—ADRIANA TRIGIANI, AUTHOR OF THE *New York Times* BESTSELLER *The Shoemaker's Wife*

"Jeremy Massey puts a fresh and intriguing spin on the Irish crime novel with the tale of an ordinary man drawn into a deadly conflict with a Dublin mob boss. *The Last Four Days of Paddy Buckley* is both a cleverly constructed thriller and an unforgettable story of friendship, love, and loyalty. It's sharply written, darkly comic, and full of heart."

—HARRY DOLAN, AUTHOR OF THE *New York Times* BESTSELLER *Bad Things Happen*

"[An] intelligent and suspenseful debut novel. . . . A hilarious funeral home scam and a quirky dead body mix-up add to this exciting, morbid tale."

—*Publishers Weekly*

"Highly readable and entertaining . . . the novel benefits especially from Massey's mostly restrained, deadpan Irish sense of humor."

—*Kirkus Reviews*

"[Massey's] dark and zany humor is anchored by some serious reflection."

—*Library Journal*

The Last Four Days
of Paddy Buckley

The Last Four Days
of Paddy Buckley

JEREMY MASSEY

RIVERHEAD BOOKS
New York

RIVERHEAD BOOKS
An imprint of Penguin Random House LLC
375 Hudson Street
New York, New York 10014

The Library of Congress has catalogued the Riverhead
hardcover edition as follows

Massey, Jeremy.
The last four days of paddy buckley : a novel / Jeremy
Massey.
p.   cm.
ISBN 978-1-59463-344-7
1. Undertakers and undertaking—Ireland—Dublin—
Fiction.   2. Organized crime—Ireland—Dublin—
Fiction. 3. Threats—Fiction.   I. Title.
PS3613.A81934L37   2015   2014043564
813.6—dc23

First Riverhead hardcover edition: May 2015
First Riverhead trade paperback edition: May 2016
Riverhead trade paperback ISBN: 978-1-10198-338-6
International edition ISBN: 978-1-59463-485-7

Printed in the United States of America

BOOK DESIGN BY NICOLE LAROCHE

For my father
&
For Zeb

The Last Four Days
of Paddy Buckley

There's a Mickey Mouse clock hanging in my kitchen, probably still ticking. I've taken quite a bit of stick about it over the
years. Mickey Mouse on its face, with his big open smile and wide
eyes, walking in place with boundless joy and enthusiasm, surrounded by numbers. My friend Christy used to shake his head
when he'd see it. "The clock's got to go, Paddy," he'd say. It's probably not the right clock to have on your wall when you're forty-
two years old; but for me, Mickey's the patron saint of getting out
of the soup with your spirit intact. No matter what's thrown at
him, no matter how hairy things get, his happy demeanor never
fades. He walks away with a whistle and smile every time.

I've been to quite a few funerals in my time. More than most
people, having been around the trade all my life. My father was
a coffin maker for one of Dublin's largest undertaking firms, and
I followed him into it, ending up making the arrangements and
running the funerals. I always liked listening to the eulogies delivered after the Mass was finished and the congregation was

settled back into their pews waiting for a few words. A few years ago, I stood at the back of the church with my boss, Frank Gallagher, listening to a guy talk about his brother, who'd died at the age of twenty-eight in a drowning accident. Everyone was pretty cut up over the loss, but this guy, beleaguered though he was, had a glow about him. Probably a few years older than his deceased brother, he stood at the pulpit with his John Lennon glasses and long hair. He told the church that we were all in a dream and that his brother had woken up. This misery of a gig called life is just a dream from which we all eventually awaken, he said. Nobody gets left behind. Even the most horrible dreams end. And I never forgot it.

My life had become pretty miserable towards the end—a nightmare, if you like. I'd gone from being a contented forty-year-old with a pregnant French wife to a disillusioned widower with nothing to wake up for except other people's funerals. My wife, Eva, died of a brain hemorrhage while standing in line at the supermarket in her thirty-sixth year. What do we do with that one, Mickey? Whistling and smiling didn't cut it. After that, enthusiasm seemed impossible.

For a guy who wanted nothing more than to escape his grief, I probably had the worst job in the world. But I buried myself in it, nonetheless, if you'll forgive my saying so. I worked the week. Seven days. Frank Gallagher didn't want to give it to me at first. It wasn't the money—he'd have had to give it to somebody—he was worried about me running myself into the ground. But I assured him it was what I wanted. I needed to help other people deal with their grief so I could escape from mine. For two years I tried this, until I couldn't sleep anymore. Until I arrived at the last few days of my life. Until a set of circumstances so outlandish, so surreal, and so dangerous could only result in one thing: my death. My awakening from the dream. And my subsequent funeral. And cremation. And all the tears and regret that go with it.

But not from me. I'm gone beyond it, where all the madness, the chaos, the seemingly endless pain is behind me, and I find myself in a place of tremendous peace and understanding, of rest. And from this perfect, still place, I have total recall of my last days. I remember every single moment.

Monday

ONE

October 13, 2014,
7:45 a.m.

T he insomnia had become chronic. It was so bad that it had dragged me from delirium and hallucinations to sudden lucid periods of prolonged focus and back again. I didn't spend much time in bed those last few months, but when I did, in the hope of sleeping, my thoughts were always with Eva. Sometimes I'd even be able to conjure up her image. I'd cling to the moment as I'd study her sitting on the edge of the bed beside me. The chestnut brown of her irises. The little twitching of her nose when she smiled. The sexy gap between her front teeth. The curves of her shoulders and breasts. I'd want to sigh deeply and never breathe again. Then, when I'd reach out to touch her, she'd disappear.

The only detail that remained was my feelings. And memories. But no such luck this morning. Nothing for me to fix on but my desperate longing.

Mondays had ceased to punctuate the beginning of the week for me, as I'd been working solidly for six months now. Even at night, I'd take the calls—death didn't keep banker's hours—and out I'd go into the darkness of Dublin, past the stinking Liffey, the drug dealers and prostitutes, the drinkers and poets, to the freshly bereaved. Sometimes there'd be a corpse for me to take away, other times not. But every time there'd be death. The tapestry of days and nights, and weeks and months, had blurred together into one gray grieving mess of funeral after funeral after funeral, each one a secret candle of remembrance for Eva.

I put on my overcoat in the hallway and checked myself in the mirror. Gray suit, blue shirt, navy tie. More and more, when I looked in the mirror now, I saw my father staring back at me. Shay Buckley had dropped the body at sixty-three—car crash: quick exit. I'd inherited his twinkling green eyes and his dimples, but it was the grayness in the hair that had me seeing his ghost in the mirror this morning. He'd had two streaks of light gray running the length of either side of his otherwise black mop of hair since he was in his thirties, which won him the moniker of the Badger. On my fortieth birthday, I thought I'd escaped the same fate, but in the last couple of years, the little flecks of gray above my ears have grown into more pronounced lines continuing down to the back of my neck. But nobody calls me the Badger, probably in deference to my father.

I MANEUVERED SLOWLY down through the traffic in my brown Toyota Camry past the redbrick houses on Crumlin Road, past the drifting pairings of strung-out junkies with their sunken eyes and Borstal marks, and the unemployed builders and plumbers outside the job center, dragging the last from their cigarettes. Further down, over the Grand Canal, past the rusted swings and graffitied walls of Dolphin House, I watched a three-legged mongrel hobbling after a bearded old man while I remembered my father and the little tricks he'd taught me. My mother died when I was only four, taken out by cancer, so it had just been ourselves, and we were extra close. Back when Gallagher's made their own boxes, Shay had been the chief coffin maker. He'd started out as a carpenter, but ended up finding his groove in Gallagher's loft and worked there until his death. He was the rock of calm in my life. The world could collapse around him and he wouldn't blow his cool, having a veritable tool kit for any situation he found himself in.

When I was seven, I broke my arm after falling out of a tree. I remember writhing in agony while gingerly cradling my crooked forearm and he sitting me down and looking me in the eye. "Patrick," he said, "I want you to focus while I tell you about something very important: Independent Channel 24." His calm was contagious. He had both my attention and curiosity.

"What is that?" I said.

"It's a place in your mind where the pain goes away."

"What do I do?"

"Listen to me. Your arm is broken, but you are not your arm, Patrick. Remove yourself from it. You have a sense of pain, but you are not your sense of pain."

Even back then, I figured my father was part druid. I held my arm, still feeling the pain, but my awareness was completely away from it now, centered instead on his words and where they were bringing me. "Now, remove yourself from your body and observe this situation between us from another perspective." Shay had helped me when I was even younger to create an imaginary sanctuary I could retreat to for relaxing and healing, and in there, he'd trained me to see myself objectively, to see the bigger picture that I was just a part of. For years after my mother had died, I'd lay in bed at night while my father guided me down twenty-one imaginary steps to the sanctuary we created together, a tranquil place, and I'd watch myself down there, removed from my body so I could see myself safe in fields of barley under the shelter of old sycamore trees. Independent Channel 24 was more radical, yet still an extension of what he'd already taught me, so I could quite easily project my imagined self to a place where I could watch myself beside him.

He must have noticed a shift in me. "Where are you now?"

My sharpened and hungry focus was informed by two things: my extreme pain diminishing and my believing in my father. I nodded to a spot beside the branch I'd fallen from. His eyes twinkled. "You've just accessed Independent Channel 24." There were other channels for other situations, I learned later, but it was number 24 that I had full understanding of at the age of seven.

I DROVE THROUGH the open cast-iron gates of the head office in Uriel Street, in the Liberties—the oldest part of Dublin. The building itself was Victorian, a robust example of the period with its solid walls made from Dolphin's Barn bricks—the Irish wonder brick of the nineteenth century—and its grand doorways and window frames painted ivy green. The bricks were practically black, having collected countless decades of soot and sulfur. Frank Gallagher had considered having them cleaned but figured in the end they were a nice reminder of what Dublin used to look like, and he'd made sure the rest of the building was always immaculate, from the paint on the doors, window frames, and gates to the gold-leaf Gothic lettering of the Gallagher's sign. It was a sizable block, housing the two-story building that made up the offices and embalming room, a long row of stables that used to accommodate the horses the firm used back in the 1930s and '40s, a gravel car park, and the garage and loft, which housed the fleet and coffins, respectively.

Inside, Frank Gallagher was sitting behind the desk in the front office, writing. I sat down opposite him and checked the list of runners for the morning's work.

"Anything doing?" I asked. Frank pulled a sheet of paper off a notepad in front of him and handed it over.

"The artist Michael Wright, dead in the Royal Hospital in Donnybrook. Cancer. His wife is waiting in their house on Pembroke Lane."

"Always plenty of cancer to go round," I said, noting the address.

Frank sat back in his seat and considered me. We were the only two in the room.

"How much sleep did you get last night?"

The question made me smile; its mirthless quality wasn't lost on Frank.

"Would you try sleeping tablets?"

"I don't want to medicate. Besides, I don't mind not sleeping."

"You've got to get a balance back in your life, Paddy. Working around the clock is not the answer." Frank got up from his chair. "Have a cup of coffee with me before you go out to that family."

Apart from the engraving of nameplates for the coffins, there was little work done in the back office. It had only a wooden counter, some stools, a kettle and cups, and a door out to the yard, which was the main entrance for staff. Jack, a young driver who'd been working with the firm for eighteen months, stood at the counter, drinking tea while reading the *Daily Star*. He was about a strawberry short of a punnet, but lived in his heart and had access to everyone else's as a result.

I sat on a stool while Frank went about getting the coffee together. As he did with everything else in his life, Frank insisted on what he considered to be the best, and in the case of coffee, it was French roast from Bewley's on Grafton Street, which Frank claimed had the best coffee in Dublin. He ground the beans prior to each serving in a little electric grinder, made the coffee extra strong, and served it black. As he focused on the coffee, I took a good look at him. Frank was in his sixties now and was to me the epitome of the perfect undertaker: always dressed somberly in beautifully tailored suits—three-piece in the winter months, two-piece in the summer—and always well groomed. He was the fairest man I'd ever met, and was known for it throughout the trade. In all the time I knew him, he'd never once veered from what he knew was the righteous path, and he demonstrated this in all aspects of his life. In fact, Frank was my external moral compass. If ever in a moral dilemma, I'd need only ask myself one question: What would Frank do?

"How does he do it?" said Jack, shaking his head at the newspaper.

"Who?" said Frank.

"Vincent Cullen," said Jack, pointing to a picture of him outside the Four Courts. "He got off again."

Frank smiled at me and got back to the coffee. It was no

surprise that Vincent Cullen had got off. He was Dublin's most heavy-duty criminal and had a knack for avoiding prison, mostly due to very effective intimidation of witnesses and jury members. Jack, and a good portion of Ireland with him, loved to marvel at the antics of the Cullen brothers through the safe window of a newspaper.

Frank slid an espresso in front of me. I downed it in one and rose to my feet.

"See you in church," I said.

TWO

9:40 a.m.

Though the address was only a hop across town, I traversed a Georgian wonderland to get to the Wrights' house, which was tucked away behind the landscaped lawns, wrought-iron railings, and manicured hedges of Wellington Road. There weren't as many pained expressions on this side of town as there were in Crumlin, and there was a wealth of stylish people with fine pedigrees and polished dreams, carrying their takeaway lattes under well-seasoned plane trees, gently swaying in an autumn that had only started undressing.

The same setting at nighttime wasn't so pretty. From Thursday through Sunday between nine at night and six in the morning, the city center took on the milieu of an open-air mental hospital. Every second or third shopfront on Grafton Street framed at least one splurge of vomit, and it was the same for the Georgian doorways on Leeson Street and Harcourt Street and around the walls of Trinity College. There were drunk people everywhere—laughing, singing, shouting, fighting—and thieves alive in the shadows. Even the buskers had to watch their money.

But by Monday morning, the madness receded, the only evidence being the last few standing revelers and the crusted vomit sneered at by the mocking light of day; the only witnesses, the slumbering homeless being woken from their cardboard beds by the nagging seagulls and choking fumes from the idling buses and gridlocked traffic.

I pressed the intercom button and waited in the lane. It was October and the wind still had a warmth to its breeze. I closed my eyes for a moment and listened to the sound of the leaves and dust swirling around me. It was so comforting that I considered curling up on the ground and falling asleep.

"Hello?" came a female voice over the intercom. I opened my eyes and moved closer to the buzzer, any notions of sleep fast disappearing.

"Mrs. Wright, it's Paddy Buckley from Gallagher's."

The door in the wall vibrated.

I pushed it open and walked across a little stone garden to be met at the sliding doors by a woman dressed in a dark green cashmere skirt and jacket, and a crimson silk blouse. She had her hair up in a loose bun and wore reading glasses over baby-blue eyes. I gauged her age to be early fifties. In a certain light, she might even pass for late forties. She offered her hand.

"Hi," she said in a soft English accent, "I'm Lucy."

I took her hand in mine. "Paddy."

"Come in, Paddy," she said, while moving back from the door. I stepped over the threshold and watched her slide the door closed.

"Let me take your coat."

I took it off and handed it to her. She had a gracious quality about her, particularly apparent when she moved. She hung the coat up and led me into the kitchen, where I sat down at the table. She leaned on the back of a chair briefly, with the hint of a smile.

"Would you like a cup of tea or coffee?"

I let a little smile settle in around my eyes.

"A cup of tea would be lovely," I said, and opened my briefcase, taking out an arrangement form and pen. Lucy put the kettle on and sat down in the chair next to me, not opposite or at the end of the table, but right beside me. The atmosphere in the house was a relaxed one. The kitchen had a bohemian character, and the fixtures, cupboards, and tiles were of another time, a forgotten era of quality and craftsmanship. There were framed oil paintings and curious mementos littering the room, and a wooden antique clock above the doorway. The farmhouse table we sat at was bathed in sunlight and pretty shadows from the philodendrons growing on the sill beside the sink. Whether she was aware of it or not, Lucy had a soothing effect. She made me feel comfortable in a way that had me wondering if the warm breeze had followed me in.

"You're not in a rush, are you?" she asked.

"Not at all," I said. Expressing the company's sadness for the loss a family had experienced was something I normally didn't do. If it had been a child who had died, I would have, because of the intensity of the loss and grief. But with someone who'd run the full course of life, it was different. To extend sympathy to a family you didn't know when you were charging them for your services could be perceived through a cynical lens as feigned or insincere, though, of course, I *was* sympathetic to their loss: This was evident in my thoughtful manner and dealings with them.

Lucy considered me for the first time.

"You have kind eyes, Paddy," she said, making me melt more into my seat. "They cancel out the roguishness in your smile."

"Not completely," I said, letting it surface briefly. I could quite happily listen to her talk in that accent all day long.

"You'll have to tell me how a funeral works over here. I've buried both my parents in London, but I understand things work a little differently in Dublin."

"They do. Tell me, was Michael Catholic or Church of Ireland?"

"Catholic."

"Are you thinking of using St. Mary's on Haddington Road?"

"Yes."

"Okay. The funeral is usually made up of two parts: the removal the evening before and the funeral itself the following morning. Would you like to bring Michael home from the hospital, or do you think you'd prefer to remove him to the church from one of our funeral homes?"

"Oh," said Lucy, as she took her glasses off, resting the end of one of the temples between her teeth while looking off to her left, unaware of me studying her. She was utterly feminine and, in any man's book, beautiful. Her gaze lent the mundane and ordinary an intimate quality, imbued by a subtly seductive charisma.

"Let's bring him back here," she said, looking directly at me.

"Perfect. This is Monday. We could bring him back to the

house here in a few hours and then, if you like, we could go to the church tomorrow evening, say at about half past five?"

Lucy nodded.

"The prayers at the church last between fifteen and twenty minutes. When they've finished, everyone will walk up to the top pew and sympathize with you, and then we'll bring you home afterwards. Then on Wednesday morning, I could have a car pick you up here at half past nine or so and bring you around to the church for the funeral Mass at ten o'clock. Are you happy with ten o'clock Mass?"

"Perfectly happy."

"And then to the cemetery or crematorium, and the car will bring you home after that. That's pretty much how it will happen."

"Okay," said Lucy, as she got up and moved to the counter to prepare the tea. "That all sounds pretty straightforward." She brought the teapot and cups to the table along with the milk and sugar. She poured two cups out and settled back into her seat.

"Shall I tell you about Michael?"

"Please," I said. Usually, when the bereaved talk about their loved one unprompted, they unwittingly give out most of the details needed, such as the deceased's age, place and time of death, and whether or not the family have a grave. I don't normally write anything down while they talk. I remember the relevant information and write it down afterwards.

"God, I don't know where to start, really. First of all, this is a release for Michael, I can tell you that. He's been in such dreadful pain for so long now that, in a strange way, I'm happy his suffering is over. He's been in that hospital for three years. Up until seven years ago, he was as strong as an ox, so young, so free-spirited. But then he had a stroke, his first one, the first of five. Just when he'd recover from one, he'd be hit by another, paralyzing him even further. He's only seventy-two but looks more like he's lived a hard ninety years. And, of course, the cancer finished him. He got it only last year. When I heard that, I thought: Why is he being put through this? It'll kill him. And it did, along with the strokes. Each one made him worse. He lost the power of speech on his third stroke. He hasn't spoken in years. There's only twelve years between us, Paddy, but for the last five, it was more like nursing my father than my husband . . ."

I was surprised. In a business where I learned people's ages every day, I'd become so good at guessing them that I was seldom off by more than a year or two. Sixty years old and looking this good? It was clear that Lucy Wright had been favored by nature, having had her aging process seemingly arrested at the age of fifty. She was much too beautiful to ever have been touched by a plastic surgeon; even her hands looked like those of a younger woman. It was so remarkable I felt compelled to say something but, given my position and circumstances, I said nothing.

"The last few years, Paddy, have been so difficult. To watch him deteriorate like that, unable to converse with him, wondering if he's able to hear the words I whisper in his ear . . ." She stopped momentarily, bringing her hand to her mouth in an effort to calm herself. I pulled out my spare handkerchief and handed it to her. She took it and rested it against her eyes for a moment.

"I'm sorry," she said, her voice trembling for the first time since we'd sat down. She cried silently for a moment.

There are a few cardinal rules in the undertaking game. One of them is to let the bereaved be bereaved. They're supposed to be upset. Another is that the undertaker never gets upset, but remains professional at all times. Being an undertaker is like being a rock: a rock of sense in a time of confusion, a rock of dependability in a time of abandonment, a rock of sympathy, of understanding, of accommodation. But at all times detached. The undertaker is never party to the grieving process; we are there to enable the family, to facilitate them in grieving. If we become involved emotionally, then we're of no use to the family.

I knew all this; by now it was second nature to me. I'd never crossed the line before. But for the first time in all my years making arrangements, I felt like reaching out and taking Lucy's hand and telling her that I understood what she was feeling, that to cry was okay. But I didn't. I kept my hands to myself.

She pulled my handkerchief away from her eyes.

"You must go through an awful lot of hankies," she said, and followed it with a laugh, a natural laugh that kept on going. I laughed along with her. It was a welcome release from the pain and stress of the situation, and we were both comfortable enough in each other's company to not want to stop it. When it came to its own end, Lucy let out a sigh.

"That's the first time I've laughed in such a long time."

"Me, too," I said.

"I don't know how you do your job, Paddy," she said. "Have you ever lost someone?"

I nodded.

"My wife, two years ago." Instinctively, Lucy reached over and put her hand over mine. I opened my hand and tightened it around hers while we both looked into the pools of each other's sorrow for a minute, saying nothing.

"Does it get easier?"

"Sometimes," I whispered. I let the moment last another few seconds before letting go of her hand.

"But we're here to talk about Michael," I said, bringing it back to the business at hand. "Tell me, would you like to put a death notice in the paper?"

"Yes," said Lucy, as she put her glasses back on. "I have this prepared here. You might have to change it a little to put it into the proper format."

She handed it to me and I looked it over. She'd put in everything relevant: the date of death, where he was from, who he was, and the fact that he was married to Lucy and had one daughter. Save for the name and date being in the wrong place, it was perfect. Also on the piece of paper was the mobile number of the doctor Michael had been under, Dr. Brady, and the number of the grave in Glasnevin Cemetery.

"It's perfect, just a little restructuring to do and putting the funeral arrangements along with it. Which paper would you like me to put it in?"

"*The Irish Times.*"

"Okay," I said, now making a note of all these details. "How many are in that grave in Glasnevin?"

"Two, I think. Just his parents."

"Plenty of room. Would you like any flowers, Lucy, maybe something for the top of the coffin?"

"Yes, I would. Could I have a bunch of white lilies with some green?"

"Of course. What would you like on the card? 'In loving memory,' or maybe something more personal?"

"Oh, let's see, definitely something more personal . . ." She removed her glasses again and looked off out the window. A moment passed and then her emotion found its way to the surface again. She brought the hankie to her face and let it absorb the tears before taking it away, her lip quivering.

"I could have danced all night," she managed to say.

I nodded as I watched her continue to battle her tears. I put my hand around hers and squeezed it tightly until she nodded that she was okay. I wrote the card inscription down on the sheet and decided to leave the questions for a moment.

Even though her face was tearstained and upset, Lucy remained as beautiful and graceful as when I'd first come in. She reached to the back of her head and pulled out the two pins that were holding her hair up. She gently shook her head, letting her hair loosen and fall to just below her shoulders.

"I've not been myself at all over the last three or four weeks. I've been forgetting everything: to feed the cat, what day of the week it is, and even more important things like paying credit-card bills and turning the immersion off. There's nothing we're forgetting, is there?"

"Did you think about how you wanted Michael dressed?"

"No, I didn't," she said, and got up from her chair. "Come upstairs with me and we'll find something."

I followed her upstairs. Because her husband had been living in the hospital for the last few years, the smell and look of the bedroom were entirely her own. It had been a while since I'd been in a beautiful woman's bedroom. The thin white linen curtains were drawn, infusing the room with an incandescent light that pervaded every last particle of dust. As I stood behind Lucy and breathed in the air of the room, I became a little intoxicated by the sheer womanliness of it all.

The wardrobe took up a whole wall. Its doors were of the sliding kind and it was divided in the middle by a large mirror. Lucy opened the left side to reveal about twenty suits hanging neatly together and seven or eight pairs of well-polished shoes on the floor. She rested a hand on one of the jackets before dropping her head and bringing her free hand to her face. She wasn't crying like before, but she was clearly upset. I wanted to hold her, to comfort her, to let her cry on my shoulder, but I restrained myself. Lucy dropped her hand away from the suit and started crying more openly. Then, in a single movement, she turned and rested her head on my chest, putting her arms around me and holding tightly as she continued to cry. I brought my arms up around her back and held her. I rubbed her back gently and let my face move down to the top of her head. She stopped crying after a few minutes, but she didn't seem to want to move away.

I hadn't been this close to a woman since Eva died, and it was beginning to take its toll. I'd found Lucy attractive the moment I'd laid eyes on her and now, having her this close to me with her hands around my waist and the smell of her perfume clouding my senses, I knew that if I didn't get out of the embrace within another minute or so I was going to have a full-blown erection.

I moved my hand up her back and patted it a few times.

"You're all right," I said, but she wasn't budging. I repeated the exercise, but still she stayed there. I felt my pulse quickening and all sorts of pleasurable rushes throughout my body, and then it happened, swelling up to being as stiff as a steel rod, it protruded away from down beside my left leg and stuck into Lucy's waist.

She moved her head away from my chest a little and looked down. She touched it with her hand. I was overcome by a terrible sense of shame.

"Lucy, I'm dreadfully sorr—" She brought her hand to my mouth and pressed her fingers against my lips, stopping me from talking, and then moved her mouth to mine. The satisfaction rushed through me as we both settled into the kiss.

I let Lucy set the pace initially—I didn't want to lead her into something she might later regret. The feeling of attraction, it appeared, was mutual. I ran my hands down her back as the kissing became deeper, our breathing more erratic. I unbuttoned her blouse and unzipped her skirt and felt the silky smooth skin of her hips and buttocks. She hurriedly undressed me before pushing me back on the bed. The feeling between us was primal. I looked at her as she sat astride me, taking me inside. Luscious and ripe, she was utterly gorgeous.

For the next little while, I slowly worked the rhythm to bring us both closer to climax. And then I noticed a change in her. I thought maybe I was hurting her because of the way she was groaning and grabbing my neck with every inward thrust, so I pulled back a little, but she continued even though I'd stopped going so deep. By that stage, my own horses had broken away from me and, while holding her hips, I came deep inside her. Then, as she seemed to reach orgasm herself, she opened her mouth wide as if in extreme pleasure, but made no sound. I stopped moving and studied her. She looked into my eyes and emptied her lungs with one long blow and then collapsed on top of me. And something left her. Something definite. Something infinite. Something vital. She was dead. I rolled her off me and held her face in my hands.

"Lucy?"

The notion that she'd died wasn't one I was willing to consider. It was simply too preposterous to have happened, to even imagine.

"Lucy?" Still nothing. I checked for her pulse. There was none.

"LUCY?" I shook her. I shook her hard. This was absurd. It couldn't be. But it was. It took another minute before it sank in: Lucy Wright was dead. I sat on the side of the bed with my eyes as wide open as they'd ever been. I couldn't believe it. Lucy had gone. Passed on. Just like her husband. Just like Eva. Just like twenty-two other souls in Dublin that day. And I was alone again.

I noticed a little pill bottle on the bedside table behind the alarm clock. I picked it up and examined the label. Warfarin. It was full. My aunt had suffered from angina before she died, and she'd been taking warfarin. I checked the name. Lucy Wright. Then I heard Lucy's voice playing back in my mind, telling me that she'd been forgetting things. Even important things, she'd said.

I put the pills back on the table and looked at Lucy's remains. Death by fucking. There'd be no talking my way out of this one. *No, Your Honor, it was her idea. Her husband had just died and she thought it would be a good idea if I followed her upstairs to her bedroom and give her the ride, make her feel a little better.* No, this was something I was going to keep to myself. Forever. Nothing would be gained by telling anyone about this—at any time, for any reason. There was going to be a postmortem, that much was certain, and if they were thorough, it would be clear that she'd had sex prior to death. But one thing at a time: I had a mess to clean up.

I walked into the en suite bathroom and ran a green facecloth under the tap. I washed her genitalia thoroughly before toweling her dry. Then I dressed her. For an undertaker, dressing a remains, sometimes by yourself, is part of the job. Within five minutes, I had her dressed exactly as she'd been when she first walked into the room and had her lying on the floor as if she'd just fallen after having her heart attack. Then I fixed the bed and made sure there were no hairs left on it. I got dressed, straightened the towel in the bathroom, and brought the facecloth downstairs with me and put it in the inside pocket of my coat.

I walked back upstairs, going over the story again and again: I'd been sitting there in the kitchen with her, taking down the details, having a cup of tea, just like we had been, then when it came to the part where I asked her about the clothes, she said, "Just a minute, I'll go and fish something out," and then she went upstairs on her own while I went about writing everything we'd been discussing onto the arrangement form, and then after what seemed like three or four minutes, I heard a bumping noise upstairs. It sufficiently alarmed me to go up and investigate, and upon finding my way to the bedroom, I discovered Lucy's body on the floor. I checked for a pulse, but she seemed to be dead. I came down to the kitchen and phoned the doctor immediately. It sounded a lot more plausible than what had actually happened. I ran the story around in my head until I was as familiar with it as I was with the truth.

I read Dr. Brady's number off Lucy's notes and punched it into my phone.

"Hello?" came the voice at the other end.

"Dr. Brady?"

"Yes?"

"This is Paddy Buckley from Gallagher's Funeral Directors."

"Hello, Paddy, what can I do for you?"

"I'm out at Michael and Lucy Wright's place in Pembroke Lane, and there's been an . . . incident. I was making arrangements with Lucy for her husband's funeral, and when she went upstairs to get her husband's suit, she dropped dead . . ."

"What!"

"She dropped dead. I heard a thump so I went up to see was everything okay and I found her lying there . . . dead."

Dr. Brady's voice was filled with levelheaded alarm.

"Are you sure she's dead?"

I've been around dead bodies all my life, I think I'd know when one of them's dead. "Pretty sure, Doctor, yeah."

"Is there any other family there?"

"No, I'm here on my own."

"Have you phoned for an ambulance?"

"No. You're the first person I've rung. It literally happened a few minutes ago."

"Okay, phone for an ambulance and wait there. That's all you can do."

"Okay, will do. Thanks, Doctor."

I ended the call and noticed Lucy's glasses and my handkerchief on the table. I put my hankie back in my pocket and looked around for anything else I might have missed. It had all happened so fast. My hands were shaking, and I was beginning to feel nauseous. A low panic was rising inside me. A little voice piped up in my head. It said, *Keep moving, Paddy. It was her time, just like it was Eva's time. Everything's going to be okay. Just keep moving.*

I phoned for an ambulance. Then I phoned the office and told Frank the same story I'd told Dr. Brady. Frank expressed his surprise and told me he'd free me up from any other work while I dealt with it.

Then, as I was sitting there waiting for the ambulance, a cat strolled in from another room and mewed hello. It was a long-haired gray Persian with yellow eyes. It brushed against my leg, purring furiously. I saw that the bowl in the corner was empty so I got up, opened a few cupboards, and found the cat food, which I poured into the bowl before filling a saucer with water and placing it down beside the food.

While I was still there on my hunkers, watching the cat tear into its meal, I heard the sliding glass doors open and close. I stood up just as a woman walked into the kitchen and stopped by the door.

My heart started to pound. I knew immediately that this was Michael and Lucy Wright's daughter, Brigid. I remembered reading her name in the death notice, but apart from having registered to myself that she existed, I'd given her no further thought.

And now here she was.

I was sure it was her because of the resemblance to her mother, only Brigid was thirty years younger and even more attractive. She wore jeans, a blue T-shirt, and a tweed sports jacket. She had shoulder-length wispy brown hair, dark brown eyes, and a purity and savvy to her stare that froze the moment for me, stretching those small few seconds into what felt like minutes.

"You must be the funeral director," she said.

"That's right. Paddy," I said, preparing myself to tell her of her very recent bereavement.

"I'm Brigid," she said. "Is my mother here?"

"Yes . . . Brigid, will you sit down for a minute, please?" I gestured to the nearest chair at the kitchen table and we both sat down a few chairs away from each other. A little knot formed in my throat.

"Brigid, your mother went upstairs twenty minutes ago to get a suit for your father to be dressed in, and . . . there's no easy way to say this . . . she collapsed and died while she was up there . . ."

Brigid brought her hand to her mouth as the blood drained from her face.

"I've been on to Dr. Brady and there's an ambulance on its way. I'm so sorry to have to tell you. I can hardly believe it myself, I can't imagine how hard it is for you to hear it like this . . ."

"Where is she?" She barely whispered the words as the tears began to spill down her cheeks.

"In her bedroom," I said. Brigid got up from her chair and crouched down as if reacting to a searing pain deep in her solar plexus.

This was a first for me. Usually the family were the ones to tell the undertaker of their bereavement. I stayed sitting on the edge of my chair as Brigid stood up and walked around in confused little circles.

"Oh, God," she said, holding both hands to her face now, leaning back against the wall and sinking slowly to her knees. I could see her hands were trembling. She looked into my eyes.

"Can I see her?"

"Of course . . . would you like me to bring you up?"

She nodded. I helped her up from the floor and led the way upstairs. I stopped just inside the bedroom door and gestured for Brigid to step in ahead of me. She moved past me and got down on her knees beside her mother's remains. Instead of breaking down like I thought she might, she smiled at her mother with a serene sadness while tears streamed down her cheeks. I stepped into the bathroom and picked up a box of tissues, which I handed to her.

She pushed her hair behind her ear before pulling a tissue out and wiping her tears.

"Soul mates till the end," she said, with a bigger, braver smile. "It's so romantic."

"I'll leave you with your mum, Brigid. I'll be in the kitchen," I said softly, and walked quietly down the stairs, letting out a long soundless whistle.

Another dream over. Lucy had woken up. As I sat on the couch in the living room, I took in the large collection of photographs on the wall detailing Michael and Lucy's life together. It had all the hallmarks of a charmed life.

The turnabout in the last hour had been surreal. And now here I sat looking at the gallery of two lives that had ended, just minutes ago in Lucy's case. And her daughter sitting with her remains upstairs, thinking it was romantic. If she only knew the truth: that the man sitting downstairs, who'd presented himself as an innocent witness and caring facilitator, may as well be the grim reaper himself, not only dealing in death but bringing it everywhere with him as if it were an infectious disease.

I was torn on my culpability. On the one hand, of course, if I'd maintained a professional code of behavior, Lucy would be alive and well. But on the other, on a level not subject to roles and conduct and societal dictums, what had happened up to the point of Lucy's passing had actually been quite beautiful and tender, maybe even healing. If she hadn't died, it would just have been one of those spontaneous encounters in life that had been noncommittal and serendipitous. But she had died, and now I had a big fat lie to peddle.

The ambulance arrived and I opened the door to the paramedics. The driver was a middle-aged man with a gray beard and pudgy face. His partner was a raven-haired, freckled woman in her twenties with a lively intelligence in her eyes who was clearly the leader of the two. I recognized her face from a hospital mortuary somewhere.

"You're from Gallagher's, aren't you?" she said.

"That's right," I said. "Paddy Buckley."

"What happened here, Paddy?" she said.

"The woman who lives here, Lucy Wright, went upstairs to get some clothes and dropped dead while she was up there. I'll bring you up. Her daughter's with her," I said.

"What's the daughter's name?" she asked.

"Brigid."

As soon as we reached the door of the bedroom, the raven-haired woman took control. Like most paramedics, she had an impenetrable calm and a pragmatic bedside manner. Brigid was still seated by her mother's remains.

"Hi, Brigid, is it?" said the raven-haired woman. "I'm Robyn, Brigid. Do you mind if I take a look at your mam?"

"Go ahead," whispered Brigid, and she got up from the floor and stood back while Robyn leaned down and checked for a pulse.

"Yeah," Robyn said softly, "she's gone."

They brought in the stretcher and placed Lucy's remains on it before covering her with a white sheet. Robyn explained that Lucy's remains would be brought to Clondalkin hospital, and then Brigid and I stood by the door and watched them leave with Lucy. The low panic was rising again. I had to get out of there.

"Brigid, this has obviously changed everything for you, and you'll want time to digest it. Is there anyone you'd like me to call for you?"

She shook her head. "No."

"Maybe I could come back later in the afternoon to discuss the funeral. Would that be okay?"

She looked like a little girl lost at a fair, shocked and aware that she'd been left alone, but secure enough in her own skin to be able to deal with it. There was nothing I could do for her.

"That's fine," she whispered.

And I was gone.

THREE

12:25 p.m.

I pulled up outside the mortuary at Clondalkin hospital, one of the biggest and busiest in Dublin. Because there were no autopsies done on Sundays, there was always a double load waiting after the weekend for Eddie Daly, the man who ran the mortuary and opened up all the bodies for the pathologists to work on. He was standing outside the front doors in his stained white coat, smoking a cigarette when I got out of my Camry. I nodded at him. As always, he wore a jaundiced, suffering smile.

"Eddie, how you getting on?"

"Struggling, and yourself?"

"Keeping busy. Listen, I've just come from a house off Wellington Road where I was making arrangements for a man with his wife, and when she went upstairs to get the clothes, she dropped dead."

"Lucy Wright."

"That's her."

"She's inside."

"I know you're up to your bollocks here, Eddie, I thought I could save you and the pathologists some time. She had angina, she told me herself before she went upstairs, so no need for a postmortem."

"She's down to be posted in the morning, Paddy, and that's the end of it. It's not up to you or me anyway, you know that."

"Who's down to do it?"

"Norman."

"Is he inside?"

"You don't want to see him, Paddy, he's like a bear with a sore prick."

"Maybe I can cheer him up," I said.

Norman Furlong looked like a bully chef. His flopping ginger mane and mustache lent a flamelike effect to his already fiery character, augmented by his pink skin and bulging gray eyes. Most undertakers I knew were intimidated by him to the point of staying well out of his way, but I hadn't a problem with him. And despite the fact that I'd never particularly warmed to the guy, today I simply had to talk to him.

The PM room was off limits to nonstaff. Written in black and red on the door was: NO ENTRY—RESTRICTED PERSONNEL ONLY. I pushed the door open and stuck my head in. Norman was standing over a remains cut open from neck to navel.

"Norman," I said, like we were buddies.

He looked up from the remains and focused on me with fire in his eyes.

"What are you doing in here?"

"Just passing by and thought I could save you some time. Lucy Wright had angina, so no real need for an autopsy."

"Get the fuck out of here," he said.

"I'll leave you to it," I said, and walked out of the room.

When I got back outside, Eddie was still there. "You didn't come up here especially for that, did you?" he said, flicking the butt of his cigarette away.

"No, I've to visit my brother-in-law, he's up in St. Michael's. My jammer all right there?" I said, pointing to my car.

"Work away."

"What time will she be done in the morning?"

"She'll be clear at lunchtime," said Eddie, walking back inside. I'd known well before I'd driven up there what I was going to be told, but I'd no choice but to try. With disgrace only a whiff away, I decided to walk around to the petrol station and buy myself a pack of cigarettes. My old reliable: Carrolls Number 1. I hadn't smoked in three years—I'd even managed to stay off them while dealing with Eva's death—but now that I was on the short end of the plank, I'd take whatever mercies I could get my hands on. With my DNA lining Lucy's birth canal, and the postmortem scheduled for less than twenty-four hours away, the awaiting indignity felt more than a little disquieting. I sparked up a smoke and turned my thoughts to what they craved most: shelter.

FOUR

1:40 p.m.

The feeling of the upright oversize coffin around me was comforting. It felt like my own wooden cocoon, tucked away behind a hundred other upright coffins waiting to be lined up in the loft.

Since my father died, Frank Gallagher brought in the boxes, and Jack put the handles on and lined the insides with padding and white silk in between doing funerals and deliveries. I felt closest to my father up there in the loft. I'd spent countless hours with him there over the years. When I was a young boy, I used to sit up on his workbench amidst the tools and sawdust while he made the boxes and engraved the nameplates with a special little hammer and chisel. But everything had changed now. Gallagher's outsourced its boxes; the nameplates were engraved by machine. And my father had long since left the loft, and Dublin, and life, for that matter. And now so had Lucy Wright. If there had been handles on the inside of the lid of the coffin I was sitting in, I would have pulled it shut, and probably wouldn't have heard Christy calling my name from down below in the garage.

"Up here!" I shouted back.

He arrived at the top of the creaking old stairs, wheezing.

"Where are you?"

I walked out from behind the coffins and stopped by the dilapidated wardrobe. Nailed to the front of it was a print of an out-of-shape Grecian female nude, smiling out from the picture like a comely Mona Lisa. It had been there since my childhood, and probably long before it, but today, as I looked at it, I saw Lucy Wright's face in there, beckoning me back to Pembroke Lane.

"What's going on?" I said.

Christy had an arrangement sheet in his hand, and going by the shininess of his bald head, he was flustered. He cut a humorous figure: thick-lensed glasses, pear-shaped trunk, and an endearing overbite.

"This one's coming in from England in the morning and I've never brought one in before. Will you give me a hand?"

"Sure," I said, and looked over the arrangement sheet. Christy had graduated from the garage as a driver at Frank Gallagher's suggestion and had been straddling both departments for a few months now. His inherent politeness made him eminently suitable for the funeral business, and after an endless stream of compliments about him from families when they paid their bills, sometimes months after the funerals, Frank decided to exploit Christy's charms beyond the atmosphere he created in the limousine.

The remains in question was one Dermot Hayes who'd been living in Manchester, where he got hooked on heroin, ending up overdosing at the age of twenty-seven. As he was originally from Walkinstown, his family, who still lived there, wanted him brought up to Gallagher's Walkinstown funeral home on Tuesday morning after his remains landed in Dublin airport.

"I've talked to the Hayes family but not the undertaker in Manchester," said Christy.

"Then let's give him a ring," I said. I looked at the form and recognized his name. I phoned Kershaw's Funeral Directors, and after being put through to the boss, Derek Kershaw, I traded the relevant information with him and ended the call. I ticked the applicable boxes and handed the form back to Christy. "Never as complicated as you think," I said.

"You're a pal," said Christy.

I'd known Christy ten years, since his days as a chauffeur, when he drove for the Spanish and Australian embassies whenever they had visiting dignitaries. He used to drive with Gallagher's in a casual capacity when he was in between jobs. After Christy's three years of part-time work, Frank offered him a full-time position, and Christy jumped at it. He was without a doubt the best driver Gallagher's had ever had: conscientious, dependable, polite, and mannerly. He was, as Frank often remarked, cut out for the funeral business like few others before him. Our friendship extended to our free time, too. We'd even organized a betting syndicate with a few of the lads from the yard, Christy and I being the horse-racing lovers in the group. Christy had a niece named Aoife, who was a stable hand in a prominent stud in Kildare, and for a slice of the action, she fed us inside information she gleaned from other stable hands, or grooms, or trainers, or even jockeys. Over a two-year period, we'd worked our seed money from two grand up to twelve.

When we'd place a bet at the track, we'd generally lay down between five hundred and a grand, with our horse usually running at short odds, and we'd each take home between four and eight hundred on the day if we were lucky. There were five of us in the group: Christy, Jack and Eamonn from the yard, Aoife down in the stud, and I. Every month we'd have an outing, and more often than not, come away with our pockets lined.

But my mind was far away from horses today; it was focused on the funerals of Michael and Lucy Wright, and Dermot Hayes.

"Overdose or suicide?" I said.

"Suicide by overdose."

"Did he leave a note?"

"Yeah, apparently he did."

I pulled out my cigarettes and lit one. I could see Christy's disappointment even though he tried to conceal it. When I'd given them up three years ago, I convinced him to do it with me and had made him feel we were in it together. Now that I'd broken the arrangement, I could sense he felt betrayed.

"You're smoking," he eventually said.

I nodded, blowing smoke out through my nostrils, feeling like a defector.

"You know they'll kill you."

"And get out of this kip sooner?"

Christy shrugged like it meant nothing. "Fuck it," he said.

"Fuck it," I said, letting a smile sink in.

"What happened in Pembroke Lane?"

"She went upstairs to get the clothes and dropped dead while she was up there."

"And where were you?"

There were secrets to tell good friends and secrets to keep to yourself. The Lucy Wright situation fell into the latter category. Neither Christy nor I had anything to gain from his knowing, and beyond that, considering what could be coming down the pike, I didn't want to involve him or put him under suspicion of collusion.

"Downstairs in the kitchen writing down the details. I hear a bump upstairs, a loud one, so I go up to the bedroom just at the top of the stairs and see her legs sticking out from the bedroom. I go into the room and there she is on the floor beside the wardrobe, the life gone out of her."

"Good Jaysus," said Christy. "And no other family there?"

"The daughter arrived after, so I told her."

"How'd she take it?"

"She thought it was romantic."

Christy shook his head a little. "Like the McKinleys. Remember?"

"Yeah," I said, "the McKinleys."

FIVE

2:30 p.m.

B rigid Wright was crouched on the draining board beside the kitchen sink, cleaning the windows. She'd already ironed her mother's shirts and blouses that were piled up beside the ironing board, and she'd swept the yard outside. She was doing all this to keep her mind occupied. She knew the shirts and blouses were never going to be worn by her mother again, but this, along with cleaning the windows, was helping her to process her grieving and think.

Even though Brigid had lived most of her teenage years in Dublin, the only time she'd spent there recently had been when visiting her parents. She'd been dealing with her father's imminent departure for the last few years of his life, particularly since his cancer diagnosis, so she'd less grieving to do there. But her mother, her darling mother—her friend, her guide, her fairy godmother, and countless other things—her passing was a different matter, and the loss she felt was massive. She hadn't expected her to die for another twenty or thirty years, much less fifteen hours after her father's death. But this was the path, and if it was to be her path, then she'd walk it with her chin up and her heart open, just like her mother always had.

It was her mother who'd counseled her through the breakup of her marriage. It was her mother who'd advised her on what paintings to include in her shows, just as it was her mother who'd taught her to always take life in stride and who'd encouraged her to be as free and independent and strong as she was.

"Nothing is forever," Lucy had always told her. And now, hours after her death, Lucy's words echoed in her daughter's ears as she continued to wipe the windows clean. Brigid was glad she'd been in Dublin for the deaths; she could soak in the freshness of their passing where it had happened, rather than traveling from London and arriving after everything had been moved and set up and organized. For once, she could plan and organize something for her mother and father, and put everything in its right place before heading back to Hampstead to collapse in a heap to wail away her lament and pour it into her pictures.

The prospect of both her parents' bodies coming back to their house to be waked rather than staying in the hospital mortuary was a heartening one for Brigid. But it was the romantic element of their dual passing she found most comforting.

Both Brigid's parents had been artists all their lives. After their funerals, she'd have to decide what to do with all the paintings in the house, both theirs and the few dozen painted by their friends and contemporaries. She hopped down from the draining board and washed her hands while thinking of her own paintings and what would be next for her now that she had a new well of pain to draw from.

Her last show had consisted of what she called her Blight Paintings, a series of oils illustrating what had actually happened in Ireland in the nineteenth century during the Famine, focusing on scenes of the food that wasn't potatoes being transported out of the country under armed guard to England, and all the Irish people being beaten away and dying because they were allowed nothing to eat other than the blighted potatoes. She'd been surprised at how well her work had gone down in London. It seemed the slight controversy the show courted during its time did her finances no harm at all. Her show sold out and managed to get the attention of the art world at large, bolstering her profile and earning power.

For her next series of paintings, death would probably be the theme. And impermanence. And maybe the state of being solitary. But not loneliness. Brigid knew her parents would always be with her now, in her heart.

SIX

4:10 p.m.

I stood amidst the swirling leaves at a door I was getting to know well, waiting to hear Brigid's voice. It never came. Instead, I listened to the door vibrating before I pushed it open. However unwittingly, I'd wronged this diminishing family, and my intentions now were strictly to arrange the ritual I'd been enlisted to carry out. Get the information, tell this woman what she needed to know about it, and leave her to grieve the loss of her departed parents.

As I approached the sliding doors, Brigid opened them, looking far more relaxed than when I'd left her earlier. Her tweed jacket was gone, replaced by a navy cashmere sweater, and her hair was back in a ponytail. I nodded hello.

"Let me take your coat," she said, just like her mother. I took it off and watched her hang it up, noticing she'd inherited her mother's grace of movement. Then she led me into the kitchen, giving me an unusually strange case of déjà vu.

"This must be a bit weird for you, having done all this with my mother earlier in the same place," she said, reading my mind while putting the kettle on.

"I think it's a bit weird for the two of us," I said, taking out a fresh arrangement form as well as her father's one.

"You look like you could do with a cup of coffee."

I'd decided before I'd come in that I wasn't going to accept any tea or coffee or anything else offered to me, and just get out of there as soon as possible. But something about the way she asked me completely disarmed my intentions.

"Why not?" I said. Brigid went about getting the good stuff together, not quite as strong as Frank's brew, but freshly ground all the same, and then sat down at the table opposite me.

"How far had you got with my mother in arranging my father's funeral?"

All sorts of unwelcome thoughts rushed around my head. I swallowed and struggled to remain calm.

"We'd pretty much covered everything. What your mother had decided upon was to have the removal tomorrow evening and the funeral on Wednesday morning after ten o'clock Mass at St. Mary's on Haddington Road. And then afterwards to Glasnevin Cemetery."

"I'd like to stick to her wishes as much as possible. Can we do that?"

"Of course," I said, wanting to accommodate her. "The only thing you need to take into consideration is the time factor. Your mother and I talked about having the removal tomorrow evening, but that was obviously before she passed on. So, bearing in mind there's to be an autopsy on her remains in the morning, I'd suggest moving the arrangements forward a day."

"Okay," said Brigid. And then as an afterthought, "Why is there an autopsy?"

It was a simple question that felt like a punch to the gut.

"It was a sudden death. Your mother is relatively young, and it happened at home. Routine under the circumstances."

"Right," said Brigid, letting me continue.

"What your mother wanted to do was to bring your father back here today and have a little bit of time with him before removing his remains to the church tomorrow. What I'd suggest, to keep in line with your mother's thinking, would be to bring both your parents back here tomorrow afternoon at the same time, have them here over a twenty-four-hour period, then bring them to the church together on Wednesday evening and have the funeral on Thursday morning."

Brigid nodded her head with somber eagerness.

"That sounds perfect," she said, as the kettle clicked off. She got up from her chair and made us both a cup of coffee. While she was pouring the water, she said nothing and neither did I. The silence was a relaxed one, and I felt no need to fill the gap with words, and nor, it seemed, did Brigid. Even when she'd sat down after putting the milk and sugar on the table, we both fixed our coffee without speaking. I watched the movement of her fingers as she stirred her coffee. She was a beautiful woman, and very much her mother's daughter. Just as my thoughts started to trace back to Lucy, Brigid broke the silence with so soft a voice that it was bordering on a whisper.

"What do you call this?" she asked. Instinctively, I leaned in a little, as she'd said it conspiratorially, and also because I hadn't a clue what she was talking about. She realized this in an instant and broke into a little laugh, bringing her hand to her nose to stifle it, making me smile.

"Sorry," said Brigid, "that silence was so nice I didn't want to offend it, and you don't know what I'm talking about anyway, do you?"

I shook my smiling head.

"What do you call it when there are two funerals together, like my parents'?" She was still smiling. I was surprised at how at ease she was. I'd been expecting her to be devastated, but she appeared to have great acceptance of her parents' deaths.

"A double funeral," I said. "I hope you don't mind me saying that you seem to be taking all this very well."

Her smile disappeared but the expression of calm and contentment remained.

"It's because they died together, Paddy," she said. "In a funny sort of way, I was sadder this morning before Mum died because I felt for her so much, having to be alone after them being with each other for most of their lives. Even though my father was very sick the last few years, they were still together and she was devoted to him: soul mates, completely. And now that she's followed him, I'm just so happy that they're together. It's the perfect ending to their romance. It gives me solace, great solace. I'll still miss them, of course I will, and I am grieving, but there's a smile between my tears."

I nodded as I listened to her, forgetting momentarily my experience with her mother and my part in her demise. When I'd been sitting at this same table with Lucy, I could have listened to her accent all day. But now, sitting here with Brigid, even though her accent was remarkably similar to her mother's, it was her voice that I found comforting.

"Have you had experience with this kind of thing before?"

"The McKinleys," I heard myself saying.

"Who were the McKinleys?"

"Well, the circumstances were quite different, really, but it's the case that springs to mind. The McKinleys were a couple, an old couple, who were well known in Dublin. They were inseparable. He was a watchmaker with a place on Dawson Street, a little man who was always impeccably dressed—he'd have his hat and black mac on even in the summertime—and anytime you'd see them around town, they'd always be holding hands: soul mates, as you say. And then she got a brain tumor and was given no hope. Months, they said. So, they sealed the windows and doors in their house, turned on the gas, got into bed, and died together, holding hands. Their children found them three days later and we looked after the funeral."

Brigid sat listening with tears filling up her eyes.

"That's so romantic," she said.

"And tragic," I said. "Unlike your parents, which is purely romantic."

Brigid nodded while still looking at me, stirring in me something I thought had died with Eva: a yearning. I looked back at her and felt my heart swelling a little. There was also a strange absence of something I couldn't quite put my finger on. And then I realized what it was. I hadn't thought of Eva once since sitting down with Brigid. It was as if she were forgotten.

I straightened the arrangement sheet in front of me and shifted on my seat, bringing us back to the task at hand.

"Your mother had agreed to arrive at the church at half past five on the evening of the removal and have ten o'clock Mass on the morning of the funeral. Okay with you?"

Brigid nodded slowly with the faintest hint of sultriness in her glistening eyes as she continued to look at me without saying a word. I felt a deepening attraction to her as each minute closed and I wondered if I was deluding myself by thinking that maybe the feeling was mutual. I felt guilty and remorseful and wondered if this was what sleep deprivation did to a man. I started running a mantra in the back of my mind: You're arranging the funeral of this girl's parents because your prick killed her mother, you fucker.

"Regarding transport, Brigid, to save you from the headache of having to drive and park, would you like me to put a car down for you on the removal and funeral?"

She nodded again.

"Yeah," she said, "do that."

I worked hard to keep my focus trained on the funeral.

"Your mother ordered a floral spray for the top of your father's coffin. Would you like me to put the same on top of her coffin?"

"That'd be nice," she said, watching me write on the arrangement sheet.

"And music, would you like me to get an organist and singer for the funeral Mass?"

Brigid thought about this for a minute, looking at me all along. I remembered her mother looking off while thinking, allowing me to study and admire her; but being here now with Brigid, it was she who was studying me as I moved through the questions. I waited for her answer while looking back into her gaze, which was a warm and comfortable place.

"Yeah, let's have music. Can I talk to the singer?"

"Of course. I'll get them to ring you. Would you like a male or female singer?"

"Which is nicer?"

"Female I find much more beautiful."

"Okay then," she said, "female."

"Your mother compiled a death notice for your father that she wanted put in *The Irish Times*. Would you like me to duplicate it and make the necessary changes for her own?"

Brigid nodded. "That'd be perfect."

"The church offering, which is obligatory, is usually about two hundred euro. Will I put down four hundred and have it paid on the day for you, or would you prefer to look after it yourself?"

"No, you look after it. Four hundred is fine."

I pulled out the coffin catalog and placed it on the table, unopened.

"And the last thing: the coffins. Do you want to take a look at them?"

"Sure," she said, and held out her hand. I passed the catalog over. Pictures of coffins often brought the finality of death tumbling home like a thumping reality check and usually turned on the waterworks, but the coffin had to be chosen.

"Did you show these to my mother?" she asked.

"We hadn't reached this stage."

She looked through them, turning the pages over one by one,

eventually stopping on a simple oak coffin. She turned it around to me like it was a menu in a restaurant.

"This one here, is it unpolished?"

"Yes, it's unpolished. That's a limed oak."

"That's the one then," she said, handing back the catalog. I put it back in my briefcase and marked down which coffin she'd selected before throwing a cursory glance over everything I'd written. I put my pen away and folded the sheet closed. I breathed easy. I'd got through it.

"That's it, Brigid," I said, intending to walk out the door in a matter of moments, but Brigid's focus remained fixed on me.

"I know my mother would have loved you, Paddy. You must have sensed that she liked you," she said. I was riveted to my seat.

"Yeah, we . . . definitely got on," I said.

She got up from her chair.

"Have dinner with me," she said, as she cleared the table of the cups.

I slammed myself hard into undertaker mode. "That's very kind of you, Brigid, but I'm on call for the night. I'll have to be getting back to the office," I said, and went about packing up my briefcase.

"Are you sure? There's a fridge full of food here and I'm going to have to throw it all out if it's not eaten."

"No, really, I can't do it, but you're very kind to ask, thank you." I rose to my feet and picked up my briefcase.

She took two wineglasses from the cupboard and picked up a bottle of red from the shelf beside the cooker. "Then have a glass of wine with me at least."

The way she said it had me wondering again whether she liked me, making me hesitate long enough for her to close the deal.

"Settled then," she said, and she uncorked the bottle. I relaxed back into my seat and rested the briefcase on the floor beside me.

"Okay," I said, swearing to myself I'd leave after one glass. "Thank you."

She sat down at the table and filled the two glasses.

"You know you don't look like an undertaker."

"What does an undertaker look like?"

She took a sip of wine, considering me. It was a Château Certan, 2006, from Bordeaux, and as far as my palate was concerned, exquisite.

"I don't know, but even five minutes ago when you were playing an undertaker, I still saw you as somehow detached from it all, like an observer, in a slightly voyeuristic sense." She trailed off, making me raise my eyebrows and smile, which made her laugh a little, preempting another of those silences.

I took a drink from my wine and savored the taste while Brigid looked at me. Apart from her beauty, her energy and humility were especially alluring: A readiness to laugh, particularly in difficult situations, had always disarmed me; and the lack of self-importance and ego emanating from her was refreshing. She didn't play on her looks, but operated instead from the seat of her character. Sitting with her now, I felt more comfortable than I had in quite a while. Lucy's effect on me earlier had been a soothing one and, of course, being around her exquisite beauty had been a pleasure, but with Brigid it was different. The harmony between us was effortless and captivating.

"What do you do?" I asked.

The cat arrived in from outside and stopped to brush against my leg. I rubbed its face before picking it up to let it rest on my lap.

"I'm a painter," said Brigid. I cocked my head to listen, as relaxed now as she and the cat were. "Six years ago, I used to share a studio with a sculptor, an old man who came to London in the seventies from India and stayed, and he told me about the seven veils."

"The dance of the seven veils?" I said.

"No, veils we use to hide and reveal ourselves. He said everyone has seven veils they use throughout their lives. When you're standing at a bus stop or waiting in line at the airport, you've got your seven veils on. Then if you pass by a neighbor on the street you know vaguely, you nod to her with six veils on. Then at work when you're around people you're familiar with but have no real friendship with, you drop down to five. With acquaintances, you alternate between five and four; with good friends, between four and three; with family, it's three veils and sometimes two, and with the one you love, two veils or, very occasionally, one. And the last one, he said, you never take off."

I had the cat purring loudly now.

"When I'm painting people, I always notice how many veils they have on. When a model is standing naked in front of you, they very often—usually, in fact—have their seven veils on. And then you might find an old woman sitting on a bench, say, fully clothed; she could be lost in thought and be wearing only two veils. But you, as an undertaker, get to see people stripped of their veils every day because death does that. It's a privilege."

I looked back at Brigid, considering what a privileged position I was in. I had the warmth and company of a purring cat on my lap, a glass of good red wine on the table in front of me, and a beautiful woman sitting opposite me who seemed, at the very least, to be a little attracted to me. And I was attracted to her. Then I considered the background to my being there, the intimacy and accidents that had brought about our getting together, and suddenly the feelings of warmth and comfort began to dissipate. I knew I'd eventually be able to forgive myself for sending Lucy on, but I'd have great difficulty in forgiving myself for bedding down her daughter in her wake. And then I considered what she'd just said about my seeing people at their most vulnerable and that it was a privileged position. And from such a position, I looked over at Brigid and made a decision.

"I've got to go," I said, putting the cat gently down on the floor and getting up from my chair. It was an abrupt end to a conversation that was only beginning, and I could sense that Brigid felt slighted. She rose to her feet.

"I hope I wasn't going on too much there," she said, following me to the door.

"No, it was a pleasure listening to you, and what you said hit a chord. It's true, it is a privileged position. When you said that, you reminded me that I have to get back to the office. I've so much to do." She handed me my coat and offered her hand.

"Thank you," she said. I shook her hand briefly while looking down at my shoes.

"If you can pick out some clothes for your parents, I'll pop around in the morning to get them if that's all right, and I'll give you the estimate then, too."

"That's fine," she said, while opening the door. The night had come. I walked out into the courtyard and headed for the road, feeling her eyes on my back. As I neared the door in the wall, something made me stop and turn around. She was still standing there under the courtyard light.

"Thanks for the wine and conversation, Brigid, it was a little slice of solace." I watched the beginnings of a smile settle around the sides of her eyes, and then before she had a chance to respond, I opened the door in the wall and left.

7:30 p.m.

It had been a long time since I'd felt anything like the increasing sense of ease that had taken seed inside me. I had the worry of Lucy's autopsy hanging over my head like a precarious guillotine, yet I was strangely free of the habitual grief that hung on me. Everything seemed possible again.

I drove back slowly to the funeral home and parked the car in the yard and went inside the office to sharpen up the Wright death notices for Tuesday's paper. The place was in darkness. I checked my watch: half past seven—still plenty of time to get the notices into the *Times*. I phoned the church to confirm the times before writing the notices into an e-mail and sending them to the Family Notices section in the paper. These were death notices, not obituaries. They were to include the deceased's name, where they were from, when they'd died, family they'd left behind, and the funeral arrangements. If the deceased were deemed important enough in society's eyes or in the eyes of the *Times* obit editors to warrant an obituary, then one would appear over the next few days. But in the case of the Wrights, there wouldn't be one. As a rule, once I'd entered the notice into the body of the e-mail, I read it twice to check there were no inaccuracies before sending it. The funeral game was one where double-checking was never enough. Check, recheck, and recheck again was Frank Gallagher's maxim. The last problem an undertaker needed was a bereaved family taking legal action for being unnecessarily upset because some detail was overlooked.

With that done, I made my way across the road to the dingiest pub on Uriel Street, An Capall Dubh, to get something to eat. There were plenty of pubs along the street, but this one was favored above all by the old lads around the area, and I found their company to be what my soul needed, most of the time. An Capall Dubh was the only pub on the street that hadn't changed its décor since the seventies. Apart from the flat-screen television mounted in the corner, it was the same as it had been for forty years.

As I grew older, I'd become allergic to the more yuppified establishments and avoided them at all costs. I yearned for the simplicity and lack of brashness An Capall Dubh offered, and so, too, it seemed, did the old lads with their working-class hearts and Old Dublin values.

While Gerry the barman organized some tea and a toasted sandwich, I sat down in my usual spot in the corner, with nothing but old guys drinking Guinness around me. I'd buried most of their relatives over the years, so I got nods of recognition from the different stools at the bar. But it wasn't their relatives that were on my mind. It was Lucy Wright and her fast-approaching autopsy. I considered it now with a relaxed and level head. Her autopsy, if it was to be carried out with no suspicion of foul play, wouldn't include any probing below the naval. People died every day in their houses and public places, more often than not with no other people around them, and when there was no question of foul play, then the autopsy would be carried out as normal. The only time this wouldn't apply would be if the pathologist was demonstrating to a student how to thoroughly carry out a full postmortem, in which case they'd investigate every orifice.

As dreams go, mine had just changed from a simple nightmare to the surreal. In all my years undertaking, I'd never even touched a family member, never mind have sex with them, and then the one time it happens, the woman in question ends up dying on top of me. And afterwards, her beautiful daughter makes my heart flutter.

Gerry placed my tea and sandwich down in front of me.

"There you are, Paddy."

"Great stuff, Gerry."

Every time I took my mind out of gear now, my thoughts conjured the image of Brigid sitting across the table, looking back at me. I definitely liked her more than I'd first imagined, but what was far more remarkable was that my mind wasn't naturally turning to thoughts of Eva. It was like I'd brought my shackles of grief to Pembroke Lane and had them unlocked by mother and daughter.

I walked back into the night, overcome by a tremendous wave of tiredness, which sent me back in the direction of the funeral home. I needed to sit down and rest. It had been a strange day.

But it turned out I was only in the ha'penny place. The night was going to get a lot stranger.

EIGHT

1:55 a.m.

I woke up to my phone vibrating in the pocket of my overcoat. I pulled it out and snapped into wide-awake mode from the armchair in the front office.

"Hello," I said, knowing it could only be one person.

"Paddy, it's Frank."

"Bring-back?"

"From Lia Fáil. Can you do it?"

"Of course."

Lia Fáil was the most decrepit nursing home in Dublin, run by the Liberties Health Service, which skimped on basics, never mind luxuries. There were no private rooms, just three floors of open wards divided into male and female. There wasn't even a mortuary, which was why bring-backs had to be done at all hours of the night. There were bring-backs and there were deliveries: the former was when you picked up a remains and brought it back to the embalming room to be worked on; the latter was when you brought a coffin to where the remains was and coffined it and left it there.

"I'll get Eamonn and Christy in to do it with you. The deceased's name is Harry Roche."

"Right. What time is it?" I said, yawning.

"Nearly two."

"Okay, see you in the morning."

I PULLED the hearse up outside the kitchens at the back of the nursing home with the two boys sitting beside me. Gallagher's fleet was made up of Mercedes hearses and limousines. Mercs had become the accepted standard in the Dublin funeral trade over the years, with most companies' fleets being made up of E-Class hearses and limos. But Frank, of course, insisted on the best, and prided himself on having the only S-Class fleet in the city, upgrading them regularly with up-to-the-minute models.

The nursing home used to be an old military hospital at the beginning of the last century. Whatever esthetic merits it may once have had had long since been defaced by an abundance of rust-covered fire escapes and a hundred years of soot. I rang the bell and waited for the night matron while Christy and Eamonn got the stretcher out from beneath the deck in the back of the hearse. The matron opened up the double doors without a word or a look at us. She was middle-aged and dumpy, and smelled of sour sweat and cigarettes. I wasn't sure if it was her job she resented or us. Either way, she wasn't happy, and if she wasn't happy, then she made sure the patients weren't either. I suspected she treated them more like inmates than residents.

She led us into the lift and pressed the button for the second floor while sighing heavily. Christy and I ignored her, but Eamonn was quite open about how much she amused him. Eamonn was Frank Gallagher's son and, as heir to the throne, had a more cavalier attitude to the whole business, not quite considering it his plaything, but he knew he could skirt close to the edge of the line and remain untouchable. He smiled at her rakishly.

"Sister, how about breakfast in the morning? You and me."

She turned around slowly and glared at him. Eamonn smiled, looking her up and down.

"I've got a thing for uniforms," he said, his smile getting bigger. As the matron turned her back on him, Christy flicked his hand out, hitting Eamonn's side, giving him a little warning nod. But it was futile.

"Did you know Jack does the ironing at night while his wife sits on the couch in front of him watching television?" said Eamonn.

"I know," said Christy, nodding to the floor. "Unbelievable."

"Unbelievable?" said Eamonn. "It's bleeding scandalous."

The matron's jowls reddened as the doors opened in front of her. I smiled as we followed her, Eamonn beside me, rolling his tongue in his cheek.

"You're in good form, Paddy," he said quietly, noticing the change in me.

"Bit of rest," I said. Eamonn and I had always had three-veils access and knew each other well as a result. He'd first started working in the yard when he was fourteen, during his school holidays. Frank had him polishing the cars, painting the walls, and doing mutes.

It takes at least three men to carry a coffin in a funeral—one at the head, two at the feet—the hearse driver, who leads the cortege, takes the head, the limo driver takes one side of the feet, and the mute takes the other. He also carries in the flowers and collects Mass cards. He's called the mute because he doesn't talk to the family; he has no need to. All he needs to do is look solemn.

I'd taken Eamonn under my wing early on and taught him everything I knew. His father was making sure he understood and could work at every level of the business, and at the moment, that meant embalming, which Eamonn hated. I'd been the embalmer for years, but was only too happy to hand over the reins to Eamonn. He was twenty-two and could probably do anything he turned his hand to, but why build a business from scratch when he'd a ready-made empire waiting for him to walk into? As close as we were, the day that sealed the bond for us happened a year ago when Eamonn was twenty-one.

Frank had gone away on business for a few days to Birmingham to source some new limousines and had left Eamonn in charge of the place for the first time. I'd been bringing a remains back from a hospital, and when I returned, I met an embarrassed and worried-looking Eamonn out in the yard.

"Can I talk to you for a minute, Paddy?" he said.

"Of course." We went into the middle office, where arrangements were usually made, and shut the door.

"You're going to find this hard to believe, Paddy, but . . . it happened—I mean, I let it happen." He looked utterly ashamed of himself and was finding it difficult to divulge his story. "I can't believe I've done this . . ."

"What happened?" I said.

"I was having a smoke out in the yard during lunch when a red Audi convertible with Northern Irish plates drove in. There were four guys in it. I knew by looking at them they were dodgy. They got out of the car and walked up to me. Three of them said nothing; one of them did all the talking, called himself John. He was older than the rest, in his forties. He looked dangerous but he was relaxed and friendly, reminded me of Dean Martin. He said I'd looked after his aunt's funeral a few months ago and that he'd heard I was a bankable guy with a lot of savvy."

I could feel where this was going. "Go on," I said.

"He said they were bringing a vanload of Armani and Versace suits through Dublin Port from England illegally and had been stopped by a customs official who wouldn't release the vehicle unless he was paid off. They would have paid it themselves, he said, but all their money was in the impounded van. He said they needed five grand to pay off the customs official, and then they'd return my five to me with another five on top of it for my trouble."

I smiled at him. "You didn't fall for that, Eamonn." The border scam was as old as the three-card trick.

He buried his face in his hands. "I did, Paddy. I can't believe it but I did."

"Oh, Jesus," I couldn't help saying. Poor Eamonn, his first day in control of the company, thinking he was the big man, swaggering so much that word of his green cockiness had got out to the wolves. Easy pickings.

"I went up to the bank on Thomas Street with them, withdrew the money, and gave it to him."

"Five grand?" I said, still finding it hard to believe. He nodded shamefully.

"I knew what was happening, Paddy, but somehow I couldn't

stop myself. My curiosity as to how it would all unfold was too great not to follow . . . and I always loved Dean Martin. The last thing the guy said to me when I'd given him the cash was 'You're well thought of in high places.'"

"Well, I'm afraid you're fucked, Eamonn. That's the last you'll be seeing of them. And your dad's five grand."

"What am I going to do?" he said miserably.

Our only chance of getting it back, I knew, was if they got greedy. The fact that it had been so easy for them could well bring them back in for more.

"There's a chance they'll be back again."

"Do you think?" said Eamonn.

"They might. That was probably the easiest score they've ever made."

"But what would we do?"

I didn't want to tell Eamonn any more than he needed to know; he was in over his head as it was. These guys were brazen and wily and lived on their wits and had already taken Eamonn to the bank.

"If they come back in, just bring them in here to the middle office and close the door, and then I'll come in and take over."

"But what'll you do?" asked Eamonn.

"See if we can get the money back," I said.

Sure enough, within another half hour they phoned the office. Frank's secretary told Eamonn that there was a John looking for him, so into the middle office we went.

"Just make sure you get them in here. No matter what they say, tell them to come in and discuss it in private. Don't tell them directly you'll give them the money, but give them the idea that you will. Can you do that?" I asked.

"No problem," said Eamonn. He took the call while I held my ear next to his to listen. With the right coaching, Eamonn was back on form, sounding perfectly confident in his compliance.

"All right, John?" he said.

"Eamonn, how's the man?" said the guy who called himself John in his silken voice.

"Good, how'd it go?" said Eamonn.

"Well, we definitely have him onside, but he's got wise to the worth of the stock we've got. He wants more money, Eamonn."

I smiled at Eamonn. Greedy bastards.

"How much more?" asked Eamonn.

"Another two grand and he'll release it immediately."

"Right then," said Eamonn. "You'd better come in so."

"Right you are. Be there shortly." And they ended the call. There was hope back in Eamonn's eyes, but he was nervous now, too.

"Okay," I said. "Now when they come back in, bring them in here and wait. Just listen to them tell you their story, then after two minutes, I'll come in and take over. You get out of the seat, stand back, and tell them I'm your associate and that I'm taking over. All right?"

"Right," said Eamonn.

I waited down the end of the yard by the stairs to the loft and watched them drive in ten minutes later in their unblemished Audi A5 coupé. Only two of them this time: a guy wearing a suit with no tie—presumably "John"—and another guy in jeans and a purple anorak. Cocky as you like. They walked out onto the street to come in the main entrance where Eamonn would meet them. When they'd turned the corner, I quickly walked up to the top of the yard and locked the cast-iron gates. Then I went inside.

I opened the door to the middle office and went in. As soon as I'd closed the door, Eamonn got up from the chair behind the desk and stood back. The two men ignored me and would look only at Eamonn.

"This is my associate, Paddy, he's taking over now," said Eamonn, stepping further back to stand at the wall.

"It's much better if we keep this between ourselves, Eamonn," said John, like he was as close as a brother to him. "Eamonn . . ." he said again, looking for eye contact, but Eamonn had shut down.

"You're talking to me now, lads," I said. Reluctantly, they turned their gaze to me. John had a fair belt of charisma about him; he was probably a traveler and knew well how to work his charms. And he did look like Dean Martin—minus the magic. He was fairly well built, too, and so was his friend, who looked more physically imposing; no surprise then who they'd picked to do the talking. Neither of them would be beyond playing the violence card if it came down to it. But I had my ace.

"We want the money back, lads," I said.

"We don't have it," he started.

"Don't even try and pull it."

"The customs official has the money—"

I cut him off fast. "I don't want to hear it. We want the money back now, or I'll have the law down here in a flash."

He looked at me, still relaxed, but no longer playing his role.

"You wouldn't like to see a man go down, would you?" he said.

"My only concern is the money. Nobody needs to go down as long as it's handed over."

"We don't have it," he said, turning his hands up, empty.

"Then get it. We're finished talking here," I said with finality, opening the door. I walked out with Eamonn close behind me. "We'll let you out the back, lads," I said, leading them into the back office and opening the door out into the yard. It wasn't until they followed us outside that they realized they were snared. No way out. John looked directly at me for a moment, fox to fox, then back to the locked gates, and then down to the ground. Dino wasn't happy. His friend waited for his move and, like an obedient watch-dog, would look only at John. After weighing up his options, John pulled out his phone and called a number. I could only hear him mumbling, but it was clear he was giving instructions. He ended the call and turned to me.

"Right," he said, capitulating. "You'll have it back in a minute." Ten minutes later, Eamonn met one of the other two thieves at the main entrance and was handed back the money, and then I opened the gates.

Frank never found out. Eamonn learned a lesson, and he also knew that I'd always have his back.

The matron in Lia Fáil led us into a ward of old men, twenty in all, most of them asleep, and stopped by the bed of the deceased. There were old screens on either side of the bed that must have been fifty years old and shielded the view only from knee to chest.

"I'll be in my office," she said, and walked out. Eamonn watched her backside sway from side to side as she waddled away.

"Would you look at the state of that," he said.

The corpse was still warm. And terrified-looking. All these guys were—dead or alive. And all so skinny—they must have been fed soup and nothing else. The funerals that followed these bring-backs were known within the company as "housers," as they were effectively on the house. Gallagher's had the contract with the Liberties Health Service, and did however many there were each year for a nominal flat rate. These were the forgotten people whose funerals consisted of veneered chipboard coffins, which arrived for the removals hours earlier than normal, and had their funeral Masses and burials before any of the company's regular funerals so they wouldn't interfere with them, timewise, as they were ser-viced by the same vehicles and men. There were seldom more than two or three people at these funerals. Most times, none. Except for Shay. And when Shay had gone, Frank.

At half two in the morning, these poor old souls got to see us at our worst: Our five o'clock shadows had doubled in length, and our dark suits and overcoats took on an even darker hue in the badly lit wards and corridors. It was always the same: These old men, scared and gaunt, would gape out from beneath their covers, looking more like concentration camp detainees than senior citi-zens in a modern republic. And they all had the same expression on their faces, which said only one thing: *Will I be next?*

We placed the stretcher on the bed beside old Harry's remains. His eyes and mouth were both wide open and he hadn't been shaved in a week. We pulled the covers off him and got ready to lift him, Eamonn at the legs, Christy and I on either side of his shoulders. Just as we went to lift him, a pocket of gas found its way up through the windpipe and escaped through the mouth, filling the air with a noxious smell, which regularly happens when a remains is lifted. But it still came as a shock to some people, and the smell was like nothing else—the worst smell in a zoo couldn't hold a candle to it. Eamonn and I were long since hardened to such smells but Christy was still a novice, and as soon as he smelled it, he hit the deck—the best place for fresh air.

Eamonn and I couldn't help laughing silently through our closed mouths, our shoulders shaking up and down. The two of us easily lifted the corpse onto the stretcher, old Harry being as light as a twelve-year-old child. We buckled the straps tightly around his torso and legs, placed the black plastic cover over him, and pulled the screens back. By this time, Christy had recovered and the three of us carried Harry out of the ward.

"I nearly brought my dinner up there," said Christy, pressing the elevator button. "As if the smell of piss and Pine-Sol isn't bad enough."

We stood the stretcher up in the elevator and sank to the ground.

NINE

3:00 a.m.

With Harry Roche's remains locked safely in the embalming room behind me, I turned my thoughts again to slumber and a soft pillow. I was about to head home when Eamonn slowed his Mercedes down as he was leaving, lowering his window.

"Back left tire, Pat," he said with a downturned smile, and drove out the gate. I looked at the tire on my Camry. It was completely flat. And then, as if on cue, the rain came down, prompting Christy to rush to my boot and open it.

"Come on, Buckley, you unlucky fuck," he said, pulling the spare out. "Let's get it changed." If it had been hailing golf balls, Christy wouldn't have hesitated to help me, such was the quality of his friendship. We battled away at the wheel with the rain bouncing heavily off the ground beside us, the pair of us saturated by the time we'd finished changing it.

"Go home," I told him. "I'll get the gate."

Christy didn't have to be told twice. He ran to his car and drove off.

Alone again, I settled into my car and relaxed, closing my eyes to listen to the rain on the roof. Memories of laughter came in and out of my mind. Lucy laughing her beautiful laugh while holding my hankie, and me laughing with her; Brigid stifling her laughter while we whispered together; Eamonn and I silently laughing in Lia Fáil; and Eva laughing the sexiest laugh I've ever heard, her hoarse and croaky voice crowning it. I imagined being away in another land with Brigid Wright, remembering the laughter from there, but I was only tormenting myself with pleasant notions that could never be.

After locking the gates and getting back in my car, I moved off down the street and failed to do something so routine, so reflexive, that I unintentionally transformed my car from an everyday object of convenience into a giant bullet. I'd forgotten to turn my lights on.

I drove down James's Street, headed for Kilmainham, my attention more absorbed in tuning the radio away from a late-night chat show than focusing on the road in front of me. Just as I tuned into some music, something ahead of me grabbed my attention. In the fraction of a second that I got to see him, I saw the trotting figure of a man holding a newspaper over his head to shield himself from the rain while he was crossing the road. But he was moving so ridiculously fast towards me that I only had time to raise my foot from the accelerator. His body was hit by the car with such a deafening wallop that he must have been thrown a good fifteen feet up in the air. I slammed on the brakes and skidded to a stop on the rainy street twenty yards up the road.

It was only as the car finally stopped moving that I realized my lights weren't on. I looked in the rearview mirror and in the dark could just make out a body lying motionless in the middle of the street. I looked at the shattered windscreen and the crumpled bonnet, and then I turned around and looked out the back window, my heart marking each moment like a pounding drum.

I got out of the car and walked shakily towards the crumpled prostrate figure. I knelt down beside it and saw a tall, well-built man, not yet middle-aged, dressed in a suit and overcoat not dissimilar to my own. The man's eyes were open and there was a little stream of blood that had trickled out of his mouth down the left side of his face. He didn't seem to be breathing. I felt for a pulse and, for the second time that day, found none. The man was dead.

Sticking out of his inside coat pocket were a bulging zip case and a leather-bound rectangular wallet. I took out the zip case and looked inside. It was jammed tight with fifty-euro notes, totaling what looked to be more than seventeen or eighteen grand. I put it back in the man's pocket and took out the wallet. I opened it up to see a large collection of credit cards. I searched for the name and saw it in raised print: DONAL CULLEN. My eyes widened with increasing horror as I looked to the face of the dead man, and then I recognized him: from the papers, outside the courts with his brother, Vincent, Dublin's number one thug.

"Oh, no." I barely whispered the words. I dropped the wallet to the ground as fear swept through me like a ghost, and I stumbled backwards to my feet. The hum of the engine running behind me never sounded so inviting. I scanned both sides of the street, both ends, to see if anyone could see me or had witnessed the accident, and I saw no one. I backed away from the body slowly. Once I got a few yards away, I turned and walked purposefully to the car. I snapped the number plate off the back of the car, quickly did the same around the front, and then got back in and shut the door. A little voice in my head made a suggestion. *Leave the lights off,* it said. I put her into gear and drove off slowly with my hands trembling. Just before I turned the corner, I noticed in the rearview mirror somebody running from a building to the body in the middle of the road. I punched the accelerator, kept my head looking forward, and a moment later I was around the corner and gone.

The voice continued. *You killed him. Not like Lucy, who happened to die while you were fucking her, this man died because you killed him with your car. You killed him by not looking. By being tired. By tuning the radio. By driving with no lights on and not braking. You took his life.*

I shook my head and gripped my face.

"Jesus Christ," I said out loud. "Oh, Jesus."

Any worries I had about Lucy Wright's autopsy disappeared the moment I'd read Donal Cullen's name. In the blink of an eye, my concerns switched from being caught out for riding a bereaved widow, a client, and sending her to the grave in the process, to being butchered alive for the unceremonious killing of the brother of the most dangerous gangster in Ireland.

By the time I'd pulled up outside my house on Mourne Road, I was numb, still not breathing normally, and living in a full-scale nightmare. I'd fled the scene, acted like a coward. Countless times had I sat with families who'd had a son or daughter killed by a hit-and-run driver, and I'd silently condemned the driver along with them. I knew well the added injustice a family felt at not having someone put their hand up and say, "Yeah, it was me, I'm so very sorry." On James's Street, I'd been fully intent on doing just that until I saw who it was. I knew it was the right thing to do. And then the fear took me. It had me by the balls and the hair and the neck, and wasn't letting go.

Eva's car, a silver ten-year-old Renault Clio, had been parked in my garage since she'd died, and I still carried the key. I opened up the garage, moved past the dusty clutter, and climbed into the little French car, praying the battery wouldn't be flat. It had been four months since I'd turned her over. I pumped the pedal, turned the key, and listened to the engine roar to life. I closed my eyes to appreciate this small triumph. I moved it out onto the street and parked it, then I drove my Camry into the same spot in the garage. I locked the garage doors and checked the damage to the car. It looked like it had killed someone.

I went into the house as quietly as I could and didn't turn on any lights. I crept upstairs to my bedroom. I left the light off while I got undressed, the room being sufficiently lit by the streetlight outside. I took off my coat and threw it to the floor and noticed a bulge in the inside breast pocket, the same one as Donal Cullen had his money in. I knelt down and put my hand in and pulled out a damp green facecloth, the one I'd cleaned off Lucy with. I'd forgotten all about it. I closed my eyes and tossed it towards the little pile of laundry in the corner before heading to the bathroom where I stripped and ran the shower. I stepped in and washed myself thoroughly and dried off afterwards with a fresh towel. I avoided looking in the mirror. I didn't want to see myself consumed by fear.

I crawled into bed and huddled in the fetal position, my mind scrambling for exits or explanations. What would Frank have done? Frank wouldn't have been in this position in the first place.

If he had filled my shoes for the day, none of this would have happened. And Frank couldn't help me with this one anyway. Nobody could. If I'd Eva here beside me, she'd hold my head in her hands and kiss my forehead tenderly and be my lover and confidante, and we'd get through it together with our bulletproof love shielding us from the world. But Eva was gone. As I lay there bereft of comfort or hope, grappling with my predicament, if I could have had the counsel of any one person, living or dead, it would have been my father.

After bringing my father to the forefront of my mind, my thoughts spontaneously vaulted back to an afternoon I'd spent with him when I was fifteen. We'd been painting the living room in the house I'd grown up in on Arnott Street at the back of the Meath Hospital, and had stopped to have a cup of tea. It was a hot day in the middle of summer and a big fly was buzzing around the room. Shay smiled at me. He had a way with all creatures, no matter what kind, like no one else I'd ever known.

Out of the blue, he said, "Make the fly land in your hand."

"Come on, Dad, the fly's not going to land in my hand."

"Why not?"

"There's no way I could get the fly to do that," I said emphatically.

"Try it." He smiled.

"It's not going to happen," I said, smiling back at him.

"Relax," he said, "and clear your mind."

I'm not sure if it was what he said or how he said it. But at that moment, I understood what he was talking about in a way I hadn't before. I let him guide me.

"Open your hand and imagine all your power, all your spirit, your essence, moving into the center of your palm. Imagine it's the seat of your soul. Everything that makes up who you are is now in that hand."

After a minute or so, there was a subtle but definite change in the feeling of my hand.

"Right?"

I nodded.

"Now allow the fly to land in your hand."

I looked at the fly, and as soon as I'd imagined it landing on my hand, it flew down and did just that. I was so astonished that my jaw dropped open. But I had the sense not to move my hand. And the fly stayed there. I looked at my father, who remained relaxed as always. Like he knew this would happen.

"You can close your hand," he said.

Slowly, I closed my hand over the fly, and it let me. Then I opened it slowly, and still it stayed there.

"Now let him fly away."

Just then it flew away, out the window. Neither one of us said anything. We drank our tea in silence while my father's eyes smiled, his head nodding imperceptibly.

Back in my bed now on Mourne Road, I stretched out my hand and imagined all that I was, my soul, my mind, the totality of me, in its palm. And after about a minute or so, I felt the change. I felt my palm pulse. Every part of my mind was focused on it. I became the process. Then the perceiving part of me left its seat behind my forehead and traveled slowly down my arm until I was in my hand, looking back at my face. And what I saw on my face was rapt focus. And then an even stranger thing happened. I detached. I was released from my body and gently floated up to the corner of the ceiling, where I rested in my suspended state. I thought I must have died, had a painless heart attack, and this was my ascent to somewhere else. But I wasn't leaving the room, and my body didn't look dead at all. It looked very much alive, still with its hand outstretched, still focused. I imagined moving my hand and relaxing it, and it did just that. I imagined changing position in the bed, and my body did exactly as I'd just imagined. This was oddly perfect. Independent Channel 24 like I'd never thought possible. All the panic and stress and fear and horror that I couldn't escape just moments ago had gone. I didn't feel any of it. I decided to say something, to see if I could get myself to talk, and then watched my mouth open down on the pillow.

"We'll get through it like this," it said. It all felt so certain, so effortless and easy, it was strangely euphoric. From this dislocated, suspended channel, I continued to watch myself watch the wall until the darkness was replaced by a room full of light.

Tuesday

TEN

October 14, 2014,
8:20 a.m.

Vincent Cullen was on his knees in the greenhouse in his back garden, planting pepper and tomato plants. He'd spent the last two hours in the outdoor vegetable patches in his back garden, weeding and planting, finding that having his hands in the soil was exactly what he needed this morning. After all, it was Donal who'd dreamed up and built the extensive greenhouse in the first place. It had been Donal, too, who'd established and expanded the vegetable garden, and planted and tended to the variety of fruit trees—apple, pear, plum, cherry, apricot, nectarine, and fig—scattered around the walled acre that constituted the back garden. Donal had even convinced his brother to let him build a chicken area at the back of the patches and raised boxes, which now housed fourteen chickens, whose eggs supplied both Cullen households. Before Donal had graced the garden with his imagination and talent for growing things, with the help of a team of gardeners, Vincent hadn't known a cloche from a cold frame, but lately he'd been getting as much satisfaction from the growing abundance in his garden as his brother had.

Seven years his junior, Donal had been Vincent's partner in crime since they were teenagers. Vincent was the leader, but Donal's enterprising spirit and fearlessness were equally responsible for the sway and influence the Cullen brothers held over Dublin. Aside from being blood and a savvy business partner, Donal was Vincent's best friend, his closest confidant, and his most trusted accomplice. Vincent knew he could rely on Donal for anything. Whether it was smoothing out a misunderstanding with a group from Belfast with his artful negotiation skills or putting together a deal with a pack of Serbs from Marseille, Donal's input into the Cullen operation matched his brother's, ounce for ounce.

And now somebody had plowed Donal down in the dead of night and robbed him in the bargain. Taken out in his prime when his star had just begun to rise.

The injustice of it deeply saddened Vincent and rankled him, fueling his hunger for retribution all the more.

The brothel on James's Street that Donal had left just prior to his death was his brainchild. Impudently called the St. James's Club, it was decked out like a five-star hotel, housing forty girls from as many different countries who were quite literally real-life fantasies for the top-end clientele. Since its doors opened four months ago, the place had become a bona fide goldmine for the Cullens, bringing in a fortune on a nightly basis. Its reputation was already luring high rollers from as far away as Stockholm, and incoming flights were being booked on a daily basis for clients across the water in London and Manchester. Of all Donal's schemes and ventures, the St. James's Club was the brightest and most flamboyant feather in his cap. It was one of life's ironies that Donal had ensured only weeks before his death that the St. James's clients would be spared being picked up on the cops' street-surveillance cameras by bribing the right officials to have the cameras permanently pointed away from the club in the direction of Thomas Street.

Death made all the bullshit fall away for Vincent. All the stuff that had taken up hours of thought and conversation only the day before ceased to be of any consequence. Matters of the heart had taken their place. He thought of his own four-year-old son, Fiach, and his wife, Angela, and cherished the fact that they were alive and in his keeping. But that didn't change the fact that Donal, who'd been around since Vincent was seven, had been robbed from him. Whoever the swine was who killed him had driven a knife deep into Vincent's heart, and it was this particular matter he was consumed with today. Every bit of power he wielded was focused entirely now on catching and destroying Donal's killer.

As Vincent finished tying up the last tomato plant to the stake beside it, Sean Scully arrived at the greenhouse door.

"Matser's here," he declared. Sean was a tall, wiry man with a permanently scheming brow and snarling nose whose loyalty to his boss was beyond question. At fifty, he'd been working with the Cullens since the early eighties and was as hell-bent as Vincent was on hunting down Donal's killer.

"Bring him out," said Vincent.

While Sean went to get Matser, Vincent wiped the dirt from his hands and got to his feet. Standing at a straight six feet, he'd the frame of a middleweight boxer. Under his T-shirt and track-suit pants, his strength seemed to brood in muscles ever ready for quelling anything that came his way. At odds with his apparent manliness was a nearly feminine aspect to his face, a prettiness to his features, his unruffled forehead and high cheekbones, but his black menacing eyes and grown-out crew cut put paid to any trace of androgyny. It was an undisputed fact in Dublin that Vincent Cullen was the alpha male of alpha males.

He walked out of the greenhouse and watched Sean escort Matser from the house over to where he now stood. Sean looked like a midget next to Matser. Six-foot-seven and thirty stone, all Matser needed to do was show up to get his way. With a cleft palate and stick-out ears, Matser was far from pretty, but what he lacked in beauty he more than made up for in brute force and determination. He'd put his life on the line for his boss more than a few times and was willing to do it again to help find Donal's killer.

"Sit down, Matser," said Vincent, gesturing to the antique bench beside the greenhouse door. Matser sat down with his elbows on his knees, eager for his orders.

"Whoever hit him took the twenty grand he'd just taken out of the club. Geno heard the bang from inside, but by the time he got out there, the guy who'd hit him was driving away with no lights on towards Kilmainham, the reg plates already ripped off the car. It looked like a dark Toyota Camry, but it was pissing rain and it was gone before Geno could get a good look. I want everyone on that street talked to today, without exception. Got it, Matser?"

Matser nodded.

"Now, if you need to use the shooter, one shot only. Two shots, people start making phone calls. Right?"

"Right," said Matser.

"Sean, get on to Gallagher's. I want somebody up here straight away."

Sean and Matser went back to the house, leaving their boss alone. As soon as they'd gone, Vincent let out a low whistle through his teeth.

"Dechtire," he said.

From the far end of the greenhouse, a large rust-colored dog raised its head and looked at Vincent. It rose and walked out slowly towards its grieving master and sat down next to him, allowing the back of its neck to be rubbed.

ELEVEN

8:45 a.m.

I'd no idea how I was still able to maintain this suspended mid-air state; it felt effortless, not to mention surreal and bizarre. But I never wanted to be back in my skin again. I felt more in control like this, more in tune with what was happening. I felt no pain. No tiredness. There was a part of me that wanted to call in sick and go to Phoenix Park or up the mountains and discover the world anew. But even more, I felt drawn to the yard in Uriel Street, and the idea of carrying on as I usually would to allay any suspicion of my culpability for Cullen's death seemed like the most intelligent course.

At a quarter to nine in the morning, I pulled Eva's car to a halt in the yard while hovering somewhere above the radio. This was the first time I'd driven her car out since she'd crossed over. I'd left it in the garage for fear I'd be overcome by the faint smell of her scent, but now with everything that was happening, my feelings and memories of Eva had been put in perspective. They were still there, but there was no more pain or expectation or longing attached to them. When I thought of Eva now, of seeing her grinning at me on Grafton Street or fitting her hand into mine as we strolled along the South Bull Wall to the Poolbeg Lighthouse, I felt nothing but fondness and gratitude. And love.

As I walked from the back office down the corridor towards the front office, I floated four or five feet ahead of my body. It happened effortlessly: Almost before I had a chance to think about it, there I was. Before my body had caught up, I joined the buzz of activity around Frank, who sat behind the main desk, with Christy and Eamonn standing by his side, looking over the list of runners, while Jack sat in the corner, listening.

"Christy," said Frank. "The Hayes remains from Manchester is being delivered here from the airport in an hour's time. Can you bring it up to Walkinstown before lunch?"

"Sure I can, yeah," said Christy.

Over at the reception desk, Corrine, Frank's secretary, put down the phone and turned to Frank.

"Vincent Cullen's brother was killed last night . . ." The very mention of Cullen's name silenced the room.

We'd got the call. Of course we had. It stood to reason. But the fear that had entered the room by Cullen's name being uttered didn't touch me. It should have, but I was impervious to it.

"They want somebody up to the house in Terenure straight away to make arrangements," Corrine said.

Just as she said the last word, my body stopped at the old grandfather clock by the parlor door. Frank's face lit up as he looked at me.

"Paddy, right on cue. Vincent Cullen's brother is dead. Can you go up and make the arrangements?"

I watched myself looking back at Frank. And then the words came.

"I'll just get a coffee," I said, unwilling to commit to anything.

"We're doing Donal Cullen's funeral," said Jack, with so much pride you'd swear we were burying Bono.

I moved towards the back office again, wondering would the fear find its way into my removed state now there'd been mention of the lion's den. I searched for any sign of it, any trace, and found none. I was fear-free.

As I was tire-kicking my fearlessness, Frank came in holding out the address on a bit of paper. Even though I was feeling invincible, I figured it was probably better if I stayed away from Cullen. He did have a reputation for being impossible to lie to, after all.

"Frank, is there any chance you'd go up and make those arrangements yourself? I'm feeling a little odd this morning." I looked at myself along with Frank. The picture of health.

Frank smiled at me.

"To Vincent Cullen's? There's nobody I'd send up there but yourself, Pat. And you look good to me—in fact, I don't remember seeing you as relaxed."

He handed me the address as well as the keys to his Mercedes.

"Take my car up," he said, and left the room.

TWELVE

9:25 a.m.

The Dublin I knew was different from the one sold on the tourist brochures. The Dublin I knew had teeth and needles and lots of tears. It wasn't devoid of smiles or charm, but it had more than its fair share of deviants. It didn't lack magic, and it had its heroes and class acts, but for the most part, it was dirty, depressive, and corrupted. Drimnagh, the suburb where I lived, with its terraced houses cramped side by side and its dreary simili-tude, was right beside Crumlin, a well-known breeding ground for villains and thieves that was the birthplace of the Cullen broth-ers. But Vincent Cullen didn't live there anymore. He'd moved to the more affluent suburb of Terenure, with taller trees, bigger houses, and loftier ideas. Comprising every class and creed, Teren-ure played all houses to all men and was renowned for its Edward-ian architecture. Cullen's house was one of its finest examples.

I stopped the car outside Cullen's electric gates and got out. The house was on a two-acre plot and was well hidden behind a high stucco wall. All I could see from the gates was a long drive lined by white oaks. I pressed the intercom on the wall and waited. This was it. Time to sit down with the man. My task was simple: take down the details for the funeral. Nothing more. I'd sit with Cullen, nod at all his requests, then split, and go about implementing them, just like I always did. I'd walk through it by treating it just like any other job.

The gates leaped back from me, continuing steadily away until the path was cleared. As I got back into the car, I clocked the little camera on a pole by the nearest tree. Seen and attended to, and silently ushered in.

The house was enormous. It was magnolia white with large shadowed windows and a steeply sloped roof with wide eaves, and was beautifully sheltered by a scattered assortment of giant trees. I parked on the gravel drive, and as I got out of the car, the front door was opened by a young man in a tracksuit.

"From Gallagher's, right?" he said.

"That's right," I said, and followed him into the house. In the front hall, the young man disappeared but two old men dressed in suits stepped forward. This was Old Dublin reaching out to me, these old guys with their weathered skin and Brylcreemed thinning hair. Without opening their mouths, their stoic faces spoke a thousand words of endurance and loyalty, and of another Dublin in a simpler time. One of them took my coat while the other knocked on a door off the darkened hallway, which was opened by a slim man around the fifty mark, also dressed in a suit, only this guy looked dangerous. He had a devious face and lucid eyes. When he saw me, he moved towards me with his hand outstretched.

"Sean Scully," he said.

"Paddy Buckley, from Gallagher's," I said, shaking his hand.

Sean nodded towards the door he'd come out of and led the way in.

This was the test. This was make or break. I was about to meet the man whose picture I'd seen in the paper a hundred times, the man whose very name instilled fear throughout the city, the man who, by all accounts, never missed a trick. And I didn't doubt it. My salvation, I hoped, would be served through my removed state.

I walked through the door, moved to the center of the room, and waited. It was a big study with mahogany paneling, chesterfield couches and chairs in front of the fireplace, a large antique desk by the window, and a bookshelf lining one of the walls. The room was lit solely by daylight.

"This is Paddy Buckley," said Sean, before sitting down on a seat in front of the desk.

Vincent, who'd been standing by the fireplace, stepped forward and clamped his hand around mine, which nearly disappeared in his. He was a big man in his late forties. He wore a suit with an open-necked shirt, and he smelled of oil, leather, and menace. His broad forehead was underpinned by hard-boiled black eyes and an equanimity loaded with malice and fortitude.

"All right, Paddy," he said.

"Hello," I said with a nod.

"Sit down."

I sat down in the chair beside Sean's, took out an arrangement form that I placed on my closed briefcase, and uncapped my pen. Vincent moved behind the desk but remained standing. He stayed there saying nothing for a few moments, just jingling the change in his pockets. The two men looked directly at me with no emotion, no apparent expectation, just indifference. I was a little thrown. Usually, I'd be the one opening the proceedings as people would have no clue where to start—I was the one with the questions after all—but with Vincent Cullen, I thought it would be wiser to wait to be dealt with. I observed all this from just above the three of us, where the top of the wall met the ceiling.

"How long are you in this game?" said Vincent eventually.

"The undertaking?"

Vincent nodded.

"Twenty-odd years," I said. Vincent nodded again while continuing to look at me.

"Right," he said softly, and then as an afterthought: "Will you have a cup of coffee, Paddy?"

"Yeah . . . thank you," I said. Vincent glanced at Sean, who got up and left the room, and then he stayed standing for another few moments before sitting down in his chair, relaxing a little.

"There's going to be a lot of publicity surrounding this funeral. I want everything to go off smoothly with complete precision. Understood?"

"Yes," I said, my pen still at the ready. Sean came back into the room and sat back down. From my aerial perspective, I could see that the top of Sean's head was practically bald; only the little tuft on top gave the illusion that his hair was only receding.

"Now, you want to ask me a few questions," said Vincent.

"Just a few details I need. Now, when were you thinking of having the funeral?"

"Thursday. We'll go to the church Wednesday evening."

"Okay. Do you want ten or eleven o'clock Mass on the Thursday morning, in Pius X, is it?"

"Twelve o'clock in the Pro-Cathedral."

"Right," I said, making a note of everything. "Mr. Cullen, your brother is lying in St. James's at the moment; do you want to have the removal from Donal's house or would you prefer to use the funeral home?"

"The funeral home. I want complete privacy while Donal is there; no other funerals are to be going out of the place. Clear?"

"Absolutely," I said. The young man in the tracksuit who'd opened the door to me came in carrying a tray with a cup of instant coffee on it. He placed it on the table beside me.

"Do you want milk?" he said.

"Just a little sugar," I said, and added it myself from the bowl on the tray.

"Thanks, Richie," said Sean, and Richie left us.

"How old is Donal?" I asked, looking at Vincent, having no problem watching myself keep my composure.

"Forty-one" came the answer.

"Is he married?"

"Yes."

I wondered where the wife was, as, technically, she was chief mourner, but I didn't question it.

"Does he have any children?"

"No."

"Did you think about a death notice for the paper?"

"That's taken care of," said Sean.

"Right," I said. "There's an offering for the church, it's usually two hundred—"

"Make it a grand," said Vincent, cutting me off. I wrote down the details as the two men continued to stare at me.

Before I could get another question in, Vincent started tapping the desk with the nail of his index finger, slowly and deliberately. I decided against asking anything further and waited. From my perched position, I looked at Sean to see his reaction, but he was giving nothing away, wearing the expression of a man fishing happily on a lake.

"Tell me about the embalming, Paddy," said Vincent.

"What do you want to know about it?"

"The process, how it works."

"Well, basically, it's a small injection to delay the decomposition of the remains."

Vincent just looked at me, letting the ticking of his desk clock punctuate the silence.

"A small injection," he repeated back to me.

"Yeah," I said.

"Save the granny speech, Paddy, and tell me how it fucking works." There wasn't the slightest change of emotion in Vincent's voice. Sean was almost smiling, looking at me while barely nodding his head, as much as to say, *Spit it out there, man, we're not precious.*

These were the kind of details nobody needed to know and even fewer wanted to know. A frank, unvarnished explanation would be upsetting to most people, especially when the imagined remains in the conversation was their relative; plus, the sugar-coated one-liner that I'd just proffered usually sufficed whenever a family member asked about the process. But these were no ordinary family members. These were guys who didn't mind killing people to get what they wanted, and they dealt in nearly as much death as I did. To them, death was part of the deal. Besides, who was I to deny Vincent Cullen?

"All right. The process happens in three stages. First of all, you've got to find one of the body's six main accessible arteries. There's one just on the inside of each upper arm near the armpit, there's another on either side of the neck, and another at the top end of each leg, just beside the groin. The underarm ones are what you'd usually work off. You make an incision a little over an inch long, find the artery, and cut an opening in it. You then put in an L-shaped tube pointed in towards the body and tie it off with a bit of ligature. Through that tube, you inject what we call arterial fluid, which is a pink chemical formula that clears any discoloration in the skin, like at the end of the fingernails or at the back of the neck or the ears, wherever the blood might have collected. The arterial fluid clears that away completely; you can actually see the collected blood disappearing. This is all being pumped around the artery system by an electric pump. After that's cleared—"

"How long does that take?" said Sean, no longer almost smiling but focusing fully, along with Vincent, on what I was telling them.

"Not long, maybe ten, fifteen minutes, depending on the condition and size of the remains. After that, you stitch up the arm and get out the trocar, which is a long, hollow, needlelike instrument about two feet long and twice as thick as a pen with three or four little holes at the pointed end of it. If you were to draw a triangle using the base of the sternum and the navel as the base and draw the top over the body's left side, the top of that triangle is where you make the incision with the trocar. The electric pump that the trocar is connected to by a long tube is now turned to vacuum. You puncture all the vital organs with the trocar and remove the blood, which works its way through the pump machine and out through another tube into a five-liter glass jar. You get the most blood out of the heart and lungs, and the rest of it from the abdominal and thoracic cavities. When you've finished that, you disconnect the trocar from the electric pump and attach a pint bottle of formaldehyde to the end of the tube and briefly go through the organs again, emptying the bottle, letting the formaldehyde work its way into them, putting a stop to any further decomposition . . . and that's basically it. After that, you could have the remains on display for months if you wanted to."

"When you puncture the organs, does it take much effort?" said Vincent. He asked as if he'd done it before and was looking to have his procedural style validated.

"Yeah, you've got to get your back into it," I said.

Vincent gently pinched the stubble on his chin while continuing to look at me, along with Sean, both apparently grateful for the candid explanation.

I watched myself sitting with them from my viewpoint up at the ceiling, and as Vincent seemed to navigate our meeting into another pocket of silence, I let my attention wander.

Down in a darkened corner at the other end of the room, I noticed a shimmering, like a pair of orange jewels. After another moment, it became clear what it was: a dog curled up like a sleeping fox but with open eyes that glimmered.

For the first time since I'd been in my dislocated state, I felt enveloped by a rush of fear, not because I'd sighted the dog, but because the dog had sighted me in my suspended, shifted state and appeared to have been looking at me there for quite some time.

And then, as if I were inhabiting two spaces at once, I felt the disconcerting sensation of shifting uncomfortably in my chair and being slapped back into my body simultaneously. I tried to repeat my dislocating trick but couldn't. I was locked inside my skin again. The shock of the sudden change brought about the beginnings of a panic attack, which I found almost impossible to mask.

How could the dog have spotted me, and was there even a dog there in the first place? Compelled to check, I turned around in my seat and looked to the end of the room where I saw the same dog rising to its feet, staring at me now, at my face, in my chair.

I turned back around to Vincent, who'd noticed the change in me and was quite at home in the silence again. Even though I'd been sitting here all along, being this close to Vincent in the firing line of his stare was a new experience, and a very unsettling one. Sean, too, seemed to be studying me, wondering where my panic had come from.

The dog, up on all fours now, walked over to my chair. Still looking into my eyes, it began to sniff around my face, its snout twitching from side to side. I'd never seen a dog like it. Its eyes had an almost human aspect to them, only with something stranger still. And its markings were unusual: rusty like a fox, with a white chest and bushy tail, but with an added blackness through its coat. It was bigger than a fox, reminding me more of a wolf, but clearly it was neither. The dog's nose was now an inch from my cheekbone.

Even as it invaded my space, I didn't mind the dog so much; in fact, I'd always had a great affinity with dogs. It was being back in my body with my fear and guilt and pounding heart, and being this close to Vincent with his penetrating gaze, that had brought on the panic.

I could feel the sweat collecting at the top of my brow and dripping down both sides of my face, which I wanted to wipe off, but didn't dare.

"What's the story with the dog?" I said, still looking at its ever-watchful eyes.

Nobody said anything for another minute or so, and I had no more questions to ask.

"She's smelling your fear, Paddy," said Vincent, practically in a whisper. "Dechtire," he said. "By my side."

The dog licked its lips and moved to Vincent's side.

My eyes darted from the dog to Vincent, to Sean, and back down to my briefcase. I could hear how irregular my breathing was, and I was squirming in my seat. I took out the coffin catalog, which I held out to Vincent, whose gaze now lowered to my trembling hand. Each moment was getting worse. As I tried to control the shaking in my hand, Sean reached over and took the catalog from me with a slight mocking smile and slowly started leafing through the pages, never once looking down at them, but continuing to stare at me all the while.

Desperate, I looked to the floor, feeling the burning heat of Vincent's disapproval along with my shame and the river of sweat collecting on my collar. As irrational as I knew it was, I was convinced that somehow Vincent knew I'd mowed his brother down and that he was about to announce it to me. I waited, knowing full well the funeral arrangements we were making had come to a grinding halt.

When Vincent spoke, he spoke much slower than he had up to this point.

"We'll come down to the funeral home later, Paddy, and finish the arrangements then. All right?"

"Okay," I said, my mouth so dry I'd whispered the word. I accepted the catalog back from Sean and put the arrangement sheet away. Both Vincent and Sean were on their feet before I'd closed the briefcase. Sean held the door open as I walked out of the room with my head bowed, and then he closed it behind me.

I felt like I'd just been squeezed through a mangle. Was this what I'd been reduced to: a muddled, sleep-deprived mental patient with the biggest secret in Dublin? I couldn't keep it to myself any longer. I had to tell someone.

THIRTEEN

10:50 a.m.

I closed the door to the back office behind me and sank to my knees, gripping my hair in despair. Vincent Cullen was going to check up on me, that was a certainty. I could only hope he'd write me off as a pathetic loser, but after my panicky display in his study, how far would his suspicions extend? I'd never felt guiltier than I had in his study, and there was no explanation for my collapse into panic, unless he'd put it down to the dog. Maybe he'd just request to have somebody else run the funeral. But considering the way my luck had been going, I wasn't expecting him to let me off the hook.

I needed to talk to Christy, to tell him what I'd done, to share the burden of my horrible crime, which I hoped would alleviate some of the mortal fear I found so impossible to shake. The relief of owning up, of admitting the truth, couldn't be mine. It was a road I knew I couldn't go down. Never in my life had I shirked the blame when it was mine. I'd always put my hand up no matter how severe the repercussions would be. But now something had changed in me. I don't know if fear had taken hold of my soul or if I was frightened by the hellish consequences I'd face if I admitted everything. I only knew that with the Lucy Wright situation and the far larger one of Donal Cullen, both of which I was one hundred percent culpable, I couldn't take the rap. It would destroy me.

Corrine arrived in with an empty cup and stopped in her tracks. I was no longer sweating like I'd been up in Cullen's house, but I still must have looked like I'd run all the way from Stephen's Green.

"Are you all right?" she said.

I took out a cigarette and lit it.

"I'll be all right in a minute," I said. Corrine was a smart woman. She didn't ask questions. She kept to herself and never got involved in anyone's dramas, preferring instead to live her life privately away from the land of funerals.

"If you mind the phones for me, I'll make you a cup of tea," she said.

"Deal," I said, and moved out towards the front office.

"Oh, and Paddy!" she shouted after me. I cocked my ear. "Eddie Daly was on. Lucy Wright is clear."

"Great," I said. Incredible how inconsequential it seemed now beside the Cullen conundrum. Granted, Lucy's death was on my head, but the price for my crime, had I been made pay, would have been my reputation. Not my life.

I popped my head into the middle office to see Christy on a call. I signaled for him to join me when he was finished, and then went to answer the ringing phone in the front office.

"Gallagher's Funerals, good morning," I said.

The voice on the other end was frantic.

"Hello, who am I speaking to, please?" It was an English accent, and familiar.

"Paddy Buckley here."

"Oh, yes, Paddy. I talked to you yesterday . . . this is Derek Kershaw in Manchester . . ."

"Everything all right, Derek?"

"No . . . no, I'm finished. I'm afraid I've made the most dreadful mistake . . ."

"What happened?" I said.

"I've sent you the wrong body . . ."

"That's not good, Derek. The Hayes family is expecting him up at the funeral home at lunchtime. How soon can you organize a flight?"

"No, it's quite irredeemable . . . there's another remains whose people didn't want a funeral at all, just a straightforward cremation without a service . . . she had no family, just a nephew who hardly knew her . . ."

Kershaw had been drinking and was slurring his words.

"Derek, can you organize a flight today?" I said clearly.

"I've not only sent you the wrong body," said Kershaw, in tears now, "I've cremated your man . . ."

Something inside me came alive. Ordinarily, this would have been enough to send the whole office into complete turmoil, me included, but a deep equanimity took a grip of me in an instant, and for the first time since I fell back into my body at Vincent Cullen's, it felt like I belonged in my skin again.

In every industry, horrible things go wrong every day, things incendiary enough to close down a business; and more times than not, somebody manages to keep a lid on it; and nobody the wiser. By some crazy cosmic decree, this happened to be a week full of lightning strikes in the same place, and I, for some unfathomable reason, was attracting them. Yet paradoxically, instead of being fried to a crisp, I'd been thrown into the eye of the storm.

I listened to Kershaw's defeated whimpering in my ear. I looked at the crimson wool fabric on the carpet. I watched Corrine's hand steadily place the mug of tea down on the desk in front of me. And I saw the grandfather clock keeping time as it had for forty years in exactly the same place.

It was then that I realized everything was perfect.

I turned away from Corrine, who'd just answered another call, and lowered my voice.

"Derek, let me understand you. You sent us the wrong body and the Hayes remains we were expecting you've cremated in Manchester. Is that it?" I asked in a calm, level voice.

"That's it," Derek whispered.

"Who knows about this?"

"No one, just my son and I," he said.

Christy came in from the middle office and sat down in front of me.

"Right, keep it to yourselves. Tell no one. Can you do that?"

"Yes, but what good—"

I cut him off. "Just give me an hour. Don't do anything or tell anyone. Sit tight. I'll ring you back in an hour." I put down the phone.

"What's going on?" said Christy, with a lowering brow.

I winked for his complicity.

"Corrine," I said, "has the Hayes remains been delivered?"

"It's in the side parlor," she said, sipping her tea while studying the *Times*'s Simplex crossword.

Christy followed me into the side parlor where the closed Hayes coffin rested on a bier. I closed the door behind us and spoke very quietly.

"Now, I need you to keep a level head and your mouth shut when I tell you this."

"What?"

"Kershaw has cremated Dermot Hayes in Manchester."

"Stop it," said Christy.

"I'm telling you," I said.

"None of your fucking messing now, Buckley," said Christy defensively, but he knew by my eyes that I was serious. He brought his hand to his head and sat slowly down on the couch.

"Mother of fuck," he said, before looking at me suddenly. "Who's he sent us?"

Within a minute, we had the screws out. I lifted the lid off the coffin and we looked inside. It was a plump old woman in her eighties, minus her dentures.

"Oh, Jesus," said Christy. "What the fuck are we going to do?"

"Keep it down."

"Paddy, this could close us down. Do you realize that?"

"No, it couldn't. It could close Kershaw down. Now, if you relax for a minute, we can make it so nobody gets closed down."

Christy wasn't one bit happy.

"How are we going to do that, Buckley?"

FRANK GALLAGHER SPENT a large part of each day up in his office, writing letters, doing the books, and looking after business in general. He was involved in a handful of community projects around the areas in Dublin he had funeral homes, as well as being a prominent figure in the national and international funeral associations he belonged to. He took these involvements seriously and gave them considerable time and energy.

In contrast to Vincent Cullen's dark mahogany study, Frank's office was oak paneled and well lit, with paintings of monasteries hanging on the walls along with framed black-and-white photographs of state funerals of prime ministers and presidents the firm had handled over the years. Frank was fond of smoking cigarillos while up there, often spending the day working under the slow-moving layers of smoke they lent the room. The baroque music he had playing in the background—Bach—put the finishing touch to the atmosphere he found best for letter writing, which was what he was in the middle of when I knocked on his door.

"Come in," said Frank.

I leaned my head in.

"Frank, just to tell you, I've had a look at the Hayes remains from Manchester, and it's a closed coffin."

He looked up from his letter for the first time.

"There's nothing Eamonn can do, no?"

"No," I said. "Tissue gas has set in. It's definitely a closed case."

"Okay, get on to the family and advise them accordingly."

"Will do," I said, and left him in the smoke.

FOURTEEN

11:45 a.m.

Christy and I stood outside the Hayeses' pebbledash house with its hodgepodge of round and square windows, waiting to be let in. Christy looked like he had the weight of Dublin's troubles on his shoulders. It was going to be a big funeral, and they'd expressed how much they wanted an open coffin, and Christy had wanted to make all their wishes come true.

"What has you so relaxed?" he said accusingly.

"It's a closed coffin," I assured him.

"This mightn't wash at all," he said to the ground.

The door was opened by old Mr. Hayes, a bull of a man in his early seventies.

"Ah, Christy," he said warmly. "Come in."

We followed him inside and were led straight into the living room where the whole family was gathered to remember Dermot, twelve of them in all, every one of them an adult. Our visit was unannounced and they were wondering what we were doing there.

"Sit down, lads," said old Mr. Hayes. Christy sat down on the arm of the couch while I stayed back at the wall. It was Christy's funeral, so it was up to him to sell it. Often there were times when a family would be advised to have a closed coffin for genuine reasons, and they nearly always took the advice. But if a family insisted on an open coffin, it was their call at the end of the day, and who were we to stand in their way? We were just there to advise them, only today we had to go beyond advising them: We had to convince them.

"Will you have a cup of tea?" said old Mr. Hayes.

"No, no," said Christy. "Just a quick word and we'll be on our way."

"There's no problem, is there?" said the old man.

"Well, I wouldn't . . . no, there's no problem, but we've just collected your son's remains from the airport, and . . . well, we've had a look at the body and it's not really suitable for viewing . . ."

"What are you saying, son?" said old Mr. Hayes.

"Well, we're here to recommend having a closed coffin. It's our opinion that you'd be better off remembering your son as he was. It would be extremely distressing to do otherwise," Christy said plainly.

The change in the room was immediate and severe. Some of them moved around on their feet like they'd been hit with news of another death. Others just looked at Christy with resentment. As if it was something he'd done.

"I've come home from Brussels for this," said one of the sons, an executive type who'd done well for himself. "It's Dermot, Dad, he's dead, and we're expecting him to look dead. The coffin stays open."

The mother started whimpering in her chair.

"Thomas," she said to her husband, "I have to see him." The old man put his hand on his wife's shoulder.

"What's the problem exactly, Christy?" he said.

"To be perfectly frank with you, tissue gas is the problem," said Christy. "Rapid deterioration and swelling of the body and severe discoloration of the skin . . ."

"I don't care what he looks like," said a determined sister. "I'm saying goodbye to him, Dad."

Then they all started. Christy just sat there with his head getting shinier while the noise in the room got louder and more aggrieved. He snuck a glance at me that said it all: *We're fucked.*

In any arrangement situation, you learn pretty quickly who you're talking to. Very often you find yourself in a roomful of family members, all of them adults, and nine times out of ten, there's just one person making the decisions. Sometimes it takes a few minutes to figure out who it is, other times it's clear immediately. In the Hayes house there was only one boss, and with everyone directing their pleas in his direction, there was no figuring out to be done. I leaned in close to old Mr. Hayes and whispered in his ear.

"Mr. Hayes, may I have a word with you outside?"

"Certainly, son," said the old man. I nodded to Christy briefly before he and I walked out of the room ahead of old Mr. Hayes, leaving them all silenced behind us.

It was a small house, and I needed privacy with the old man. Without any prompting, he led us out of the little hallway into the kitchen before closing the door behind us. This was delicate ground and, to an extent, sacred. I had to be careful with what I said, as whatever picture he bought into would stay with him for the rest of his days. *Tread softly,* I told myself.

"I'm the embalmer," I said. "Now, it's your call, let me say that before I tell you anything, but before you make a decision, I think you need to be fully abreast of the situation. I've worked with Gallagher's all my life. I've buried my father and my wife, so believe me, I know the territory well, not to mention how important this is to you. But I also know what viewing a remains in Dermot's state can do to a family. Christy mentioned that tissue gas has set in. It has and it's at an advanced stage. When that happens, there's nothing anyone can do to stop it. There's no process to arrest it, embalming can do nothing. To give you an example of how drastic the change in appearance is, just a few years ago I buried the brother of a retired army captain from Inchicore. Tissue gas had set into his brother's remains and it was a nasty case, so bad that the body had blown up like a balloon and the skin had turned a putrid green. The face had split open and gangrenous flesh had been exposed. I implored the captain to have a closed coffin, but he insisted on having it open, convinced he knew better. After seeing the state of his brother's remains, he demanded that the coffin be closed at once and afterwards developed a twitch under his right eye."

Old Mr. Hayes winced while he listened.

"Now, I simply can't dissuade you enough, but if you insist on coming down yourself to decide, then so be it. But please understand that the dignity of the dead stops me from describing the state of Dermot's remains to you. I can only appeal to your higher sense to treasure your memories of him as they are. It's your decision, Mr. Hayes."

The old man held his emotion while he reluctantly shook his head, gripping my arm with gratitude.

"I don't know how you do your job, son. Fair play to you." He wiped his face briefly and then walked back inside to his family. Christy and I waited out in the hallway with our ears pricked up.

"There'll be no further discussion," declared the old man. "The coffin is staying shut."

FIFTEEN

12:20 p.m.

With all of the problems I had on my mind, it was a blessing to have been able to put the Hayes predicament into check and refreshing not to have been morally compromised by the circumstances. To choose between the Hayeses having their already upside-down world turned inside out and being able to bury their son and grieve normally was no choice at all. We'd prevented a disaster, enabled the proper path of grief, and saved a man's livelihood in the bargain. But Dermot Hayes's coffin wasn't in the ground yet.

I had promised to get over to Brigid Wright to pick up her parents' clothes, but the Cullens and Hayeses had kept me from her. And now I'd Kershaw to assuage before I could do anything.

I opened the Hayes sheet in the comfort of the middle office and dialed Kershaw's number. He answered it himself after one ring.

"Hello, Kershaw's?" He was a little less frantic but no less relaxed, and still drunk.

"Derek, it's Paddy Buckley here."

"Yes?"

"You're clear, as long as you don't mind sending out that other crowd the wrong ashes."

"... What?"

"I've convinced the Hayes family to have a closed-coffin funeral. Now, as it stands here, Christy Boylan and I are the only ones who know about it, is it still yourself and your son who know about it at your end?"

"Yes, yes, it is, oh, my God ... how did you ... thank you ... thank you ..." Kershaw was overwhelmed with relief.

The door opened and in popped Christy, pointing out front urgently.

"Vincent Cullen's standing out there with two of his men."

"Listen, Derek, I've another family here, I've got to go. Remember, not a word to anyone. Good luck."

I put the phone down and exhaled. I'd planned on getting up to Brigid Wright before dealing with Cullen, but I could scratch that now. She'd have to wait.

I checked myself for the fear. The experience with the Hayeses had given me some of my confidence back, and getting the all clear on Lucy Wright's postmortem had also given me a boost. Even still, I'd be better equipped to deal with Cullen if I could get out of my skin again. But I'd no time to try that. I had to meet him in the flesh.

Vincent Cullen stood in front of the main desk, wearing an overcoat like his brother's, while Sean Scully and Richie flanked him.

"Mr. Cullen," I said as I approached them, noticing that the menace I'd seen earlier on was largely absent now, replaced by an unexpected warmth that seemed to be directed at me.

"Nobody calls me Mr. Cullen, Paddy. It's Vincent."

"Vincent," I said, never happier to be on first-name terms with anyone. "Come and I'll show you the coffins."

Leaving his men behind, Vincent followed me out past the back office into the selection room where the range of coffins and caskets were mounted and on display. He walked up and down each line of coffins, considering each one as if he were a furniture critic, and then stopped at the most expensive casket in the room.

"You had a situation in here a while back, a few lads in trying to scam Gallagher's son," he said, letting the words hang in the room. Then I saw him smile for the first time. "I heard you sorted it out fairly nicely."

I had no clue where he'd been getting his information from, but whoever had filled him in had done a top-class job.

"It's true," I said, wondering what else he knew.

He turned to the oak casket.

"This Irish?"

"Yes, it is, down from County Louth. Solid oak," I said.

"That's the one then, in the mahogany. Now show me the parlor," he said, walking out of the room ahead of me.

While Vincent looked over the front parlor, I sat down on the couch to take down the remaining details I needed.

"Vincent, did you think about transport on the removal and funeral?"

Vincent continued to face the painting on the wall he was inspecting, depicting fishermen at sea at night dealing with a violent storm.

"Five limousines for both days," he said, moving on to take a closer look at a marble-topped table.

"And what about clothes, do you want Donal dressed in a suit?"

"Yeah, call by in the morning and I'll have it ready for you." He was back on the move again, only now his focus was on me.

"I've a question for you now," he said, placing his right foot up on the bier in the center of the room. I looked up from the arrangement sheet to see him no longer smiling.

"You were in An Capall Dubh last night, weren't you?"

I got flashes of being in his study with him earlier, awash with fear.

"Yeah, I was," I said.

"Didn't see any strangers there, did you, maybe someone who looked out of place?"

The memories rushed at me: the old guys at the bar; Gerry pulling pints; the crunching thump of Donal hitting the windscreen.

"No. Just the usual crowd, you know."

Vincent sat himself down beside me on the couch, taking up more than his fair share of space, stretching his arm so it reached around my shoulder and crossing his legs in such a way that his foot leaned against my shin. I tried to remain calm, but I was unnerved by how close he was to me.

"And what time did you leave at?" he said softly.

"Jesus, you've got me thinking now," I said. "What time would it have been? It must have been about half nine or ten."

"And straight home to bed then, yeah?" said Vincent, almost whispering, well aware of how close he was to me.

". . . Yeah, I went home then," I said hesitantly.

"Good," said Vincent, and he smiled again before rising to his feet.

"I hear you've got a syndicate going here," he said. If it had been anyone else, I would have shown my astonishment and asked how they knew, but this was Vincent Cullen. If he'd told me my wife's maiden name at this stage I wouldn't have been surprised.

"Yeah," I said. "We like to keep an eye on the horses."

"Well, I'll give you a winner you won't need your pals for. Liberty Girl, running down the Curragh on Saturday week, a rank outsider."

The extent of the U-turn was profound and unexpected, considering my earlier performance with him. Still, I was intrigued to know who he'd talked to.

"Liberty Girl, thank you."

Vincent smiled magnanimously. I appreciated the spirit of the gesture; it wasn't every day I got a tip like that. I walked out ahead of him into the front office only to see Frank entering the office from the corridor.

"Paddy." He smiled regretfully. "I heard about the flat tire."

I was taken off guard. "Huh?"

"Three o'clock this morning after the bring-back . . ."

Vincent appeared behind me, making Frank instantly raise his hand in apology.

"Oh, I didn't realize you were with Mr. Cullen, I beg your pardon," said Frank, and he continued on towards Corrine's desk.

I turned around to face Vincent, whose eyes were darkening with anger.

"What's this about three o'clock this morning?" he said evenly.

"Just part of the job. I didn't want to bother you with details of other funerals—it's something I never do. I had to bring a remains back from a nursing home last night, a call that came in well after hours, and when I got back, I had a flat."

Every word I'd just told him was true and I knew he could feel it.

"That Merc yours?" he said.

"No, it's Frank Gallagher's."

"What do you drive?"

"A Renault Clio," I said, deadpan.

"Out in the yard, is it?"

"It is, yeah."

The change in Vincent hadn't been picked up by Corrine or Frank, but his men were watching us like a couple of surveillance cameras. No doubt they were well used to the implications of such a shift in their boss's behavior. I wasn't used to the silent staring games, but neither was I nervous because I knew I'd been truthful with him except for the omission of details of the bring-back, which I believed he appreciated.

"I'll be on to you," said Vincent, before turning and walking out the front door, his men following after him.

Frank looked up from his desk. "Well?"

"A hearse and five for removal and funeral, and a mahogany casket."

"Excellent," he said.

SIXTEEN

2:15 p.m.

I'd been through half the coffins in the loft by the time Jack wandered up, and I still hadn't found a casket for the Cullen job. Ninety-odd percent of the funerals we did were furnished with coffins rather than caskets, the latter being significantly more expensive, but we still stocked them. And I couldn't find one anywhere. Of all the funerals I'd ever looked after, there was none I could less afford to balls up than Cullen's.

"Are you looking for a flat-lid for that houser?" said Jack.

"No," I said, "a mahogany casket for Cullen."

"You won't find a mahogany casket up here," said Jack. "The last one went out in August."

"Don't tell me that, Jack."

"We've oak caskets, there's one up in the selection room, but no mahoganies."

I pulled out my phone and sat down by the workbench, in need of a very good turn. I punched in the numbers and waited.

"Hello, Conway's," said a deep male voice in a County Louth accent.

"Liam, it's Paddy Buckley here from Gallagher's."

"What can I do for you, Paddy?"

"Sorry to be asking you at this stage of the day, Liam, but I've a big favor to ask."

"What do you need?"

"A mahogany casket."

"Today?"

"Today."

"Out of the question. I'll be heading across to the UK early Friday morning with a load, I could drop one into you then."

"Nah, it's today I need it . . ."

"Sorry, Paddy, not happening."

"It's for Vincent Cullen's brother," I said, knowing well the effect it would have.

Silence of the golden kind.

"Why didn't you tell me it was for Cullen in the first place, you prick?" said Liam. "I'll be down this evening with it."

"Thanks, Liam. See you later." I might as well have said *abracadabra*.

I pulled out my smokes and mused on the black-and-white nude on the wardrobe, her Rubenesque figure and comely smile the antidote to many an ail. But not mine. Here I was, up in the loft with Jack, whose sole noble concern was tacking a crucifix and nameplate onto old Harry's coffin, while my own mind was filled with maintaining deceptions. Brigid Wright was still waiting for me, I knew, and I felt a growing reluctance to go out to her. I was out of the woods with her mother's autopsy; she'd never be made to suffer the truth now of Lucy's far from romantic exit. Yet still I faltered. I was attracted to Brigid, deeply attracted to her, but I knew I wouldn't be able to pour out to her what she'd stirred inside me. However attractive she was, I could never build something special on foundations of duplicity.

And on top of that, as well as my second meeting with Cullen had gone, I still felt a burning need to confess to Christy what I'd done.

"Jack, can you do something for me?"

"Sure," said Jack, ever willing to help anyone out.

"I have to go up to Walkinstown to see the Hayes family. Could you head around to Pembroke Lane and pick clothes up for me?"

"Certainly," said Jack. "Now?"

"If you can, Jack, yeah. They're for Michael and Lucy Wright. Their daughter will be there. Tell her I'll see her when I bring their remains out this evening at half six or so."

When Jack had started in the yard, I'd given him enough money to get him going in the syndicate, and no matter how many times I told him to, he never forgot it, claiming me afterwards as his number one ally. He rubbed his hands together as if relishing the task.

"I'll leave them in the embalming room for you," he said.

CHRISTY WAS SO NERVOUS he was chewing the inside of his bottom lip. The Hayeses agreeing to a closed coffin had sent him into a terribly stressed state, and he wouldn't be able to sit still till the grave was filled in. As Christy saw it, I was the cause of his trouble. I'd shifted the blame from Kershaw to ourselves and, in doing so, had gone against the grain and raised Christy's blood pressure considerably. He gripped the wheel tightly as we drove up Windmill Road. Never a better time to take his mind off it.

"I've something I'm going to tell you, and when I say you have to keep this to yourself, I mean you can never tell another soul, all right?"

"Right," said Christy.

"I knocked Donal Cullen down last night and killed him."

Christy stayed looking at the road ahead while a sarcastic curl took hold of his mouth.

"You're in flying form, Buckley. It's lovely to see you back in the game, but I've had enough of your bollocks for one day."

I turned around in my seat.

"Christy, I'm serious. After you left me last night, I headed home through Kilmainham, and when I drove down James's Street, I hit him."

"Fuck off," said Christy, not having a bit of it.

"Christy, I'm deadly fucking serious. Look at me," I said. He turned his head briefly to smile at me then turned back to the road.

"You won't get me, Paddy, no matter how hard you try, so give it up, I'm not buying it."

"I didn't have my lights on, and I was shattered tired. I was tuning the radio; I'd taken my eyes off the road . . . I didn't even see him."

"You've put some thought into it anyway, fair play to you, but fuck right off, Buckley, you're beginning to annoy me."

With Christy in this mood, there was no talking to him. I'd have to take another tack.

OF GALLAGHER'S six premises, the funeral home in Walkinstown was the busiest. Purpose-built in the seventies and freestanding on the corner of a busy intersection, it had become a landmark in Dublin 12 and was known to everyone within a five-mile radius as Gallagher's corner. We'd come up to make sure the Hayes coffin stayed shut and to make the family feel fussed over.

During the three days it usually takes to have an Irish funeral, a family's emotions are prone to peaking at a number of stages, and the triggers that precipitate these crescendos are well defined and known to anyone working in the trade. One of the more pronounced ones is when the coffin is removed from the funeral home or house or hospital and put in the back of the hearse and taken to the church. When the coffin is open with the family sitting around the parlor and the undertaker comes in to tell them it's time to go, knowing that this is the last time they'll ever see their loved one, the emotional upheaval that follows can be quite upsetting to witness, never mind experience. And it's not unusual for family members of an emotionally delicate disposition to throw their arms around their loved one, sometimes even trying to pull them out of the coffin, often screaming proclamations of undying love, unbreakable bonds, and intentions of following soon after.

The danger with the Hayeses was that at the last minute, if the father was momentarily absent, the mother or one of the sons or daughters would get their way and have the coffin opened. Usually we stayed out of the parlor to give the family as much privacy as possible, but on this occasion, we stayed at the back of the room for the duration of the family's time in the funeral home. To my relief and particularly to Christy's, not a word was said to us, and old Mr. Hayes's order went unchallenged.

We were due at the Assumption church in Walkinstown at five o'clock. At five minutes to the hour, we carried the coffin out of the parlor and placed it in the back of the hearse, Christy visibly relaxing as he firmly shut the back door and knocked on the side of the hearse to send it on its way. The Hayes family, tucked in the back of their limousines, was ferried down to the church behind the hearse. Their focus was safely on their grief and the coming prayers, well away now from the fact that they were denied their open-coffined farewell.

I'D TOLD CHRISTY I needed to pick something up at home, knowing full well there was nothing else I could say to him that would convince him of my guilt. He pulled up outside my house.

"Come in for a minute, I've something I want to show you."

"Buckley, if this is more of your messing—"

"Christy, I want to *show* you something . . . all right?"

Reluctantly, he gave in to the sense being made to him.

"Fair enough," he said.

I led him in through the kitchen and down the step into the darkened garage, and turned on the light. There was my Camry. If he'd seen a child getting shot beside him, it could hardly have had a more profound effect on Christy's composure. He winced as he slowly placed one hand on his belly and the other to his mouth. The shattered windscreen sparkled like a thousand diamonds in front of us, and the bonnet was even more crumpled than I remembered. Christy just looked at me, bereft of anything to say. All he could do was look increasingly pained.

"I didn't see him. I didn't even brake till after I'd hit him," I said.

"Jesus H. Christ," said Christy, saying each syllable with whispered emphasis. "Did you stop?"

"Of course I did. I got out and leaned down over him to see was he breathing, but he was gone. He died instantly, I'd say. I took out his wallet, which was hanging out of his coat, and it was then I saw his name. Now there was no way I was hanging around there—"

"Fuck no," said Christy emphatically.

"For what, a slow death? Accident or no accident, Cullen would have me killed. No thanks. I got back in my car, left the lights off, and came back here. And I didn't sleep a wink. Not a wink."

"And nobody saw you?"

"I don't think so. I looked around and the street looked as dead as he was. When I was nearly out of sight, somebody rushed out of a building to his side, but he couldn't have seen me or got the reg."

"Holy fucking Mary," Christy said to the car. "And what about Cullen, how are you getting on with him?"

There was a part of me that wanted to tell Christy about my Independent Channel 24 experience. My father had taught only me about it, and I'd never shared my knowledge of it with anyone. Even though it had taken up quite a bit of the last twelve hours and had in some ways been my saving grace, telling Christy about it now, on top of what he was already struggling under, would be unfair and unnecessary.

"Started off shaky when I went up to the house. Man, was I scared in there, but then when he came down to the yard, he was all over me, like best buddies. I don't think he knows, though."

"Paddy, you wouldn't be standing here talking to me if the man knew. But if you get as much as a dirty look, skate the fuck out of town immediately."

"I already got one."

"What?"

"Frank nearly let it out earlier on," I said.

"Does Frank know?"

"No, he doesn't, but he came into the front office talking about me getting that flat at three in the morning after me telling Cullen that I went straight home after the pub . . . and Cullen overheard it."

"So what you tell Cullen?"

"I told him it was part of the job and I didn't want to bring him in on other funerals I was looking after."

"Did you tell him you were in the pub?"

"No, he told me, that's what has me shaking. The fucker knows everything."

Christy's shock was now replaced by deep concern.

"You should never have made those arrangements, Paddy. What possessed you to go up?"

"I don't know, Frank insisted on it, and I felt strange this morning, and numb, so numb I couldn't feel a thing, so I just went up. I was getting on grand till I spotted his dog at the end of the room, and whatever that did to me, it put an end to my numbness. All I could feel then was panic and fear."

"Fear of the dog?"

"No, of Cullen and the other guy in the room, Sean Scully, who were both playing silent staring games, and I had this notion that I couldn't shake that Cullen somehow knew that I'd killed his brother and was about to tell me . . . it was terrible, my whole body was trembling and I was sweating like a horse."

"Paddy, call in sick, that's what you do, I'll look after the rest of it for you."

It was comforting to have Christy's understanding and concern, but that's all he or anyone else could give me.

"No, he'd seek me out, I know he would. And this is where he'd come to," I said, indicating the car. "I've no choice but to see it through."

Christy's eyes widened behind his glasses as it sunk in that this wasn't a family like the Hayeses, whose trusting nature could be manipulated. We were dealing with the violent world of Vincent Cullen and the terrifying and bloody implications of such a man's vengeance.

"I'm shoulder to shoulder with you, Paddy," he said.

SEVENTEEN

6:30 p.m.

I'd often remarked to myself, countless times, in fact, how strange it was to see the remains of someone I knew. Most of the people we buried were unknown to me, and when I'd dress a remains, or embalm them, or even close the lid of their coffin, I was always aware that I could get no real sense of how they looked when they were alive. The animating feature had gone; Elvis had left the building. But when it's someone you know, and you see them laid out, expecting them to look at rest or asleep, you get a nasty jar when they don't look like themselves at all. There'd been cases in the past where a family member had insisted that it wasn't their father or mother in the coffin when it absolutely was. Something happens to the face, it collapses a little. All that's left is a husk.

When I saw Lucy Wright's remains laid out on the embalming room table beside her husband's, waiting to be dressed, I was filled with memories of her living beauty; of her laughing heartily, making me laugh, too; of her standing by the counter, making tea;

leaning on the chair, smiling, disarming me completely; holding my hankie to her eyes, containing her emotion; and of her legs opening while taking me inside her. I wondered if her ghost was near, and what she'd think of everything now that she'd awoken from the dream.

Eamonn opened and closed the scissors while raising his eyebrows at Christy.

"Polikoff Special, Christy," he said, winking at me. The Polikoff Special was one of the tricks of the trade that gave Christy an uneasy feeling going out on funerals, particularly ones he'd arranged himself. To facilitate the path of least resistance in getting a garment on a remains, the back of it was cut open right up to within an inch of the neckline. Then it was just a matter of placing it over the head, putting the arms in the sleeves and tucking the back in to where it originally belonged. I'd bought a relatively cheap suit in England years ago under the Polikoff label, and the inside lining came apart in the same week of my buying it. After that, whenever I'd put a blade to a suit in the embalming room, I'd always preface the cut with the words "Polikoff Special." I showed Eamonn when he first started embalming, and he took it as his own.

The trousers were always a cinch to get on and needed no cutting. One man lifted the legs while the other pulled the trousers up to the waist. We had Michael Wright's remains dressed and coffined within minutes.

And then Lucy. Eamonn was about to cut her blouse and cardigan up the back, but I raised my hand.

"There's three of us here, just as quick to put them on her," I said, and started lifting her shoulders. Eamonn was slightly taken aback as I'd rarely not go for the Polikoff, but Christy moved in immediately.

"Bang on, Buckley," he said, and helped me dress her without tearing anything. We lifted her from the table into the coffin then, and I fixed her hair. It was common practice within the firm to administer only the smallest amount of makeup, so I put on just the subtlest hint of rouge around her cheeks to raise her color slightly. As corpses go, she looked dignified and composed.

I opened the embalming room door out onto the yard where the two hearses were waiting in the darkening evening. As I turned on the deck lights in the back of the first hearse, a white articulated lorry slowly maneuvered its way through the gates.

"I thought Conway's only delivered coffins down here on Saturdays," said Christy from the door.

"They made an exception today," I said.

"That's a first," said Eamonn.

"It's for Cullen."

Eamonn let out a little chuckle.

"Amazing what a bit of fear does to people, isn't it?" he said, closing the lids on the coffins.

"Amazing," I said, looking at Christy.

I LED THE WAY out to Pembroke Lane, Christy and Eamonn each in a hearse behind me. The nearer I got to Brigid Wright, the more my heart swelled, never mind that I was bringing her parents' remains home for her to grieve over. When I stepped back and looked at it, it all seemed a little twisted, but I hadn't wished for it or invited it in, and the chemistry between us didn't have a switch

I could hit, nor did it seem right to hand the funerals over to Frank or Christy. The moments I shared with her mother in the kitchen were golden to me, and I felt duty-bound to carry out the funerals as originally intended, all the more now that I'd met Brigid. To honor the Wrights and atone for my role in Lucy's death, the least I could do was bury them well. I'd keep my feelings in check and my heart hidden.

After pressing the buzzer, I felt the door shake and hum before I pressed it open and walked through to the open front door. I expected there to be a crowd rallying around Brigid by this stage, but she was on her own.

"Hi," she said. "Come on in."

I followed her through the living room into a bigger room, a study with wall-to-wall bookshelves. Brigid pointed to where she wanted the coffins.

"There and there, I was thinking. What do you think?"

"Perfect," I said, and it was. I'd been in many beautiful houses making arrangements in my time, some of them opulent beyond belief, but what the Wrights had done in their home no interior designer could do. They had class. Not manufactured or emulated, but genuine, and they were artists. The room was filled with the smallest, seemingly effortless details. The little framed charcoal sketch fitting snugly between bookshelves; the old rug on the floor, probably woven in the west of Ireland with colors to paint the night red with; and countless other inimitable touches.

"We'll bring them in. Do you want to wait in the kitchen, and I'll come and get you when we're ready?"

"Sure," she said, and then disappeared back through the living room.

We wheeled the coffins in one by one and left them on their trolleys, side by side, just in front of the fireplace. Christy got out his screwdriver and opened the lids, resting them against the books while Eamonn and I fixed the hair and clothes on Michael and Lucy, respectively, and adjusted their heads on the little pillows beneath them. We did this deftly and without a word as we always did when in someone's house. Everything in its place, both men nodded silently to me and walked out of the house into the night and away with their hearses.

I knocked gently on the kitchen door and walked in to where Brigid sat at the table, looking at me expectantly.

"Can I go in now?"

"Of course."

I stayed in the kitchen while she went in, her scent still alive in the room and doing a number on my senses. She looked even more gorgeous than she had in my head all day. Her hair was half up, half down, and she wore a white linen blouse with jeans and knee-high brown leather boots. I sat down at the table with my stomach aflutter, wondering should I have gone with the boys and left her alone to grieve her departed parents. I knew from compiling the death notices that there weren't many relatives on either side, certainly no sisters- or brothers-in-law, nor were there nephews or nieces; surely, though, she'd be expecting someone. The reason I'd hung around was to give her the estimate—at least that's what I'd told myself. I could've given it to her when she'd let me in, but I didn't. I'd kept it till after, when we'd be alone. Shaking my head at my inner machinations, I pulled out the envelope containing the estimate and placed it on the table in front of me. I'd no further business there.

I rose to my feet and walked inside to tell her I was on my way. I stopped at the door to see her turning around to look at me from the chair she'd placed between the coffins. She'd lit a pair of candles on the mantelpiece, which gave the room a soft, glowing light. I was going to tell her that I'd left the estimate on the table for her and that I'd see her tomorrow, but as I stood there looking at her in the flickering candlelight, her eyes glistening with sorrow and love and longing and loss, I found myself completely disarmed by her beauty and wanted nothing more than to stay there looking at her.

"I'll leave you, Brigid," I said softly.

"Are you on call?"

"No, I'm off duty," I said, delighted to be able to tell the truth.

"Then stay awhile."

"You've probably got people coming over; I'd only be in the way."

"There's nobody coming over. Can you do something for me?"

"Sure."

"Pour two glasses of wine and bring them in."

I sourced the wine, a 2010 Châteauneuf-du-Pape, walked back in, and handed her a glass. She took it in both hands and sipped from it while looking up at me. It didn't seem odd that the silence was comfortable. As if appreciating the taste of the wine, she closed her eyes and rolled her head back on her shoulders. The desire to reach out and touch her, to kiss her and undress her and explore her body, was becoming more difficult to resist and I had to battle it. Why couldn't I just take her away from her dead parents, from my dead life, to a place where nothing mattered, where we could love each other freely and just start again? She was beautiful and wonderful and obviously aware of the burgeoning feelings between us, and maybe waiting for me to make a play, however small—a sign, a gesture—to let her know that I liked her, that I was willing to acknowledge the obvious, however bizarre the situation.

I took my glass and walked to the couch, where I sat down and looked at the floor. As much as I liked her, I couldn't help vacillating between warning myself against what seemed to be growing between us and feeling like an intrusive pervert. I didn't want to hurt or confuse her or lead her somewhere I knew I could never go myself. I was dancing close to the fire as it was, but toying with something sacred, something that was in my custody, however briefly, that I was honor bound to protect, went against the grain of my character, never mind my duty.

I drank down my wine and felt a wave of tiredness and regret sweep over me. After five minutes of looking through the floor into my soul, I sat up, put my elbows on my knees, and looked over to Brigid.

"I feel a strange kind of comfort when you're here," she said quietly, still looking at her father's remains. "I don't know if it's because you were here when my mother died or because you were the one to tell me that she'd died or if it's because of something else, but that solace you talked of before you left the last time"—she turned to look at me—"I feel it whenever you're around me."

"I feel it, too," I said, willing to confess that much at least. She closed her eyes.

"Just the strangest circumstances," she said, so softly I could barely hear her.

I wanted more than ever to embrace her but, like opposing magnets, felt myself polarized and negated from being able to do so.

She got up from her chair and walked into the kitchen. I checked my watch: half seven. Time to go. As I was getting out of my seat, Brigid walked back in with the bottle of wine, not stopping until she was standing beside me, refilling my glass.

"Stay a little longer," she said, sitting down on the couch beside me. I sat back down, finding myself closer to her than ever before. There was no denying it: She was doing to my heart what only Eva had done before her. And it was becoming pretty clear that the feeling was mutual. Sublimation was futile, regardless of how compromised my morals were.

"I've been thinking," she said, with no more than three veils on. "Tomorrow evening when the coffins are in the church for the prayers, nobody will know which coffin is which, will they?"

"You're right. No one will know, apart from those close enough to read the nameplates."

"Would it be odd if we were to place a picture of them on top of their coffins while they're in the church?"

"Wouldn't be odd at all," I said.

"I think I'd like to do that. Will you help me pick out the photographs?"

"I will," I said, and placed my glass on the floor before following her out to the wall with the photographs. There must have been fifty or sixty in all, a lot of them black-and-white. Michael looked like Richard Burton in many of them, and Lucy looked as beautiful and bohemian in them all as I'm sure she had throughout her life. Brigid stood with her weight on one hip, holding her wine with her head to one side, nearly swaying in relaxed consideration. She had a sensuality to her movements that was both sultry and alluring.

"Your father reminds me of Richard Burton," I said.

"He always did me, too," she said softly with a smile. "And he had a similar voice, but with an Irish accent, of course."

It was a little spooky standing behind Brigid while being smiled at by Lucy, albeit from pictures of her, but not so much that it was off-putting.

"I think that picture of my mum is possibly the one," she said, pointing to a color photograph probably taken five years ago. I'd always paid particular attention to women's hands, and Brigid's had an elegance to them, along with a vitality that made them even more attractive. I got a flash of her hand taking coins out of a purse to give to a five-year-old for ice cream.

"She looks beautiful. And maybe that one of your dad." I pointed to one that looked like it had been taken around the same time. Our proximity, not to mention the swelling intimacy, had brought our voices down to whispers.

"That was the year before his stroke. They'd go well together, wouldn't they?"

She rolled her head back on her shoulders again, closer to me than ever now. We were centimeters from each other. I cupped her elbow in my hand, and she moved back into me so that I could touch and smell her hair. She turned slowly in my arms, and then we kissed. It was soft and exquisite and dizzying. There was an unspoken understanding and tenderness between us that transcended the myriad reasons I shouldn't be anywhere near her. I knew I was getting into something that would ultimately lead to

130

pain for both of us; I simply couldn't undo what had happened with Lucy and the lies it had precipitated, yet neither could I deny the potency and immediacy of the feelings between Brigid and me. She broke out of the kiss and looked at me. I felt like I was made of endorphins.

"Is this two veils?" I said.

"Getting there," she whispered, and we kissed again. I moved my hands down her sides, over her hips, and just as they reached her jeans, the doorbell rang. We both sighed through our noses as the kiss ended.

"Saved by the bell," I said, only half joking. She smiled while fixing herself up.

"I've no idea who that could be."

While she went to open the door, I put my coat on. The sound of a sympathetic male voice came traveling in from the front door: the priest. I fixed my tie and moved out to the hallway where Brigid stood with the priest from Haddington Road church.

"Hello, Father," I said, offering my hand. "Paddy Buckley from Gallagher's." The priest, bent over with age, smelled of altar wine and decaying teeth, and had little tufts of unshaved stubble under his nose and at the sides of his mouth.

"Hello, Paddy," he said, with a gaping smile.

"I'll leave you to it, Father. I know you've things to discuss with Ms. Wright."

I turned to Brigid, taking her hand briefly in mine.

"I'll talk to you tomorrow, Brigid," I said, moving to the door. She looked back at me a little disappointed, but also with the yearning that had been awakened in us both.

"Goodnight," she said.

BY THE TIME I got home, I was exhausted and still slightly love drunk. I rested my head down on my pillow and was fast asleep in moments. And then I dreamed, not of Brigid, but of being back on James's Street, driving, just as I had been on Monday night, only in the dream it was twilight and the road was flooded with rain, my car cutting through it like a slow-moving speedboat. I gripped the wheel, focusing madly on the street outside, filled with the dreadful feeling that something horrible was about to happen. I searched and scanned the street, but it was deserted. And then, just as I neared the accident spot, I noticed the church to my left had its doors open with the most beautiful pink and yellow shafts of light beaming out onto the street accompanied by strangely familiar and comforting music. This reduced the dread factor before replacing it with feelings of warmth and curiosity, which were dashed quickly by the dark figure rushing across my path from the other side of the street like a racing squirrel. I pounded my foot to the brake and pulled the wheel down, but to no avail: I kept careering towards him at increasing speed. I frantically looked to the floor and saw that there were no pedals anywhere, just carpet. I swerved again but the wheels stayed locked on course, moving ever closer to Donal's figure. And then, just at the unbearable point of impact, I sat bolt upright in my bed, saturated with sweat. There was a fleeting moment where I thought it was just a dream, but then reality came rushing, and I collapsed back on my bed. *It's over,* I told myself, *and there's nothing you can do to change it. Just bury him well.*

Wednesday

Wednesday

EIGHTEEN

October 15, 2014, 9:30 a.m.

I f it weren't for one significant detail, being embraced into Vincent Cullen's world would have been a warm if slightly disquieting experience. But what I'd done had left me feeling like a fraud, a wolf in sheep's clothing, and not much of a wolf at that. If I was to be found out, I knew my days would end with a torture motif. And that was my sobering and very present reality.

I stepped out of the hearse to see Richie waiting by Cullen's front door, squinting at me. I noticed there were more cars than yesterday. Apart from Vincent's maroon Jag parked nose out, ready to go, there were two Subaru Imprezas and a navy Range Rover.

"He's waiting for you round the back," said Richie.

"Okay," I said, not sure if I was to walk through the house or around it. Richie jerked his thumb towards the side of the house like he was talking to a moron.

"Go round the side."

I walked by the front bay windows around the side of the house, where I saw a hardwood kennel with a pitched tile roof and red door standing proudly beside a coal bunker. It was so grand, I had to look twice to make sure it was for a dog, which on closer inspection it must have been as the floor inside was lined with straw.

It was a big back garden and well loved. There were plum trees and apple trees and an abundance of roses and flowers. Vincent stood over by the greenhouse talking with another man. He waved me over. I was down to drive the hearse for the ten o'clock Mass in Walkinstown and had timed it so I'd have plenty of margin in making the twenty-minute trip from Cullen's.

Reaching the greenhouse, I stopped dead as I recognized the man sitting on the bench, smiling warmly at me. I'd made arrangements with Chris O'Donoghue seven years ago. A big round man with Celtic coloring and penetrating mystic blue eyes, Chris had come into Gallagher's in Uriel Street unannounced after his three-month-old son had suffered a cot death, and I'd looked after the arrangements for him. It was policy in Gallagher's not to charge for baby funerals, so I'd done everything for him gratis, Frank Gallagher believing a family suffering the loss of an infant had more to be troubling themselves with than having to consider what nobody should ever have to: buying a coffin for their baby. Out of the thousands of funerals I'd arranged over the years, there was only a handful that stood out in my mind, and my experience with Chris was one of them.

"Chris," I said, breaking into an easy smile. "What a surprise."

Chris got to his feet and ignored my outstretched hand, pulling me into an embrace instead. We slapped each other on the back affectionately.

"Good to see you," he said, and then pointed at Vincent. "When

Vincent phoned me yesterday asking about you, I was only too glad to tell him what kind of man he's dealing with."

"I'd never have put you together," I said.

"He's my accountant," said Vincent. "You'll have a cup of coffee, Paddy," he said then, more as a statement than an invitation.

"I'd love to, Vincent, but I'm driving a hearse on a ten o'clock Mass and—"

"You'll have a cup of coffee, Paddy," said Vincent again.

"Well, I'll have a quick cup then."

"Sit down," said Vincent, gesturing to the bench. Chris and I sat down as Vincent looked to the back door of the house where Richie stood, playing with his phone.

"Richie," said Vincent, no louder than he'd been talking to us. He held up three fingers. "Coffee."

"Do you have a garden at home, Paddy?" asked Vincent.

"A small one," I said. He reached down to beside the greenhouse wall and picked up a potted sapling.

"Here," he said, handing it to me. "It's a medlar tree, good for October planting."

"Thanks, Vincent," I said, touched by the gesture.

"Get your hands in the dirt, Paddy. It'll pull you into your boots."

As I wondered was this kindness because of my sweaty panic yesterday, the dog came to the door of the greenhouse and fixed her focus on me. I was glad to be able to return the dog's interest this time without the fear and panic. I leaned forward, nodding her over and watched her come willingly. I rubbed behind her ears and the side of her snout, listening to her groan as she moved her face to facilitate a good scratch.

Chris looked up to Vincent, who matched his surprised expression.

"She likes you, Paddy," said Chris, looking increasingly confounded.

"Do you think?" I said, enjoying the interaction as much as the dog.

"I've never seen her like that with anyone," said Vincent.

"Neither have I," said Chris.

I didn't understand what the big deal was. I'd always had a way with dogs, as did many people.

"Who's a good old bowler?" I said to the dog.

"That's no ordinary bowler," said Chris, looking to Vincent, who gave him silent permission to continue.

"What kind of a dog is it?"

"It's a K1."

"Never heard of it."

"Nor are you likely to again," said Chris, like he was holding a precious secret. "A K1 is a hybrid never believed possible before, but with the patience and tenacity of a Scottish friend of ours, it was brought into being twenty years ago. What you're looking at there is a mixture of wolf, fox, and Alsatian."

I was able to see little bits of every breed mentioned.

"Dechtire here is expecting eight pups in a month's time."

"Could you put me down for one?" I said, making both men laugh, but the joke was lost on me.

"I'll leave Chris to explain the story to you, Paddy. I'll grab you some clothes for Donal." Vincent walked away while Chris momentarily held my arm.

"What I'm about to explain to you, Paddy, is highly confidential and can't ever be talked about to anyone. All right?"

"All right," I said, massaging the dog's chest.

"Wolves have been crossed with plenty of dogs over the years, Alsatians among them, but never with a fox. It's still thought to be impossible, and if it wasn't for Angus Fitzconor, what's standing there beside you probably still wouldn't exist."

Richie arrived with a tray of coffee and biscuits, which he set down on a little table beside the bench.

"I'll leave that there with you, gents," he said, and left us.

"Thanks, Richie," said Chris, picking up a biscuit.

"Who's Angus Fitzconor?" I said.

"A stubborn bollocks and a great man; a man who's become very dear to Vincent and me. He was a prominent figure in Glasgow in the seventies, responsible for a large portion of the prostitution and racketeering, building himself an empire and the fortune to go with it. He retired in the late eighties, leaving his sons to look after his business interests, which they'd largely legitimized by that stage, leaving Angus free to go to the Highlands, where he lives today in an old castle. He embraced the country life and got stuck into managing the hundreds of acres he had, getting to know over the years where the different birds had their nests and where the foxes had their dens. He became one with the place.

"One morning in 1990 he heard shots fired and went out to investigate. He found the hunters in question, made it clear to them they were never to trespass again by shooting over their heads, and sent them on their way. Then, while taking a walk later, he came across the fox they'd killed, or the vixen, to be precise, and took in her kits, four of them, and decided to raise them himself."

I sipped my coffee while listening to his story, occasionally looking down to Dechtire, who was practically purring beside me.

"And that's when he got the idea. He'd a friend with a pet wolf and so organized himself a couple of wolf cubs that he put in with the fox kits."

"I wouldn't have imagined wolf cubs would be that easy to come by," I said.

"When you've the wealth and connections of the Fitzconors, Paddy, getting what you want can be very easy. But that's where Easy Street ended for him. From there on in, he came up against headache after hurdle. It nearly proved impossible. Angus had believed that the reason there'd never been a successful cross between the two breeds was because the animals were natural enemies. A wolf would normally kill a fox on sight, and a fox would never knowingly cross a wolf's path.

"He separated the male and female wolf cubs and put them with the fox kits and watched them grow. When the time came, the wolf bitch wouldn't let the fox anywhere near her, nearly killed it at one stage; and the wolf successfully covered the vixen, but nothing came of it. But Angus kept at it, and even though he was getting nowhere, he still believed it possible. Then on a spring morning in '92, the biggest, meanest-looking fox he'd ever seen came out of the woods and just stood there, staring at the wolf bitch caged in her pen. Angus called him Zulu because whatever it was about him, he had that wolf bitch hypnotized. He let her out and watched her vanish into the woods after the fox, only to return two days later, panting and pregnant. She gave birth two months later to five of the most beautiful little pups he'd ever seen."

"That's some story, Chris. How come I've never heard of them?"

"It doesn't end there, Paddy. The offspring ended up being too highly strung. One in particular, which Angus described as the most demonic animal he'd ever encountered, killed another one of the cubs in a fight. After that, he had to intervene in their scraps. So to introduce a little street savvy to the mix, he added the Alsatian, a champion dog from a top breeder in Mělník in the Czech Republic. But take a look at something that's always intrigued me. See Dechtire's eyes? They're the same as a fox's. They've survived each cross, they're serpentine."

I looked into the dog's eyes and noticed for the first time that they had vertical-slit pupils, like a cat's.

Vincent arrived back with a garment bag and picked up his coffee from the tray.

Chris continued his story. "But the most remarkable thing about the dog turned out to be not its eyes, but its intelligence, along with how well it bonded with its master. The connection is nothing short of extraordinary."

"So they're bright," I said.

"Beyond bright," said Vincent. There was clearly much more to the story, but as interested as I was, I had a hearse to drive and was out of time.

"I'd love to stay longer, but I've got to go," I said, picking up the plant Vincent had given me. He handed me the bag of clothes.

"Will you see his shoes in the coffin?" said Vincent.

"No, but I can still put them on him. It's up to you."

"Put them on him. Let's have him fully dressed."

Chris got up from the bench.

"I'll walk you out, Paddy."

As I moved away from the dog, she grunted urgently for my attention and succeeded in turning all three of our heads. She looked at me and licked her lips quickly, as if she wanted another scratch. I smiled and winked at her affectionately.

"Dechtire," said Vincent, in a commanding tone, and she turned from me and moved to his side.

We left Vincent with the dog and headed for the hearse.

"So how much are you selling the pups for?" I asked him.

"A hundred grand, sterling."

I smiled at him.

"Come off it."

"We could probably charge double that and not meet the slightest resistance."

"Who pays that kind of money for a dog?"

"Mainly Saudi princes and sheikhs, and people with money to burn, who, like yourself, have an affinity with dogs and an appreciation for the kind of bond I'm talking about. The potential is vast, Paddy."

I opened the hearse and put in the clothes and plant.

"What do you mean, exactly?"

Chris leaned in close to the hearse, resting his arm on the roof, and changed his tone to conspiratorial.

"You know what kind of guys these are, right?" he said, with a backward nod.

"Of course."

He lowered his voice even further. "Two years ago, Vincent and I were away on business together, so Donal was left in charge.

Vincent had a warehouse over by the North Wall filled with electrical goods, that kind of thing, and had five rottweilers guarding it at nighttime. The old guy who looked after it used to drink in The Port Jester after work—rough house—he was a simple little guy who took pride in his work and used to talk in the pub about how secure the place was because of the dogs. Anyway, to prove a point or to just shut him up, one of the younger guys in the pub hopped over the gates one night with nothing but a spade in his hand and killed every one of the dogs, leaving them in a pool of blood. The warehouse was well monitored with cameras and Donal watched the footage a couple of times. One tough bastard the guy was, a total animal. Donal makes enquiries and finds out the guy's into hard-core porn, so he gets information to the guy through his dealer that the warehouse is a distribution center for porn and snuff movies, and that a key to the place is kept hanging on a hook above the door in the outside jacks in the yard. It took nine days for the guy to come in, but he did come in. Now bear in mind Dechtire's been with Donal all this time. He takes her everywhere with him—she was there with him the morning they found the dogs dead, she inspected it in detail along with Donal, and is with him each evening while he waits for your man, right?"

"Go on," I told him.

"So, the night in question, Donal has Dechtire waiting in the toilet for your man, and come half one, the guy hops over the gate, walks down to the jacks, opens the door to get the key, and Dechtire springs out on top of him, pushes him to the ground, and bites the Adam's apple out through his neck in a matter of seconds."

"Killing him?"

"Stone dead. Now, as gruesome as it is, that's not the extraordinary bit, Paddy. Here's the thing: Donal had been in a fight in Limerick three months prior to the North Wall incident, which he ended by biting the Adam's apple out of the guy's throat, killing him. With Vincent out of the country, Dechtire spends her days and nights with Donal, during which time they bond and deal with the North Wall situation together. And that's just one story."

I was horrified but intrigued.

"So Donal showed her what to do?" I said.

"He did no such thing, Paddy. This is the connection and potential I'm talking about. Beginning to see the possibilities?"

I was enjoying the story about the dog as much as I was appreciative of the conviviality and trust between Chris and me, but before I could enjoy another moment of either, the thought of my forgotten hearse-driving duties drained the blood from my face. I checked my watch: 10:30.

"Oh, Christ," I said.

NINETEEN

10:30 a.m.

There weren't many things that annoyed Frank Gallagher, but hearses arriving late for funerals was at the top of the list. At twenty past ten, when Paddy hadn't answered his phone, he'd begun to suspect things weren't running as smoothly as he'd like, but now, standing outside the church at half past ten with no sign of a hearse, he was becoming furious.

He tried phoning the church to see if he could get anyone to go out to the altar and alert the priest to the problem so he could help by stretching the Mass a little, but nobody answered the phone. He'd have organized another hearse to come up in its place if there was one available, but it was a busy morning and they were flat out. They were just going to have to wait for Paddy.

Christy and Jack, who were with him, were no happier than Frank was. Nobody wanted to be left explaining to a grieving family surrounded by hundreds of mourners why the hearse hadn't arrived.

The priest had just finished the Mass and was stepping down

past the altar to stand by the coffin to say the closing prayers. The sacristan stood beside him, tending to the incense and holy water. These prayers seldom took more than five minutes, ten at the most. Frank prayed with every bit of faith he possessed that the priest would take it past the ten-minute mark, long enough for Paddy to pull up outside.

The generally accepted cue for the undertakers to walk to the top of the side aisles and stand in waiting was the priest's starting of the closing prayers. Frank turned to his men, grim-faced.

"Right, we're going to have to go up. We'll take this as slowly as possible."

Christy and Jack followed Frank up the left side of the church so slowly that hardly any of the mourners even noticed them moving. Christy, for his part, was extremely apprehensive about dealing with the Hayeses under such circumstances, but was more worried that Paddy had come unstuck with Cullen in some way, and played out all sorts of unwelcome scenarios in his head, his sunken cheeks the only outward sign of anxiety.

Once at the top of the aisle, the three men stood still with their hands clasped behind them and their faces drawn.

They'd hoped that one of the family would take to the podium to say a few words about the deceased's short life, which would have added another five minutes and possibly saved them, but nothing of the sort happened.

The priest took the holy water from the sacristan and walked slowly around the coffin with the sprinkler, shaking the water onto it. He followed that by doing a similar ritual with the thurible, which he used to shake incense at the coffin with a practiced hand before passing it back to the sacristan and getting back to his prayer book.

"May the martyrs come to welcome you and may the angels lead you into Paradise and may you have eternal rest," he said, before making the Sign of the Cross and turning off his mike. He stepped down off the altar and proceeded to walk past the coffin a few feet down the center aisle, stopping to wait for the coffin to be turned and wheeled down behind him.

As the organ music piped up to see them out of the church, Frank moved to the coffin much slower than he usually would with added dignity and piousness and took longer, too, in what appeared to be a heartfelt genuflection, emulated precisely by Christy and Jack. Then they turned the coffin around on its trolley so the feet were facing the priest. Just as the priest was about to continue towards the door, Frank moved to the family and took old Mrs. Hayes's hands in his.

"Mrs. Hayes, would you like your sons to carry Dermot out on their shoulders?"

The old woman nodded her weeping head. Frank then turned to the sons and took his time about telling them what their mother had decided before guiding them out of the pew and placing them around the coffin according to their height: tallest at the back, shortest at the front. Once they all had their positions and the coffin was raised onto their shoulders, Frank gave the priest the nod to go on, following after him at a snail's pace, flanked by Christy and Jack, whose eyes, along with Frank's, were riveted on the space outside the open doors that was still horribly vacant.

As the Hayeses carried the coffin behind him, Frank mentally went through the route from Cullen's house to the church to appease his tortured mind and fervently prayed Paddy was only moments away. *Jesus, get him here, I'm begging you, roll that hearse up outside the doors, please, Lord, I implore you, let me see that hearse outside.*

TWENTY

10:41 a.m.

I hadn't stopped once since leaving Cullen's house. Breaking five red traffic lights, driving on the wrong side of the road, and three times touching on 140 kph, I managed to squeeze the twenty-minute journey into an even eleven minutes. By the time I got to the church, I was sure I'd be pulling up to a mob of angry mourners, but as I approached the doors of the Romanesque monstrosity of a church, it was miraculously free of people. I slunk past the main doors as the coffin was being marched down the steps and inched to a stop as if it was as methodical a proce- dure as the tightly linked cogs in a clock keeping time. I killed the engine just as Frank turned the handle on the back door and opened it up for the coffin, which was slowly pushed up to a stop just behind my head.

I got out of the hearse only to be immediately met by Frank, who took a firm grip of my arm and led me around the corner to the side of the church, where he stopped short of pinning me to the wall.

"Are you trying to give me a fucking heart attack?" he said, barely able to contain his anger.

"Frank, I'm sorry. I couldn't get away from Cullen."

Frank was incredulous.

"I don't give a shite who you were with, Paddy. You should have been here at ten past the fucking hour. Why didn't you answer your phone?"

"It was on silent. He's a tricky bastard, Frank; he tells me when I can come and go. I'm sorry."

He straightened his coat with a yank. "Don't ever do that to me again," he said with finality, and walked back around the corner. I gave it a minute before following after him, moving around to the back of the hearse, where Christy was placing the family wreath at the head of the coffin while Jack placed the other flowers on either side of the coffin. Christy raised his eyebrows at me while exhaling through puffed cheeks.

Before we could say a word to each other, our attention was seized by old Mrs. Hayes making her way up to Frank, who was standing on the other side of the hearse, collecting Mass cards from the occasional mourner.

"Mr. Gallagher," she said. "I've rosary beads here. Is it possible to have them put in the coffin at this late stage?"

"Of course it is," said Frank, his calm restored. "Have you them there? I'll look after it myself."

She handed him the beads.

"We'll just have to take the coffin inside the church again."

"Thanks very much," she said, and moved back to her family. Christy was beside Frank in a matter of seconds, holding out his hand.

"I'll look after that for you, Frank."

"You can give me a hand," said Frank, and then looked to Jack. "Keep an eye on things out here, Jack, we're taking the coffin back inside for a minute."

"Right you are," said Jack.

Christy kept his hand held out, the panic coming alive in his eyes.

"Here, Frank, Paddy and I'll look after that, you can stay out here."

Frank ignored him. He moved to the back of the hearse and took out the spuds holding the coffin in place. I knew Frank well, and once he'd decided on something, he generally stuck to it like glue.

"Paddy," he said. "Give us a hand getting this inside."

Christy's eyes were darting all over the place. I winked at him as we took a grip of either side of the coffin while Frank took the head. We carried it inside and placed it on the trolley and then wheeled it over to a quiet alcove. I took out my screwdriver, opened the four screws holding the lid down, and opened it a crack. I stretched my hand out to Frank.

"I'll just slip them in," I said.

Frank wasn't in the mood to be challenged. "No, take the lid off the coffin."

I took the lid off to reveal the dead old woman. Frank's jaw dropped slowly open. Christy stood there looking awkward and ashamed, sinking lower in his shoes by the second. And I just waited. Frank brought his gaze up to mine.

"What the fuck is going on here?" he said, with contained righteous anger.

"We weren't just sent the wrong body," I said. "Kershaw's cremated Dermot Hayes over there."

"And whose decision was it to wing it?" said Frank, with scrutinizing eyes.

"It was mine," said Christy, taking the proverbial bullet. Granted, it was his funeral, and because of that, he felt responsible, but it was the caliber of his friendship that informed his spurious confession.

"It was mine," I said. "It was mine all the way."

TWENTY-ONE

12:40 p.m.

The boardroom in Gallagher's was a long room seldom used for anything but the storage of neglected ashes and the odd meeting Frank might have with his lawyer or accountant. I sat at the end of the long oak table by the boxes of ashes, looking at Christy through the film of dust on the antique mirror spanning the length of the wall. He didn't want to talk to me. Having positioned himself half a table length from me with his face cupped in his hand, he was completely despondent, blaming himself for listening to me and veering from Frank's code of rectitude at all times, at all costs.

If the Kershaw situation had happened in any other week, I probably wouldn't have gone down the route of deceit, but the die had been cast with the Wright and Cullen situations, so I did it as much to validate and bolster the desperate measures I'd been forced to take as to keep the Hayeses from a tainted grieving process and Kershaw out of the soup. But this was little comfort to Christy with his job on the block and reputation tarnished.

"Christy . . ." I began.

He raised his hand to silence me without looking up and then let it drop in his lap.

"I feel like a bollocks," I said.

"Don't," he said flatly. "I'll be able to pick up some work with the embassies."

I emptied my lungs. "What a monumental fuckup," I said.

"The beads," he said. "Those fucking rosary beads . . ."

Before I could respond, Frank came in, looking even more deflated than Christy, but with an anger on him. He dropped himself into the chair at the head of the table and looked at me like a betrayed and disappointed father.

"How much did you make on this, Paddy?"

I thought he knew me better than that, but then I suppose he thought he knew me better, too.

"You think I did what I did to make money?"

"Well, why else would you have done it? Surely you wouldn't have hung me out to dry for nothing?"

"I didn't make a penny on this—it never even crossed my mind . . ."

"So you put my business on the line, my livelihood, my reputation, Paddy, to cover a man in England who you've never even fucking met! Is that what you're telling me?" He stood up out of his chair, utterly indignant.

"I did it to cover the situation, Frank, not Kershaw per se, but the whole thing. I took a calculated risk, never intending to make money but to—"

"Jesus Christ Almighty, do you want to come home with me, Paddy, and start running my house and family, too?"

I felt his pain. I'd disrespected him and deserved whatever he had to mete out.

"I've no defense," I said, and looked to the table.

"There was a pair of us in it, Frank. It was as much me as it was Paddy," said Christy. Frank sat down and sighed heavily.

"Your loyalty is admirable, Christy, but misplaced. There's one to be brought back from the Mercy, bring Jack with you. Now get out of my sight."

Christy got up from his seat. "I'm sorry," he said to Frank quietly, and left the room.

In the thirty years Frank and I had known each other we'd never had a moment like this. It was a tough call for him. I'd love to have been able to talk to him about the bind I was in, but under the circumstances, he was the last person I could tell. He was having difficulty as it was; to heap any more on his plate wouldn't do anyone any favors, least of all Frank himself.

"What would your father think?" he said, in nearly a whisper.

"I'd imagine he'd be concerned, like yourself. The truth is, Frank, I've felt him closer to me this week than I have in years. I know how out of character all this seems, but I'm having the strangest week I think I've ever had. I feel like I'm halfway down a birth canal. And I've been asking myself what would Shay think, and I think from where he's at he'd have perspective on it like you can't have when you're seeing it from just one angle. I'm not saying what I did was right, but I did it to facilitate a normal funeral, a normal grieving process. And I know what it's done to the dynamic between you and me, and I can't express just how sorry I am about that. For what it's worth, I have more respect for you than any living person I know. And that's the truth."

He sat there continuing to look at me, considering what I'd said. He took out his brass case of cigarillos along with his matches. It was a meditative technique I'd seen him use countless times when big decisions had to be made. He selected a cigarillo slowly and methodically, tapped it three times against the case, and lit a match, puffing out the smoke while sucking the flame against the tobacco. They were James Fox's finest cigarillos. I knew this because I picked them up for him from Fox's on Grafton Street whenever he needed them. It smelled so nice I pulled out a cigarette and joined him. As smoking moments go, it was a perfect one.

The anger that had been so tangible when he'd first entered the room was gone. All I could feel exuding from him now was his inherent kindness. But I knew he wasn't given to sentimentality and that pragmatism and fairness would inform his decision before his magnanimity.

I was three-quarters way through my cigarette when he put his case back in his pocket, the picture of composure.

"The Cullen remains is in the embalming room waiting to be laid out," he said, with a gentleness that put the perfect end to the meeting.

I put out my cigarette and blew out the last of the smoke.

"Thank you, Frank."

TWENTY-TWO

2:25 p.m.

Donal Cullen's remains lay naked on the embalming room table stitched back together after the autopsy. The eyes and mouth were gaping, and his hair was bloodstained and dragged down over his forehead, reminding me of a medieval portrait that hung in the refectory of my alma mater, St. James's on Basin Lane. The lines on his brow suggested a keen intelligence had once worked behind it; his whole body, in fact, was as big and powerful looking as Vincent's. And his teeth were long and sharp, reminding me of the story of the fight he'd had in Limerick. I felt a shiver run down my spine as I imagined him jerking his head back after biting the Adam's apple out of the other man's neck. But regardless of my imaginings, my job was to prepare his remains for the final viewing.

I shampooed his hair, washed his face and hands, and dried them all off with a towel. Then I moved on to his eyes. I tore off a piece of cotton wool and held it between the arms of a forceps. I then pinched the eyelid and held it up while I wiped the cotton wool over the eyeball and behind the lid, removing the fluid that was making it slide open in the first place. Then I pressed the eyes closed, which would stay shut until they withered away.

I gave him a shave with an electric shaver and combed his hair neatly, messing it slightly afterwards to give it a natural look. Then came the Polikoff treatment. It was a petrol-blue cashmere Ermenegildo Zegna suit. It nearly seemed a shame to cut it, but his back was never going to be seen again. After I'd finished dressing him, I put his tie on, giving him a Windsor knot, and slipped on his black Bruno Magli shoes. I fastened the middle button on the suit and finished by joining his hands together.

I stood back and looked at him. I was both his executioner and last custodian. My father had always said the same thing when someone we knew died prematurely or in an accident: *It was their time.* And this, undoubtedly, was Donal's. That didn't take away from my part in it, though. Surely every hit-and-run driver went through a similar justification process. Moved by the hand of God to take back another of his children, having no choice in the matter, like a pawn in a grander game I knew nothing of. I placed my hand over Donal's and looked at his dead and composed face.

"I'm sorry," I whispered. "If we could only switch places."

TWENTY-THREE

4:50 p.m.

Eugene Lyons sat alone at a table in a darkened bar on Thomas Street in the heart of the Liberties, calling for his second double vodka and tonic. He'd good reason to celebrate but, as was usually the case with his little celebrations, it was a solitary affair, for if anyone else was made privy to the reason, they'd balk. He drained the last of his drink as the fresh one was placed down before him, and swished the vodka around his badly receded gums. His eyes fixed on the barmaid's rear end as she retreated to the bar.

"Thanks, darling," he called after her.

Geno was a creepy little man in his fifties with a ferretlike face, bad breath, and a penchant for silk suits. As intensely devious as his innate expression was, he'd been dealt a gift of sorts by fortune in the shape of a nasty childhood accident involving his left eye and a cast-iron radiator that resulted in his eye being removed and replaced by a glass eye, which lent his face a spurious benevolence, allowing him to access positions that would have otherwise been denied him, his role in Cullen's brothel among them.

Geno had been managing the St. James's Club since its doors had first opened, having met Donal at a poker game a few months prior where he talked himself up as a manager of lap-dancing clubs in Liverpool. For a man whose primary urge in life was to rape, managing Cullen's club was a dream come true. And now, with Donal out of the picture, he could start bringing his fantasies to life on a daily basis if he felt like it.

It was only a matter of time before he'd take his place beside Sean Scully in Cullen's empire. With Donal gone now, the opening was there for him, and he'd take full advantage of it. He'd make himself indispensable to Cullen. He'd become more valued than Scully. Maybe even Donal.

In the eyes of Vincent, Geno considered himself to be something approaching a hero. Having given Donal the night's takings as well as a newspaper to shield his head from the rain on Monday night, it was Geno who'd rushed out, too late as it happened, to the side of Vincent's slaughtered brother. Just as it was he who rang Vincent at ten past three that same morning with the news of the hit, snatch, and run, as he'd come to call it in his own mind as well as to the girls in the club. If it wasn't for him, he'd told them, they wouldn't have the make of the car that hit him.

He'd never tell anyone he'd taken the money, just as he'd never talked about other moneys he'd lifted in the past or women he'd raped. As Geno saw it, he did exactly what Donal or Vincent would have done if they'd been in his shoes. He'd kept his eyes open, used his head, and taken his chance when he saw it. Donal wasn't going to be needing the cash, that was for sure, and what was twenty grand to a man like Vincent Cullen? Sure he'd lay more than that on a single trip to the bookie's office. And who-

ever had knocked Donal down deserved the added charge for running off in the first place.

Monday had been quite the night for opportunities. Donal getting killed hadn't just created a golden opening for rapid ascension through the ranks, but with Donal gone, the girls no longer
had their protector. So after alerting Vincent to the news, Geno
began his reign of rape on the young Polish beauty he'd had his
eye on since she'd started three weeks ago. Twenty grand in his
pocket, the promise of promotion, and the prospect of anal rape
all made for a powerful aphrodisiac. By the time he'd finished
with her, the girl was in a quivering heap. If they weren't whimpering and trembling by the end of it, he hadn't done it right.

Geno finished his drink and left the bar and walked up
through the drizzling rain past the deal-yelling stallholders of
Liberty Market on Meath Street towards the funeral home. He'd
dressed in his favorite suit for the evening, a black three-piece silk
number he'd bought in Bangkok, which he'd complemented with
a black shirt and red tie. It was, he believed, fitting funeral wear.

He let a gob of phlegm exit the side of his mouth while squinting his eye at the few people gathered outside the funeral home, a
few faces he even recognized from the club. He moved past them
like he'd never seen them before, went into the crowded funeral
home, and made his way towards the front parlor.

TWENTY-FOUR

5:10 p.m.

Standing with my back to the wall and my head bowed in the candlelit parlor, I listened silently along with everyone else to the music Vincent had selected, Pergolesi's "Quando Corpus Morietur." Of the hundreds of people gathered in the funeral home and the street outside, Sean Scully was only allowing twenty in the parlor at any one time, under orders from Vincent, who sat with his legs crossed in the chesterfield armchair by the head of the casket. The candlelight gave the room a medieval quality, brought to life by the faces of Matser and Richie, the dutiful executioners; the brutal crown of Vincent, whose thoughts seemed to pulse with dreams of bloody vengeance; and the ruthless head of Scully, the ever-vigilant gatekeeper. In a room full of dark secrets—fuller, no doubt, than any other space in Dublin—mine was unquestionably the most coveted, and looking increasingly safe as time ticked by.

But it was the effect of my secret that I was faced with now. The loss and misery I'd created were here before me, all around me, my feelings of remorse made all the more palpable by being steeped in the devastation I'd caused.

As if to trump my hidden lament, a woman in a black dress who'd been sitting on the couch approached the casket, holding her trembling mouth, barely containing her tears. She had raven black hair flowing over her shoulders, skin like marble on a pretty but deeply pained face, and a sizable baby growing inside her. With her free hand, she gripped Donal's arm as the tears erupted, spilling fast down her cheeks and over her fingers.

"What am I going to do now?" she said to Donal's remains. Vincent's face hardened as his eyes moved from the carpet to her knees, while everyone else's moved between Vincent and the woman. She was shaking the arm now, not caring about her place, or Vincent, or the scene she was creating. I noticed the wedding ring on her finger and heard the echo of Vincent's curt reply when I'd asked him whether Donal was married.

"What'll I do, Donal?" she whimpered helplessly, while my heart grew heavier and my guilt laid anchor in her belly. Then she started wailing.

Vincent glanced briefly at Sean, making the smallest gesture with his fingers. Sean reacted instantly by placing his hands around the woman's shoulders.

"Come on now," he said, gently guiding her back to the couch where her whimpering quieted to silent crying. The urge I felt to step forward and claim responsibility was so overwhelming it surprised me. I wanted to collapse to my knees and tell them I'd hit him. It was my fault. And I'd take the blows. I'd absorb the wailing. I'd take the kicks and the beatings. As dangerous as I knew Vincent was, there was a part of him I liked and respected, which made it all the more difficult to maintain my spineless routine. I had to get out of there before I did something regrettable.

I moved to Vincent's side and leaned in to whisper.

"We'd want to be leaving here no later than half five, so bearing that in mind, we need this room cleared by twenty past so you can have a few minutes alone with Donal. Do you want me to go ahead and organize that?"

After getting the nod, I moved past Richie, Matser, a few old men and women, and Sean, who opened the door for me. As I was about to squeeze out, a small man in a black suit came in, nodding to Sean briefly before turning to face me with a squint. There was something odd about him. The skin around his left eye was fixed in a perpetual smile, and the pupil in the eye itself, which was glass, was completely dilated. This was belied by the other eye, which was devoid of any warmth, housing a pinprick pupil. He looked like he was trying to place me. Satisfied that I'd never met him, I slipped out the door into the main office and over to the fireplace.

The backs of my legs were only beginning to warm when Sean emerged from the parlor and walked right up to me.

"Can I've a word?" he said.

"Sure," I said, and I ushered him around the corner into the middle office.

"Everything all right?" I asked.

"I just want you to put me wide on something. My mother-in-law died earlier in the year—your competitor handled the job—and she was cremated. Her ashes have been sitting under my bed since—my wife wants to be close to her. Before I met you, I never gave it much thought, but now that I have you here, give it to me straight: What's in the urn? Is there coffin ashes as well as human ashes in there?"

"No," I said, relieved it was a question I could answer. "Actually, they're not ashes in there at all."

"What? Then what are they?"

"Chippings."

"Chippings?" said Sean. "Fuck's sake, go on."

"This is how it works: You get the coffin, with the remains still in it, put it in the furnace, close the door, and turn it on. It burns at a thousand degrees centigrade for an hour, during which time pretty much everything goes up the chimney. After the hour, and after it's all cooled down, you pick up what you have left, which is usually just the skull and hip bone—"

"What do you mean, 'usually'?"

"Depending on the size of the remains, you might have a couple of femurs, but if it was you or me, it'd be just the skull and hip bone left."

"Right."

"So you pick them up—they're charred but basically intact—and you put them in a grinder, turn it on, and after a few minutes, they're ground down to what appear to be ashes, but what are actually, upon closer inspection, fine chippings. And that's what's in the urn under your bed."

He smiled wolfishly and shook his head. "Unfuckingbelievable," he said, and went back in to the parlor. With Frank and Corrine manning the office, I ventured out the back for refuge from the mourning. Christy stood by the counter with a newspaper open and a cup of tea in his hand.

"All right?" he asked. He could see I was struggling.

"I feel like a swine," I said. "I'm thinking maybe I should turn myself in."

"Hang on, now," he said, closing the paper and making sure the door was firmly closed. "Relax for a minute and tell me this: Do you think you deserve to die for what you've done?"

"No."

"Then keep your mouth shut and get any notions of telling anyone out of your head. You've got immunity on this one, Buckley. Sure half the country is glad he's dead. The first time I heard Donal Cullen's name was in 1991 when he went down for shooting dead a bank manager during a robbery—an unarmed bank manager. He was a menace and a bully, and responsible for more murders and crimes than we'll ever know about."

"I've just seen his heavily pregnant wife break down in the front parlor. I'm the cause of every bit of anguish in that room."

"Paddy, you're not thinking straight. Now let's be very clear on what would happen to you if you did give yourself up. After a week or two, you'd disappear. No trace. There'd be an inquiry, it'd make the news for a few weeks, but no one would be even slightly surprised because in the country's eyes you would have effectively committed suicide the moment you'd handed yourself in. And that'd just be the end of Paddy Buckley, the undertaker. Then there'd be the beginning of Paddy Buckley, the torture victim. Remember, Paddy, not only did you kill his brother, but you waltzed into his house afterwards and drank his coffee and ate his biscuits."

"I didn't eat the biscuits."

"Fuck the biscuits, Buckley, you'd be strung up! And then

brutally murdered. You think Cullen is going to let you away with it because he's got to know you?"

I emptied my lungs. "No. But I still feel like a swine."

"It'll pass."

AFTER I CLEARED the room, only a handful of people stayed behind for the final goodbye. Feeling I should leave them alone, I made for the door, but Vincent caught my eye as I clasped the handle and signaled for me to stay. As touched as I was by the gesture, it only made me feel worse. I stood back by the door and waited.

It was the first time I'd seen Vincent's wife and son. They were perfectly cast in their roles: she, as the subservient yet strong beauty, whose hardened gaze could only be broken by the likes of Cullen; and the son, still a young boy, but with Vincent's mettle already evident in his confidence and obvious intelligence. They both sat impassively on the couch, watching Donal's wife bawling as quietly as she could while saying goodbye, leaning down to kiss Donal's lips and rub the side of his face. She probably would've stayed there all night if Sean hadn't walked her to the door and sent her out. Vincent's wife and son followed her. And then it was just Vincent, Sean, and I.

Vincent gripped the side of the casket and looked down at his brother with a tenderness usually well hidden behind his veils. He moved his thumb under Donal's chin and up the side of his face before leaning down and kissing his forehead. And then he just stayed there a minute, looking at his brother for the last time while Sean and I watched him. He turned away from the casket and made his way out the door, only stopping to briefly hold my arm.

"Thanks, Paddy," he said in a raspy voice, and he left the room, Sean following behind him, making the Sign of the Cross. As soon as they'd gone, Christy, Eamonn, and Jack came in and screwed the lid down on the casket. I stayed back by the door, holding my head in my hands, immersed in my shame. With the lid securely on, Christy moved to open up the double doors to bring the casket out, giving me a reassuring, conspiratorial wink.

"Showtime," he whispered.

TWENTY-FIVE

6:05 p.m.

St. Mary's Pro-Cathedral on Marlborough Street is the episco-pal seat of the Roman Catholic Archbishop of Dublin and practically unnoticeable when compared with its Protestant coun-terparts, tucked away at the back of O'Connell Street. But in-side, it did a little better in keeping up with its Church of Ireland sisters, having the quintessential aura of ritualistic grandeur bol-stered by ancient church art, cold tiles, and the smell of lingering incense. It was customary in Dublin for the mourners to wait out-side for the hearse to arrive, but this evening, because of the in-creasingly heavy rain, they'd gathered inside and awaited the arrival of Donal's remains in the pews in the main body of the cathedral.

Geno had gone ahead of the cortège, having got across town in a taxi, and was waiting, along with the hundreds of others, for the coffin to be wheeled up the center aisle. Now that he could practi-cally touch his new rank in Cullen's crew, he felt like he'd been waiting for Donal all his life. All the missed or pissed-away opportunities were worth it when he considered what he was poised for. To be back in Dublin after years across the water was turning out to be better than he ever could have dreamed up. The country was on its knees after the economy had collapsed and the banks had ruptured and the public was well acquainted again with its old friend Austerity, but that didn't matter. For as long as Geno was aligned with a man like Vincent, he'd take what he wanted whenever he felt like it.

At just ten past six, the priest reemerged from the porch and led the procession up the aisle. Behind him, pushing the casket in their dampened overcoats, were the four undertakers, who were followed in turn by Vincent; his wife, son, and crew; Donal's wife; and an ongoing stream of mourners.

Geno was looking at the lead undertaker again, the one with the black and gray hair. It was annoying him that he couldn't place him, as he prided himself on never forgetting a face. He thought maybe the undertaker reminded him of someone else, like an actor in the movies or someone on television; he knew he'd have remembered him if they'd actually met. He watched him as the cortège came level with his pew and passed him by, continuing along its way. Then, as his eyes followed the undertaker's back, his mind traced the hidden profile to produce a triumphant bingo call from his very recent memory: the guy who ran Donal down. His killer. The thrill that surged through him was so powerful he nearly became aroused, and the expression of glee etched itself so deeply onto his face that he was forced to wrap his hand around his mouth to hide it.

Once at the top of the aisle, just in front of the ornate candlelit altar, the four undertakers genuflected in unison and made their way down the side aisles out of the cathedral. Geno stepped out of his pew and followed closely behind them. He knew it was the guy who had run down Donal, but he had to be absolutely certain.

Outside, he lit a cigarette and leaned against the railings and watched the undertakers talking to their boss under his big black umbrella. Then the lead undertaker and his bald friend moved away and got into the hearse, the lead undertaker sitting behind the wheel.

This was arch theater. The circumstances were conspiring with him: It was dark, it was raining, and, strangest of all, Donal's killer was willingly reenacting Monday night's events for him by driving away from exactly the same angle. To complete the contrivance, Geno stepped down onto the street and stood there in the lashings of rain and watched them drive away into the night. It was Donal's killer all right. Geno had him made. He climbed the steps to the shelter of the portico and waited patiently for his ascension.

When the prayers had finished and the front-pew commiserating was coming to an end, the mourners drifted out of the church into the evening. Then, at twenty to seven, Vincent led his crew out of the church, past Frank Gallagher, through the open door of the front limo. Within minutes, the other cars were filled and inching away from the curb while the undertakers stood out on the street, their hands raised in an effort to pause the oncoming traffic. Before anyone was kind or old-fashioned enough to stop, Geno made his way through the rain to Vincent's limo and rapped his knuckles hard on the side of it. Sean lowered his window.

"What?"

"I've to talk to Vincent," said Geno.

"Talk to me, what is it?" said Sean.

"No, I've to talk to Vincent," said Geno. Sean turned to the driver briefly.

"Hang on a minute," he said, and got out of the car abruptly, taking Geno by the arm and marching him to the shelter of the front porch.

"Look, I'm going to give you the benefit of the doubt here and pretend you don't know how it works. If you want to talk to Vincent, you go through me no matter what's on your fucking mind. Now, he's in no mood for conversation so this better be good, Geno. What is it?"

Geno was breathing through his mouth he was so excited.

"I know who killed Donal," he said, as if he were holding a poker of aces.

Sean scrutinized him for a good moment before giving him a narrow-eyed nod.

"Wait here," he said, and got back into the limo while Geno stood there with all sorts of violent fantasies flipping over in his head. Maybe Vincent would give him the honor of plunging the knife deep into the undertaker, or a turn at least. Or perhaps he'd ask him to look after it altogether. The prospect of Vincent sanctioning such rough justice had him salivating.

Sean came back over to him, his impatience vanished now that his appetite for vengeance had been whetted.

"Let's get you a lift, Geno."

TWENTY-SIX

7:40 p.m.

I've only ever been rooted to the ground by a painting two or three times in my life. Vermeer's *Girl with a Pearl Earring* was one that did it. *The Meeting on the Turret Stairs* by Burton was another. And maybe da Vinci's *The Virgin and Child with St. Anne and St. John the Baptist.* I didn't live in the art world, or even on the fringes of it—the nearest I'd usually get to art was when I'd lift an oak coffin with the Last Supper carved on its side—so I didn't expect to be stopped by a painting when I stepped into the Wrights' house on Wednesday evening. It wasn't painted by any of the Wrights, either, but by Shay Mac Giolla, the celebrated artist who defined what Irish mythology looked like through a series of seminal works in the seventies and beyond. I'd known about Mac Giolla since I was a child. My father would read me tales of Irish mythology from Mac Giolla's illustrated books, and I used to get lost in his detailed pictures of heroic warriors and sultry goddesses framed by intricately woven Celtic griffins. Like most of my generation, I could spot a Mac Giolla anywhere, and I hadn't gone five feet into the Wrights' hallway when, leaning against the wall, the framed painting of Lucy as a goddess stopped me dead.

As is often the case after a removal, the house was open and abuzz with chatter, laughter, and tears, everyone smoking and drinking, artist types, the lot of them. There were bearded old men wearing ponytails and white suits; gray-haired women with clever, cultured eyes behind horn-rimmed glasses who were wearing sequined dresses; and a sweating black-haired violinist with a three-day beard and tufty eyebrows who seemed lost in and deeply saddened by the lament he was playing. There were groups of women laughing quietly with plenty to talk about in clusters in front of the photographs of Michael and Lucy Wright. But they were nearly invisible to me. I moved to the picture and leaned down to submerge myself in it. He'd captured her beauty and essence perfectly. He'd painted her wearing a translucent blue robe, kneeling by a stream, collecting herbs in an ethereal world. And she was so much younger than my memory of her.

Somebody hunched down to join me in studying the picture.

"You knew her," said the man, a friendly giant dressed in a linen suit. It had to be Mac Giolla. He looked like a character from one of his paintings: part Gypsy, part Viking.

"I did," I said. "Man, you got her."

"It's Airmed, Goddess of Healing. I painted it in '74, a year or so after my fling with Lucy. I was no stranger to strong women—I was raised by them—but she turned my world inside out and left me in a heap. It was only afterwards I realized what she'd done for me."

"What did she do?"

"She cleared whatever was blocking me. It wasn't anything

she'd said or done, it was something more latent than that, not perceptible till later. I saw the same thing with organizations or symposiums she'd joined. If they'd been floundering before she joined them, they flourished after she'd left; if they hadn't yet found their way, there'd be a blaze in the wake of their path when she'd gone. But there were always difficulties first, usually involving her leaving the company. And in each case, after the dust had settled, it always became clear what she'd done, and Lucy, of course, remained on good terms with everyone. She became a close friend of mine and a strange sort of revered talisman to the groups she'd saved. Quite a legacy."

He offered his hand.

"Shay."

"Paddy," I said, shaking his hand. "It's a beautiful tribute and a mesmerizing picture."

"Airmed's also associated with resurrection," he said.

It was no surprise to learn that Lucy had broken plenty of hearts and molds in her time. Although my ending her life had put paid to any further healing she might have done, even so, she still turned my world upside down. Mac Giolla had a shrewdness about him, a kind of Gypsy magic that made me slightly uncomfortable and stopped me from telling him anything for fear he'd be able to see through my veneer of half-truths and lies.

We stood up as Brigid came into the hallway. Her face became visibly happier when she saw me.

"Paddy," she said.

"Hey," I said softly. It was the first time I'd seen her in a dress, a little black number she wore with stockings and high heels and her hair tied loosely back off her face.

"Brigid," said Mac Giolla, reaching for her arm. "We've got to go up to the RHK for a sculpture symposium. Both your parents will be honored there tonight, you should know that."

"Thanks, Shay," said Brigid. "And thanks again for the painting, I adore it."

Mac Giolla leaned in and hugged her warmly.

"Hang in there," he whispered, and then he turned to me with a smile.

"Good luck, Paddy."

Maybe he knew I needed it. All the other artists followed him up to Kilmainham, and within ten minutes, the house was cleared. When the last person had gone, Brigid closed the door, leaned back against it, and just looked at me, her eyes full of wanting and sorrow, tenderness and curiosity. I leaned against the wall not five feet from her, looking back at her with similar feelings and my unspeakable secrets, Lucy's portrait by my knees. Gone were any notions of roles to be played and the pretense they necessitated. The longing and desire between us had been unmasked, and now that the crowd had vanished, the silence in the house seemed to swell along with our feelings for each other. I wanted to take her away from her sadness and grief and, for once, away from her parents' house.

"Do you want to go out for a drink?" I said.

CARRYING TWO PINTS of Guinness over to Brigid in the snug in Toners Pub on Baggot Street, it occurred to me that I hadn't been out with a woman since Eva had died. There hadn't even been anyone I'd fancied from afar. And now here I was, moving towards someone who'd captured my attention and burgeoning affection. Everything that had brought us both to this point felt increasingly unimportant. I only had her best interests at heart. To think that something so special and sacred could enter the realm of the sullied, regardless of what had preceded it, seemed absurd.

I rested the pints down, closed the snug door against the live music and pub chatter, and sat down opposite her. We raised our drinks.

"To life," I said, making her smile.

"To life." We each took a good drink, as if demonstrating the vitality of the toast.

"How are you holding up?" I said.

"It comes in waves. But good, all things considered."

"And how was the removal?"

"It was sad and touching. And surprising, too."

"In what sense?"

"Some of the people who came, I didn't expect to see them there . . ." She paused and looked deep into my eyes. "Can I tell you a secret?"

"Of course," I said, somewhat relieved that she had secrets, too.

"I want to tell you because I trust you, one, and, two, now that my parents are gone, nobody else knows about it, and I really feel like sharing it."

"Share away," I said. She shifted on her seat and turned the bottom of her glass while gathering her thoughts.

"One of the people there this evening was a guy I hadn't seen in a long time. Barry is his name. We met when we were seventeen. We never really went out, we just had an ongoing thing. We fit perfectly—mentally, emotionally, physically—but there was something that kept us from actually going out together. When I was nineteen, I got pregnant. He was seeing someone else, I didn't want to have a baby with him, and I didn't want to become a mother at that stage of my life. But I didn't want to get rid of it, either. I confided in my parents—they were never the kind to freak out—and for two weeks I contemplated every possible outcome. One thing I knew, and I don't know why I was so inflexible on this, but I couldn't tell Barry. Whatever I decided, I'd decide alone."

"What did you do?"

"It was my father who made up my mind for me. I remember he was smoking a cigarette in his studio, and he said, 'Abortion and adoption have just two letters in the difference, but those two letters are the difference between a death sentence and a clarion call.' I chose to heed the call. I gave the baby up for adoption."

Tears had started flowing down Brigid's face, but she remained calm.

"And I never told Barry. And to see him there this evening offering his condolences took me by surprise." She wiped the tears away with my hankie. "He lives in New York now with his wife and family. He came all the way home for this. It was sweet of him."

"So you set him free, too."

She smiled while I placed my hand over hers. "Do you regret giving the baby up?"

"A part of me does. He'd be fourteen now and I often wonder what he'd be like."

"I know what that feels like," I said. "My wife died in her seventh month of pregnancy."

Just like her mother before her, she instinctively gripped my arm. "No!" she said. "When?"

"Two years ago on the third of December." I swirled the remains of my pint around and downed it.

"How?"

"I was in Tallaght delivering a coffin when I got a call from Frank Gallagher, telling me to go directly to St. James's Hospital, that my wife had had an accident, that she'd collapsed. That's all he knew. I got in the hearse and drove back faster than I've ever driven in my life. I didn't have to use the horn once. It was as if the other drivers knew this was a genuine emergency and got out of my way as soon as I appeared behind them. I'd driven so fast that I got to the hospital before Frank, who'd only been down the road. As soon as I got there, I was taken into a private room to wait for the doctor. I think I knew then, being given the special treatment already, but I couldn't let myself think like that. By the time the doctor came out in his scrubs, Frank had got there and was standing with me, waiting. I knew by the doctor's face what he had to say, but I had to hear him say it. He told me that she'd collapsed in the supermarket, that the paramedics had done what they could when they got there as well as on the way to the hospital. And that he'd done everything that could possibly be done, but that nothing had worked. And then he tightened his lips and said the unthinkable. Eva was dead. And so was the baby. I learned later it was a brain hemorrhage."

"Oh, no," said Brigid, quite involuntarily through her tear-stained lips. "How old was she?"

"Thirty-five. Our daughter, had she lived, would have been nearly two now."

"Paddy," she said woefully, gripping my hand tight. "How long were you married?"

"Nine years."

"Your heart must be broken."

"It broke my heart, no doubt about it. In half. And you don't think you're ever going to recover, you don't think it's possible. And everything becomes very black. But there eventually comes a day when you realize you've survived it—you're no longer a victim but a survivor. And you realize you can feel again, that your heart mended, that it's possible to love."

I'd opened up Brigid's waterworks, something I'd hoped to keep her from, but as we held hands there in the little snug, sharing each other's pain, the solidarity between us brought us closer.

TWENTY-SEVEN

8:45 p.m.

Donal Cullen had spared no expense when creating his office and the corridor outside it on the top floor of the brothel. The tiles were marble, the chandeliers were Venetian glass, and the chairs in the corridor were like thrones, which made Geno smile as he sat on the one closest to Vincent's office waiting to be brought inside. It felt as if he'd inherited the club after Donal relinquished his crown, and that very soon the keys to the kingdom would be in his hands. Since Monday night, Geno's fantasies had extended beyond the realm of the sexual to the loftiest notions he'd ever held. Finally, thanks to his good memory, his patience and cunning were paying off. He'd been waiting there a while—*To show me who's boss*, he thought to himself. He'd no problem with Vincent being boss. Geno knew well he was no leader. He saw himself more as an adviser who'd get pleasure vicariously by watching Vincent implement his ideas, and that was fine. That'd be perfect. For now.

He was more relaxed now than earlier with Sean. He was over

the initial rush of excitement. He'd tempered it with his resolve and ambition, and was perfectly happy to wait until midnight if they wanted to keep him that long. The way Geno saw it, his destiny had arrived, and he'd greet it with a steady nerve.

The door was opened by Sean.

"Come in."

He walked into the office to see Vincent sitting over the side of the desk with a chair right up close to his knee.

"Sit down," he said, pointing his finger briefly at the chair. Geno sat down and placed his hands on his knees. The only light on in the room was the desk lamp, and it was shining right into Geno's face. Vincent looked into Geno's real eye, seeing past the sham warmth to the deviant at the wheel. Vincent had never liked Geno from the start, but the club was Donal's baby and Donal had recruited him, so he hadn't argued with his brother. Ordinarily, if Vincent didn't like someone, they didn't get in. It was as simple as that. But Donal had assured him that Geno had the smarts he was looking for as well as the experience, and as it was turning out, it looked as if Donal's judgment was bang on. If Geno could successfully finger the killer, then maybe he was up to more than Vincent had given him credit for.

Vincent lowered his head slightly to look deeper into Geno's eye like he was viewing the contents of the man's memory, and then turned his focus to the suit. He rubbed his hand over it as if he were caressing the neck of a racehorse and then gently stroked the side of Geno's face like he was going to kiss him. Geno looked back as neutrally as he could. Sean stood against the wall, chewing gum, observing it all coldly.

"Tell me," said Vincent.

Because of Vincent's elevated position, Geno had to crane his neck to look up at him.

"It was the undertaker."

"What?" said Sean, like he was hearing nonsense. Geno looked from Vincent to Sean and back to Vincent.

"It's him, I guarantee it."

"Which undertaker, Gene?" said Vincent.

"The hearse driver, the one who cleared the room."

"Buckley?" said Sean, no nearer to believing him.

"I'm telling you," said Geno. "I never forget a face."

"When you talked to me on Monday night, you told me you didn't see his face," said Vincent.

"I know. I saw the back of his head and only the very side of his face, but this evening when I was in the church, I saw him wheeling up the coffin from the same angle and I'm telling you, he's your man. Hair like a badger. Follow it up, I've never been more sure of anything."

Vincent looked at Geno a few moments longer, checking for any cracks of doubt on his face. It was the first time since Donal had died that he'd felt his brother's presence, to the point where it felt like he was standing right beside him. Maybe Donal was reaching out somehow, using Geno to point to his killer. Vincent imagined his brother smiling at him with a sleepy knowing wink as he'd always done when he'd delivered the goods.

"All right, Gene," he said. "Leave us."

Geno got up from his chair and left the room while Sean smiled disbelievingly with his arms folded. "Paddy Buckley?"

Vincent's expression hadn't changed from the moment Geno had come in, save for his eyes, which had got blacker. He moved away from the desk, put his hands in his pockets, and walked a few slow steps before stopping in the middle of the room, thinking all the while of Paddy's panicky state on Tuesday morning and of the way he lied to him that afternoon about what time he'd gone home on Monday night.

"He did it," Vincent said.

Sean looked at the floor searchingly, trying to find the sense in it.

"Paddy fucking Buckley," he said beneath his breath, increasingly dumbfounded.

"Will I go up and get him?"

"No. As far as that pox bottle's concerned, we haven't a clue what's going on. And for the moment, that's the way it's to stay. But as soon as Donal is buried, bring that spineless fuck in to me."

Sean just nodded while continuing to look at the floor, quietly seething that he'd been fooled by Paddy Buckley.

TWENTY-EIGHT

10:50 p.m.

The tears had stopped, and although there were undoubtedly many more in store, they'd been replaced by a mutual desire for us to be close to each other. After sharing more stories and pints together in our snug, we walked back to Pembroke Lane under the dripping maple trees in a Dublin that had just turned decidedly colder. But I was oblivious to the perils that awaited me, perfectly content in the coziness of the present and the warm possibilities it had to offer.

Armed with a bottle of red wine, Brigid led the way across the back garden to her father's loft studio that was his refuge and sanctuary when he'd been active. She had told me that he'd disappear up there for months sometimes to get lost in his work, and that on occasion, he'd cut himself off from the world for significantly longer periods, only emerging for alcohol, tobacco, and painting supplies.

It didn't look like much from the outside: darkly stained wooden walls around what appeared to be a dust-filled garage.

But once we'd shifted through the cluttered entrance, past an old MGB roadster and a collection of ladders and tools, we climbed the steps to the loft. I could see why her father considered it his sanctuary. From the moment I set foot in it I didn't want to leave. It was like the attic of his mind manifested in a studio space. It was an old building, maybe a hundred years old, and the loft itself was bigger than I'd expected. There were wooden beams protruding from the ceiling. The walls were lined with shelves crammed with books and sculptures. There were paintings hung on the little spaces of wall remaining, and others leaning against the bookshelves or stacked together, and more again sitting on easels. There was a futon covered with a bloodred blanket and a little fireplace on the back brick wall beside a bureau with a wooden swivel chair. And probably what made it most special was the window, which took up a whole wall and looked out onto the rooftops and chimneys of Wellington Road, illuminated this evening by street light and a waning moon.

Brigid leaned down by the fireplace where a little turf fire had been prepared and struck a match to it.

"My father always left the fire ready to light. That must be like that five years."

"The smell of a turf fire," I said.

Brigid smiled. "He was from Mayo and grew up with a fire constantly burning in the house. I remember him driving to the west with a trailer and returning with it piled high with turf every September."

She straightened up and opened the bottle of wine as the smoke climbed the chimney.

"It's the first time I've got any real sense of your father," I said.

"Your mother's so special, I imagined that your father played second fiddle to her."

"My father was the artist," said Brigid, filling two glasses. "Don't get me wrong, my mother's art is first-rate, but she wasn't as prolific as my father. I always thought of my mother more as a work of art herself, even though she unequivocally was an artist—some of her paintings make me cry, they're so loaded. My father's art is more serious, I suppose; there are deep-seated themes behind each painting. He drew heavily from myth and archetype, from the works of Jung and Campbell, even from fairy tales."

"Fairy tales?"

"Yeah, the feminine mysteries of life and death; the masculine mysteries of wounding and growth." She handed me a glass of pinot noir and moved to the paintings leaning against the bookshelf and leaned down to file through them, completely unaware of her allure while her attention was on the paintings. As she unconsciously pushed her hair behind her ear, my eyes traced the outline of her figure beneath the black silk of her dress tightening over her hips and thighs as she crouched.

"Here are the ones I wanted to show you," she said, pulling out three canvases and placing them side by side against the wall. They were powerful pieces all right, each one depicting a horse.

"These were the last paintings he worked on. The three stages of man: the red horse, white horse, and black horse. Shame he didn't get to finish them."

I could freely appreciate Brigid's beauty while she gave her attention to the art. I watched her hands as they pointed to the different aspects of the paintings, her contained passion as she explained the subtleties of each one, and how sexy her mouth was when she talked. As interested as I was in her father's paintings—and I was interested—the intimacy between us was active in the space between the words, where we were really meeting.

I put down my glass while she talked about the representations of intensity on the red horse, the engagement of the white, and the humanity of the black, and sat myself down on the floor in front of the paintings and crossed my legs. The warmth from the fire had removed the chill from the place, and the wine, which was already room temperature from being in the house, was keeping alive the little buzz we had in the snug. It had been a while since I'd been in the intimate zone emotionally, and now here I was in its cupped hands with a woman so exceptional it felt like a fantasy. The pillow talk I used to share with Eva had always been the most treasured part of my day, and its absence had made my grieving all the sharper. But now my heart had swollen for another woman, whose affection, though I suspect matched mine in intensity, I knew I wasn't entitled to. Yet who was to say you couldn't polish a tarnished gem?

Brigid pushed her shoes off with her toes and sat down opposite me on the rug so that our knees touched, and we settled into what was becoming one of our signature silences. The desire between us was center stage now and unbridled, any doubt or hesitancy was behind us, and we were safely hidden away up in the loft, beyond intrusion from priests or anyone else. Brigid reached behind her head and pulled out the pins holding her hair up, quickening my pulse as it fell loose and our legs folded around each other's.

We kissed slowly, exploring each other, undressing one another, and got lost in whispers and moans for the next few hours, making love again and again, drunk by the end on the love and sated desire between us.

Afterwards, spooning Brigid on the futon while she slept for what must have been the first time in days, it became clear to me how well matched we were mentally and spiritually, and physically we fit together like a perfect jigsaw, which only strengthened the bond between us and quickened the promise of love's possibilities.

It was after two by the time I felt myself drifting off. And then I dreamed the dream again: Driving through the flooded, twilit street, I moved slowly towards the accident point, only this time beside me was Lucy, even though she looked exactly like Brigid from head to toe, and she was smiling, well happy to be there with me, sitting with one leg curled up beneath her and the other bent with her knee pointed towards the roof, and wearing nothing but an open blue shirt. Her happiness was infectious and took my panic away, making me feel safe. To the left again, I noticed the church with its open doors and the light spilling out onto the street, shimmering on the surface of the shallow water. The music was a little louder this time, making me raise my eyebrows happily as I recognized what it was: cheerful carousel music; and though I couldn't see what was emitting the colorful beams of light, I knew it was a merry-go-round, and it made me smile, having both Lucy and me transfixed, until Lucy pointed across the road, and I remembered Donal. I punched for the brake with my foot as the trotting figure moved steadily into place for the killing; but there was no brake, nor could I move the wheel this time. It was locked on course. I looked at Lucy in my panic, but she just smiled serenely at me. All I could do was look back at the figure and wait, but instead of the figure remaining oblivious to his oncoming fate as he had before, this time he turned his head to look at me. And I saw that it was no longer Donal running, it was me, looking right back at me, into my eyes. The beautiful light emanating from the church was surely where my trotting self was headed, and the feeling it gave me was a strange mixture of panic and hope and horror and comfort. Just before the moment of impact, I threw myself awake, heaving my lungs up and down, my heart at full gallop, my neck and chest rushing with sweat.

It's only a dream, I told myself. *You're just processing.*

I sat there a good five minutes, leveling my breathing and calming my thoughts, before returning to the warmth of the woman beside me. I got up and put more turf on the fire, then snuggled in beside Brigid and nuzzled my face into the back of her neck and meandered my way back to sleep.

Thursday

TWENTY-NINE

October 16, 2014,
5:40 a.m.

There's nothing nicer for a man than getting his hair washed by a woman: reclining comfortably with your head craned back into a basin, warm water softly flowing over your head, and female hands gently working the lather through your hair, massaging your scalp. It spells heaven, and it's how Eva and I met twelve years ago. I'd called in to a hairdresser's salon on George's Street for a trim, and after I was directed to a basin by the guy at the front desk, Eva appeared by my side. She said the smallest hello and slowly started washing my hair. I knew she was French the moment she'd opened her mouth; she also looked like she'd just walked off the set of a Godard movie, and having her hands move over my head and through my hair made me feel as if I'd fallen into the arms of a goddess. On the few occasions I looked up, she was looking down directly into my eyes, always relaxed and at ease. Then as she cut my hair, it was more of the same: lingering looks; the way she touched my head or my chin while she made the cuts; her breast pushing against me when she cut around my ear while leaning over my head. The energy between us was smoldering and undeniable. After she'd finished the haircut, she went to lead me to the cash register, but I asked her if she'd mind washing my hair one more time. It was then that she smiled, revealing the gap between her teeth, which was the point of no return for me. She spent even longer washing my hair than she had the first time, focusing more on the massage than the washing. It was a defining moment in my life. "Have dinner with me," I said, when she gave me back my change at the register. "Okay," she replied, smiling. And I walked out of there with a feeling that never went away. Until that Monday in December when my heart was pruned in full bloom. But now the bloom was back, and love was within reach once again.

Brigid's fingers tightened around the hair on my scalp as I moved deep inside her, both our bodies utterly exhausted from the sheer pleasure of being unable to pry ourselves away from each other. Such was the connection between us that we climaxed together every time and then could somehow summon the energy to do it all again. I don't think either of us wanted to come down from that loft for at least a month, but there were funerals to attend, more tears to be shed, and I still had Cullen to contend with.

I was in the process of rekindling the fire so that Brigid could stay warm while I prepared to leave, but she insisted on coming inside and making me coffee before I left. While the coffee brewed in the kitchen, we ended up on the table, giving it one more go. We just couldn't get enough of each other, coming back for one more taste, one more fill, one last time, exhausting and energizing ourselves simultaneously.

I tucked in my shirt and buckled my belt while Brigid poured the coffee. The quality of her stare, along with each tiny movement and gesture, was informed by love. We could both feel it. This wasn't wanton lust or escapism. I was long enough around and experienced in matters of the heart to recognize the real deal when faced with it. And the truth was I felt the same way.

I downed the coffee and left with just enough energy to walk out of there, pausing in the hallway briefly to take a photo of Mac Giolla's picture with my phone. Maybe Lucy was my talisman after all.

BY THE TIME I pulled up on Mourne Road, it was half past six. The sky was cloudless and getting brighter, the buses were running, and the street was coming alive with the red-eyed brigade emerging for the day. There were two men sitting on motorbikes, talking with their helmets off right opposite my house, but apart from remarking to myself that they were there, I gave them no further thought and disappeared inside for a shower and change of clothes.

When I reemerged, there was only one man, and he was putting his helmet on. I noticed him doing it but made little of it. It was rush hour, after all, and the swelling in my heart had permeated my every thought to the point where all I could think about was Brigid and getting back up in that loft with her. I didn't care about motorbikes or guys on motorbikes, so when the very same guy followed me all the way to work but kept going when I turned into the yard, I put it down to the fact that more people than I knew the quickest route from Drimnagh.

I got myself together for the morning's funerals with a smiling dreaminess. Opening my locker and pulling out my bowler hat and leather gloves, I remembered little moments from last night like they'd just happened: holding Brigid's waist, kissing her neck, moving my hands through her hair, and inconsequential things she said. I had it bad. Gone was the worry I'd been plagued with over the last few days. It was replaced now by a state I never dreamed I'd feel again: rhapsody.

Polishing my shoes in the back office, it was the same. The idle chatter among the drivers sitting around me drinking tea went right over my head, my thoughts concerning themselves solely with Brigid and the road before us.

OVER ON HADDINGTON ROAD, as I approached the steps of St. Mary's church, I noticed another motorbike driving by, the driver looking in at me this time as he passed. I took my bowler hat off, fastened up my coat, and moved inside the church, feeling slightly unsettled. I wondered for the first time could there be a connection between the bikes and Cullen. Surely I was clear at this stage. I was considered a friend by Vincent. Chris O'Donoghue had vouched for me. I was safe. And Dublin was chock-full of motorbikes, anyway.

I moved through the people gathered at the back of the church and sidled up to Jack, who was warming his hands against the radiators amidst dozens of people who'd arrived late and missed out on a seat. The church was crammed, which stood to reason. Michael and Lucy were well-known artists, and good people, and were being mourned by the most genuinely stylish crowd I'd ever seen gathered under one roof. There were famous musicians and actors, broadcasters, and probably dozens more high-profile folk I wouldn't recognize, all focused on the two oak coffins resting side by side in front of the altar. But my focus was on Brigid, whose head was bowed in sorrow. What we had between us went far beyond any chemistry we might be sharing. We cared deeply about each other. And though the love felt all pervasive, it didn't take away from the mourning Brigid was steeped in, but rather it was a warm and utterly respectful accompaniment to it.

As the priest shook the incense from the thurible and holy water from the aspergillum, I, and the five men with me, moved slowly up the side aisles and waited at the top of the church for the closing of the prayers. As soon as the priest turned the mike off, I led the way out from the wings and picked up the photographs from on top of the coffins and placed them down beside the wreaths on the steps of the altar. I got Jack and two other men in place to wheel Michael's coffin down behind the priest. Then I took the head of Lucy's coffin with the remaining men and stopped briefly to wait for Brigid. She stood there looking at me with tears filling up her eyes, not quite sure of the exact protocol to follow, and seemed so utterly alone. If ever she needed me to hold her, this was the time—but not the place. So I extended my hand to her, which she took and let me lead her out of the pew while the soprano soared the beautiful heights of Schubert's "Ave Maria." With Brigid behind me, the flow from altar to hearse could move along unimpeded. These were automatic moments for me where my mind could freewheel, locked as I was in my funereal role, and in my mind I returned to the comfort of the loft on Pembroke Lane.

I hadn't taken ten steps down the aisle when my daydream was ended by four men who didn't belong at the funeral but were interspersed among the rest of the mourners. They were of another breed, the kind I expected to see at Donal's funeral, and their focus wasn't on the coffins or on Brigid or on the priest or on anyone else. It was firmly fixed on me.

My thoughts immediately leaped to one thing: Brigid's safety. To protect her, I had to distance myself from her completely now.

Outside, after we'd secured the coffins in the hearses, I stood collecting Mass cards while the other men went about retrieving the wreaths from the church, and, again, I clocked two wily-looking men standing together by the gate, watching me.

The voice in my head was active again. It said: *However he found out, now he knows. Paddy, you're fucked.*

Brigid was kept busy talking to a never-ending stream of mourners lining up to commiserate with her. I couldn't bring myself to even look at her now. Her worth as a pawn in Vincent's game would prove priceless if he knew of our love. And now that they weren't letting me out of their sight for even a moment, I was going to have to blank her to keep her safe. So instead of waiting to check if she was okay and see her into the limousine, not to mention stopping the traffic for the cortège, I turned to Jack, who was driving the first hearse.

"I'm going to head over to Glasnevin ahead of you," I said.

"Are you not going to see me out?" said Jack.

"I'll see you over there," I said, already walking away from him. I kept my head down as I left the church grounds and made my way to my car.

THIRTY

10:40 a.m.

Richie walked out of his mother's brown roughcast house up in Drimnagh and stopped to give the old woman a hug.

"Thanks for the tea, Ma," he said, kissing the top of her gray head. Richie had been gone from his mother's house for a good fifteen years, but that didn't stop him from visiting the old woman twice a week for a feed. His mother's was the only house on Rafters Road that had never been robbed, due to everyone in the robbing business knowing well they'd end up in a six-foot box if they even dared peer through the old woman's window. She was like royalty on that street and loved her son all the more for giving her the protection and security she enjoyed, though nobody got a bigger kick out of the fear his name instilled than Richie himself.

Walking down Mourne Road towards Paddy's, Richie slipped a cigarette between his lips and sparked it. Watching the house numbers climb the high one hundreds, he couldn't help marveling at the stupidity of this crazy undertaker or how easy it was going to be to pull him in, and when he got to thinking of what

Vincent was going to do to Paddy, the smile on Richie's face crept downward with a strange kind of malevolent pride as images of ritualistic torture flipped over in his mind.

There were only a few houses on Mourne Road with garages, and Richie knew them all. At the end of a terraced block, he stopped outside a house with a light blue door and matching garage, and smiled at the fact that Paddy's neighbor had a clear run through to his back garden, making for ridiculously easy access. Richie hopped over the sidewall into Paddy's garden and had the back door picked and opened in under a minute. Closing the door behind him, he took a long pull on his smoke, checking out Paddy's kitchen, and paused to let out a pitiful snigger when he noticed the Mickey Mouse clock on the wall. He put his cigarette out on the floor and moved through the washhouse into the garage before flicking on the light. There in front of him was the sparkling smoking gun. He took a dozen pictures of the car with his phone, went back into the kitchen for another smoke, and sat down at Paddy's table to select the best photograph to send, which, as soon as he had it, he sent directly to Vincent's phone.

THIRTY-ONE

11:15 a.m.

After the two coffins had been lowered into the grave—Michael's first, then Lucy's—the priest went through the prayers with a hundred artists huddled around him. I'd positioned myself just behind the large pile of dirt on the border of the next row of graves, allowing the widest possible view of the space around me. I couldn't see anyone watching me, but that didn't mean a thing. For all I knew, Vincent had known all along and had been playing me like the scorpion played the frog and was only now beginning to sink his sting in. Brigid stayed at the grave after the priest had finished while the mourners dispersed, and let her attention settle on me. As much as I felt pulled to her, I stayed where I was. This only made Brigid break away from the aging artists intent on minding her, and come to my side, making my heart skip as the arm of her coat brushed against me.

"I'm having people back to the house for some lunch. Can you come?" She seemed so vulnerable, as if she could collapse in a wailing heap at any moment, and I desperately wanted to make even the smallest gesture to comfort her, but I kept my hands clasped behind my back and flashed a pained smile.

"Can't. More funerals to attend."

"I missed you after you left this morning," she said, her longing for me evident to anyone who cared to look closer. I wanted to squeeze her hand, but I didn't dare. I couldn't take any chances now. Brevity was the name of the game.

"I missed you, too. I'll call you later on," I said. I let the warmth reach my eyes briefly and I winked at her. She hesitated slightly before leaning in and tenderly kissing my cheek, her scent sending my head into a spin.

"Talk to you later," she said a little wistfully, and moved back to her friends. I watched them walk away from the grave, wondering to myself whether that was the last kiss we'd ever know now that I was effectively a hunted man. I adjusted my bowler hat and turned on my heels, keeping my head down until I was in my car and headed back to the city.

I REALIZED I was in so far over my head that my only choice was to carry on. Back at the office, I stepped up into the loft and sat down on the bier, surrounded by a legion of leering coffins. What advice would my father give me now? If he were there on the loft with me and fully abreast of the lie I was living, he'd probably place his hand on my shoulder and hang his head to join me in my shame. I could hear the words coming out of his mouth: "The chickens are coming home to roost." I was a dead man.

Christy arrived at the top of the stairs with his bowler hat and overcoat on.

"There you are. Are you right?" he said.

"He knows," I said plainly.

"Who knows?"

"Cullen. He's wide."

"How is he wide?"

"I don't know," I said.

"Then how do you know he knows?" said Christy.

"I've been followed around town all morning."

"By who?"

"I don't know, Christy, a lot of motorbikes, for a start."

"A lot of motorbikes, in the courier capital of Europe?" he said, as if he were feeding back nonsense.

"And then by six men in Haddington Road church who looked well out of place. I'm being watched and they're making no secret of it."

"Are you being watched now?" said Christy.

"Come on, do you think I'm making this up?"

"I think you're being paranoid," said Christy, matter-of-factly.

"I may be many things, but paranoid isn't one of them."

"Then where are they now, Paddy? How come I can't see them? I'm after buying a bottle of milk across the road, and there wasn't a soul anywhere. Sure he's giving you tips on horses, for fuck's sake. He doesn't know a thing about it."

"Christy . . ." I said, beginning to feel exasperated.

"Relax," he said. "You're letting your imagination run riot with you. Now come on, we've to get over there."

If ever I wanted to be delusional, this was the time. It was painfully clear to me that my secret was no secret anymore, but the only way to find out for sure was to look into Vincent's eyes. Then I'd know for certain.

I STOOD WAITING on the curb outside the Pro-Cathedral on Marlborough Street, feeling like I was on the end of a wavering plank. Cullen didn't get to where he was in life by letting people get away from him. His reputation for thoroughness was legendary; I knew I was no match for him. He'd snap me in two without a second thought if he decided to. My guilt was reason enough, but presenting myself to him as an innocent on top of it was enough to incite him to wipe out my whole family, if I had one. And standing there, waiting for the limousines to roll up with a possible window into my fate, I felt blessed that I didn't. Christy was in the sacristy, handing over the church offering to the sacristan, so I was alone when the first limo pulled up beside me at two minutes to the hour. I opened the doors and stood aside. Sean Scully was the first to get out, immediately followed by Richie and Matser. They made their way up the steps, buttoning their suits closed, each one of them ignoring me completely, not giving me as much as a glance.

Then Vincent stepped out. I stood there, three feet away from him, with my hands gripped together behind my back, waiting for him to look at me so I'd know. He stopped briefly to pick a bit of breakfast out of his teeth, then walked by me as if he hadn't even seen me, continuing up the steps until he'd disappeared inside the cathedral. Never before had I been so blatantly snubbed.

The other four limousines pulled in behind the first while I stood, numb, rooted to the ground, watching the drivers open the doors for their passengers. It was while these mourners were making their way up the steps that I noticed Chris O'Donoghue moving swiftly past them into the cathedral. If I'd needed confirmation that my head was on the block, then here it was. A man who'd demonstrated such warmth and kindness to me only the day before practically skipping up the steps to avoid me. If I'd had leprosy, they'd have given me no wider a berth.

I sat in the back of the first limo alone, feeling a dreadful sinking sensation in my stomach. Christy opened the door and sat in beside me.

"Well?" he said.

"Well what?"

"Are you still being watched?"

"Worse. I'm being blanked. By them all. Even Cullen. Even Chris O'Donoghue, who yesterday had his arms wrapped around me, slapping my back, ran up the steps so he wouldn't have to talk to me."

"When was that?" said Christy.

"Just now, a few minutes ago."

Christy checked his watch.

"A few minutes ago, Paddy, the Mass had already started. He was probably concerned with getting inside."

"Just a nod, Christy, that's all I was looking for."

"I wish you could hear yourself. Back at the yard, you were complaining that you were getting too much eyeball, now you're not getting enough. Paranoia, Paddy, it has you. You're home and fucking dry, man."

Trying to convince Christy was pointless.

"Sure what could I do, anyway?" I said. "If Cullen wants to kill me, then who am I to stop him?" I straightened up and resigned myself to my fate. "I'm dead."

"Do me a favor," said Christy, with his reasonable face on. "Come inside and let me be the judge of that."

With six priests and four altar boys on the altar, you'd be forgiven for thinking the Archbishop himself had died. In Italy, the Pope had excommunicated the Mafia, but in Dublin, the treatment of their Irish equivalent was a different affair. When it came to the Gospel, the priest read the passage from Luke about the Good Thief; and in the eulogy, brief though it was, he heaped praise on Donal for the charity work he'd done over the years for the youth in Dolphin House, Fatima Mansions, and Teresa's Gardens in Dublin 8. There was nothing mentioned about the heinous nature of the countless crimes he'd been convicted of, never mind the myriad others he'd walked away from. But I suppose the Church was no stranger to honoring crooks: It had been sheltering far worse for centuries.

Looking at the collected heads around the church was like viewing a rogues' gallery made flesh. And as Fauré's *Requiem* played throughout the Mass, with a chamber orchestra brought in especially for the occasion, I couldn't help feel that this was, in a strange sort of way, my Requiem Mass. And Gabriel Fauré's music the soundtrack to my demise.

There were people crying around the church, but nobody was more demonstrative in their grief than Donal's wife. The poor woman wailed throughout the Mass, tucked away behind Vincent's crew, relegated to the third pew.

As the soprano scaled the aria "Pie Jesu" in Latin, I waited in the wings of the packed cathedral with Christy and the five limo drivers while the priests went through the closing prayers in front of the casket. For the duration of the Mass, we were paid no attention whatsoever, which only augmented Christy's reluctance to believe me. At twenty-five past the hour, Frank joined us and waited with us for our cue to step out, upon which I led the men to genuflect before turning the casket around on its trolley.

I needed to look into Vincent's eyes. There was the tiniest possibility that Christy was right. I paused in front of Vincent and leaned in for a word. He had his head bowed like a wounded emperor and his focus trained firmly on the floor. He had every chance to look up at me—it was the natural thing to do—instead, Sean reached his head out from the pew behind.

"All right?" he said quietly.

"Would you like to carry Donal out?" I said.

"No. You do it," he said flatly.

I wasted no time in getting the drivers in place and the casket raised to shoulder height before carrying it down the aisle with them behind the priests, ahead of the family.

Outside, I stood at the back of the hearse with Frank while the crowd mingled, and not a single member of Cullen's crew came near either one of us, or anyone else in the firm. I could forget about looking into Vincent's eyes. He probably never wanted to see me again and would have me done away with by people I'd never met. Maybe I wouldn't even see it coming and be woken by a bullet to the back of the head.

It was going on half past one when I drove the hearse through the front gates of Mount Jerome Cemetery. Once inside, everything slowed right down while the superintendent took over. Mount Jerome ran like a well-choreographed ballet. Its crematorium was the busiest in the country, and the cemetery itself, which was probably the prettiest, dated back to the early nineteenth century. The funeral traffic was conducted by the cemetery superintendents, who all wore morning suits and top hats. They met each hearse at the gate and, carrying their silver-topped ebony canes, led the cortège to its designated grave while the mourners walked behind the hearse and limos. I could see in the side mirror that Matser, Richie, and Sean were out of their limo and walking right behind me, only now they didn't seem to mind watching me so much. Every time I checked the mirror, I could see Richie looking in at me, deadpan.

Once we reached the grave, the gravediggers stepped aside to let me pass them and then knocked on the side for me to stop. Usually, all I'd have to do was open the back of the hearse, as it was the gravediggers who lowered the coffin into the grave—they even unloaded the flowers from the hearse while the priest readied himself for the final prayers—but today, I let them open the back. I wasn't getting out of that hearse for anybody.

On a funeral like Cullen's, it'd also be normal for the hearse driver to wait until the prayers were finished before driving off, but I'd had enough. I'd left the engine running so as not to draw any undue attention to myself while sloping off. And once the last wreath was laid on the green mat beside the grave, that's exactly what I did.

CHRISTY WAS WALKING up the yard towards the back office when I pulled up beside him. I got out of the hearse, feeling rattled and scared. With Donal in the ground now, it was business as usual for Vincent, and I was expecting to see him or members of his crew driving through the gates at any moment. Christy smiled like he hadn't a care in the world.

"No bullets in you, no?"

"Don't be starting with me, Christy. Did you not see him at the top of the church? Don't tell me he wasn't giving me a vibe."

"A sad vibe, Paddy, the man is in mourning."

"I can't believe you're blind to this . . ."

"If Vincent Cullen wanted you dead, you wouldn't know a thing about it. I'm telling you, you're clear. Your guilt is playing havoc with your conscience, that's what's happening."

Before I could answer, the door was opened by Frank, who stepped out, holding a bit of paper.

"Can you both go up to the South Circular Road to Deirdre Hennesy, who's dead in the house? There'll be no one there to greet you. Bring her back here in a Last Supper oak. Closed coffin, going to the church tonight. The key is under the stone Buddha outside the back door," he said, and handed me the address. "Take Eamonn with you, he's in the embalming room."

We headed up to Hennesy's house, which was only ten minutes up the road, with the coffin loaded behind us. There was no point in talking about Cullen anymore, not to Christy or anyone else. All the talking in the world couldn't save me now. I was deeply embedded in a fat cake of lies, and I'd been deluding myself all week, both with the Cullen situation and with Brigid, that I could operate outside the consequences of my deeds. I felt ashamed of myself for taking the road I'd gone down with Vincent, and though real feelings had developed between Brigid and me, the color of my soul had been darkening as the week went on. And deep down I knew it.

THIRTY-TWO

2:20 p.m.

T he old woman had been living in squalor and darkness, and had probably been bedridden the last few months of her life. Whoever was making the arrangements had chosen the most expensive coffin, though it didn't necessarily follow that because there was money for old Deirdre, there'd be love, too. The curtains were drawn, the walls were stained, and there were empty food cartons and unwashed dishes that must have been months untouched.

Upstairs was worse. It looked like it had been ransacked sometime last year, and there was a pungent odor in the air, which was coming from Deirdre Hennesy's bedroom. I pulled back the curtains in her room and opened a window and breathed in deeply the air from outside. It was a bad case.

Christy stayed back by the wall with his hand over his nose, while Eamonn suffered the smell and took the lid off the coffin. The mattress she'd died on was so badly dipped in the middle that the rigor mortis had locked her remains in a crawling position.

"She's not going to fit in the coffin like that," said Eamonn. The rigor mortis had to be broken. I moved to the side of the old woman's remains and knelt down by the bed, facing her feet. I took hold of her elbow in one hand and her wrist in the other, and then forced her arm open so that I'd straightened it, which took quite a bit of effort. I repeated the process with the other limbs until the rigor mortis had left her body and she was completely straightened. After that, we picked up the edges of the sheet she was lying on, hoisted her up off the bed, and lowered her into the coffin on the floor, covering her face and body afterwards with the corners of the sheet.

I moved to the wall to get the lid, and then, from the smallest glance out the window, my worst fears were confirmed. Matser and Richie were crossing the road with purpose in their step.

"Fuck," I said, feeling the horror take hold.

"What?" said Eamonn, picking up on the resigned dread in my tone. Christy took his hand away from his nose as his eyes widened with fear.

"They're here," I said.

"Who's here?" said Eamonn, while Christy moved swiftly to the window.

"Jesus Christ," whispered Christy.

"What's going on?" said Eamonn, as alarmed now as Christy and I.

"No time to explain. Hide me!" I said. And without another word, each of us grabbed the sheet covering the old woman's remains, lifted her out onto the floor, and slid her under the bed. Then I lay down in the coffin while Christy slapped the lid down on top of me, and everything went black. They lifted me up, went out of the room, and descended the stairs. I was completely hemmed in but I could breathe easily enough. I began to experience the world through sound: the creaking of the individual steps under Christy's and Eamonn's hard leather soles; Christy's voice saying: "Don't move a muscle"; the air rushing steadily in and out of my flared nostrils; and my heart pounding relentlessly like a ceaseless drum.

In the darkness, I lay there mute, expecting gunshots to rip through the wood. I pressed my feet against the end of the coffin to keep myself straight and heard banging on the front door and the words "Open up!" The coffin stopped moving and was horizontal again. Christy must have opened the door. I stopped breathing and stared wide-eyed into the blackness in front of me. I heard Richie's voice.

"Is Paddy Buckley here?"

The coffin started moving again.

"No, he's up in Clondalkin meeting a family," said Christy. I slowly started breathing. We were out of the house.

"We were told he was here," said Richie.

"No, this is a two-man job. He's up in Clondalkin," said Christy. The movement picked up.

The sounds and vibrations continued: footsteps on the pavement; the opening of the back door of the hearse; the base of the box hitting the deck; the rollers rattling beneath me, making my spine vibrate until the coffin thumped into place by the spuds; and the back door banging shut. The driver and passenger doors opened and clunked closed and the engine turned over.

"Where are they?" I said, the tips of my fingers touching the lid, ready to push it off at any moment.

"Searching the house," said Christy. "Sit tight." The hearse moved slowly down the street and then stopped.

"Why are we stopped?" I said.

"Red light," said Christy. I lay there, contemplating the power of a red traffic light, and imagined it in front of me as if it were actually there, right up close, pulsating red, stopping everything.

"They're out!" said Eamonn. "They've seen us! Fuck!"

"Hang on," said Christy. The hearse reversed two or three feet and then swung out and moved forward, slowly inching ahead. I heard the screeching of tires, the blasting of horns, and then my head hit the top wall of the coffin hard as the hearse roared up the street. Christy was an excellent wheelman and there was plenty of torque under the bonnet, but we were being pursued by men in a Subaru who wanted to kill me, and it was maddening not to be able to see them, never mind where we were going. I couldn't protect my head or hold on to anything, either. Every time Christy floored the pedal, my head would slam into the coffin wall behind me, and when he braked, he braked hard, and I had to keep my legs flexed rigid so my knees wouldn't hit the lid. The rapid accelerating was relentless, along with the swerving and bumping and braking. He must have hit an open stretch then because he gunned the engine so hard I thought it was going to pop. Instead, the speed decreased rapidly and the hearse skidded to a halt. I heard their doors opening and then knuckles rapping on the side of the coffin.

"Paddy, get out of there!" said Christy.

I violently shoved the lid away, flooding my eyes with light;

flipped myself out of the coffin; and clambered out the back. The hearse was stopped on South Richmond Street in a bus lane behind a broken-down lorry, and there were cars stuck in traffic all around us, every one of the drivers staring at us, gobsmacked.

Richie's Subaru was hammering down the bus lane towards us, Matser's huge frame nearly filling the windscreen. The three of us ran for all we were worth, leaving the hearse behind, and headed around the corner onto Harrington Street. Christy was beside me, his shirt hanging out and flapping madly along with his jacket, his face contorted with heavy panting.

"Where are we going!" said Eamonn.

"Just keep running!" I said.

I looked quickly behind us again to see Matser charging ahead in front of Richie, forty or fifty yards away. Out of the corner of my eye, down a side street, I spotted a woman holding a baby, standing by a car.

"Lads!" I said. Both men turned instantly and followed me down the little street up to the young mother, who was in the process of opening the door to her Volvo. I snatched the keys off her and hopped in behind the wheel, Christy and Eamonn scrambling in after me. The woman stood back, clutching her baby, horrified. I revved the engine alive and looked in the rearview mirror to see Matser galloping around the corner. I screeched off down the street, watching Matser diminish in size while clumsily stopping beside the woman.

I drove down Heytesbury Street at a normal speed, speechless and still breathing heavily. Christy sat beside me, wild-eyed and wheezing. Eamonn sat in the back, his eyes locked on the rear window. Now that we'd safely broken away from them, I fumbled for a cigarette and lit it with a shaking hand.

"Here, give us one of them!" said Christy, grabbing the packet. "How the fuck did he find out?"

"I don't know, but the knives are out now, anyway."

I pulled into a multistory car park on Drury Street, parked on the third floor, killed the engine, and felt my back relax into the seat behind me. There was small comfort in knowing I wasn't paranoid or mad, even if it meant Cullen wanted my life. At least now I knew he wanted to kill me.

"What does Cullen want you for?" said a shaken-looking Eamonn.

"For knocking down his brother and killing him," I said.

"Did you?"

"I did. It was a complete accident, but it was me that hit him."

"And now Cullen wants you dead."

"I'd imagine that's what he has in mind, yeah."

"So what are you going to do?"

"Forget about me for a minute, Eamonn, and think about yourself. You need to go away for a few days. Call Corrine and tell her you won't be in, and call your dad a bit later and explain the situation to him. But don't go in yourself, and don't go home. The fact that you helped conceal me won't have made you popular with Cullen. So split for a while, all right?"

Eamonn nodded numbly.

"You know how serious this is?" I said.

He nodded again.

"Right, get going."

Eamonn opened the door an inch and stopped.

"What are you going to do?" he said.

"I don't know yet."

Eamonn's chin tightened and his eyes watered slightly, prompting him to grab my hand eagerly and hold on to it.

"Seeya, Paddy," he said awkwardly. "Good luck."

"Thanks for sticking your neck out for me," I said. He took his hand back, got out of the car, and scarpered, leaving Christy and me together in the front seat.

"So what *are* you going to do?" said Christy.

"Get out of the country. It's my only option."

"With what and to where?"

"If I stick around here, I'll be strung up, so anywhere is the answer. If I can get my hands on my share of the syndicate money, that'll at least help me get out . . ."

Christy's brow lowered.

"Wait a minute, you're not saying you're going back to the yard . . ."

"Yeah, and without a bother. I figure Cullen will show up at some stage this afternoon to check it out and that'll be his last visit. If I head there at, say, eight o'clock, I can pick up the money and split."

"And how will you get out?"

"Don't know yet. Maybe west to Knock, maybe south to Cork. If I get across to Knock tonight, I could catch a flight out first thing in the morning."

Christy nodded like it was all making sense to him. "Okay," he said. "I'll see you in the office at eight."

"Christy," I said, smiling, touched by his loyalty. "You don't want to be anywhere near me. We'll say our goodbyes here and now."

"You said it yourself a minute ago, it's the last place Cullen is going to look, and I have a few quid at home I want to give you."

"I'll have more than enough—"

"You're going to need every penny you can get, Paddy, so I'll see you at eight."

"You're an awful man," I said. "In the meantime, get your family out of the house."

Christy got out of the car, gave me a wink, and walked.

THIRTY-THREE

3:30 p.m.

Now that Donal was in the ground, the theme of the day for Vincent was retribution. It was a word and concept he always liked. And it went well with another favorite. Tribulation. He stepped out of his Jag in Gallagher's yard and walked up past the stables towards the office under the hanging geranium pots while Sean and Matser drove in the gates past him in Sean's Chrysler. Vincent knew Buckley wouldn't be here. He was on the run now, running scared. He smiled as he flexed his jaw. *Run all you like, Buckley. You won't get away from me.*

He stepped into the funeral office to see Corrine sitting at her desk alone.

"Hi," he said with a friendly face. "Is Paddy Buckley here?"

The fear that often went hand in hand with a Cullen encounter was untraceable in Corrine, who maintained an air of perfect calm while talking to him.

"No, he's out with a family at the moment. Can anyone else help you?"

"Is Frank Gallagher around?"

"Yes," she said, picking up the phone. "I'll just get him for you."

A few moments passed before Frank emerged from the middle office, looking like a model undertaker.

"Mr. Cullen, Frank Gallagher," he said, offering his hand, which was accepted and shaken.

"Vincent."

DOWN THE BOTTOM of the yard, Jack was sitting in the back of Frank's Mercedes, vacuuming the carpets. So engrossed was he in his chore that he didn't notice Sean leaning over the open back door watching him until he was satisfied that the floor was clean, whereupon he raised his head to see Sean's piercing gaze and Matser behind him, leaning against a limo, peeling an orange.

"Sorry," said Jack, turning off the vacuum cleaner. "I didn't see you there."

Sean smiled at him ruefully. "I didn't mean to frighten you. Tell me, do you know where Paddy Buckley is?"

Despite the fact that Sean was quite blatantly boxing Jack in, his body language was lost on his subject, who sat back in his seat, blissfully unaware.

"No," said Jack. "I don't."

"That's what your friends came out with," said Matser, as he shoved half an orange into his mouth.

"I'm sorry?" said Jack, not sure he'd heard him right.

"Where's Paddy Buckley?" said Sean.

"I don't know where he is."

"Bollocks, if I ever heard it," said Matser, swallowing down the other half.

Jack was a little affronted that he wasn't being believed, but the penny was slowly dropping that something untoward was happening.

"I'm telling you," he said. "I don't know where he is."

In an instant, Sean's manner changed from avuncular to vicious.

"You're not telling me a fucking thing," he said, pulling Jack roughly out of the car. Jack stiffened with fear as Sean head-butted him hard in the face, which sent him stumbling backwards to the wall, terror stricken. Matser moved away from the limo and reversed Sean's car down beside Frank's.

"Give me your phone," said Sean, pulling it out of Jack's hip pocket before kneeing him hard in the groin and again in the face. Jack fell to the ground, holding his nose as the blood ran freely over his hand and down his shirt. Sean opened the boot of his car, wiping the spittle from his mouth.

"Put him in," he said to Matser.

FRANK SAT BEHIND the desk in the middle office, watching Vincent. He'd already written him out a receipt for the cash he'd been paid but Vincent stayed there, and all he seemed interested in was Paddy Buckley. Frank's thoughts had been trained solely on Donal's funeral, but the longer he spent with Vincent, the more he got the feeling that he had some niggling gripe with Paddy.

"Was everything all right on the funeral?" he said.

"It was perfect."

"And Paddy Buckley . . . you were happy with the way he handled everything?"

Vincent sat back in his chair, resting his hands together on his lap. Besides paying the bill, he'd come in to check if Frank Gallagher was sheltering Buckley, but he could see in the man's eyes that he knew nothing of Paddy's involvement in his brother's death. Here was an honest man offering a top-class service. He had no gripe with Frank. He respected him.

The way Vincent saw it, if Frank Gallagher knew that Paddy had killed a man and subsequently buried him, he'd eject him from his company immediately and have his head on a plate. The truth was that Paddy Buckley had been ostensibly operating under both men's noses as a dutiful servant and employee while behind the mask he was a conniving Judas.

"The funeral couldn't have gone off any better; there wasn't a single hitch. I've just heard that Paddy might have some information on who killed Donal, and I wanted to talk to him about it sooner rather than later."

Frank became instantly concerned.

"Right," he said, letting the weight of Vincent's words sink into the room. "Well, as soon as I see him, I'll make sure he gets on to you straightaway."

"I'd appreciate it," said Vincent, rising to his feet. Frank moved around from behind the desk and saw him out.

As soon as Vincent had turned into the yard, Frank closed the door and rested his back against it, suddenly seeing Paddy's behavior of late in an entirely different light. He remembered what Paddy had said in the boardroom yesterday after the Hayes funeral, that he was having the strangest week he'd ever had, that he felt like he was halfway down a birth canal. And now Vincent Cullen thought Paddy knew something about his brother's death. Frank was worried about him. Deeply worried. And then, as if to augment his anxiety, Corrine turned to him with an expression to match his own.

"The police have been on from Harcourt Street. One of our hearses has been abandoned on Richmond Street with all its doors open and an empty Last Supper oak in the back."

"What?" said Frank, disturbed now.

"I've sent three men up to retrieve it and do the bring-back from the South Circular. But that's not all, I'm afraid, Frank . . ."

The horror Frank felt had eclipsed his outrage. "Go on," he said.

"Paddy, Christy, and Eamonn have all been on, saying they won't be in for a couple of days. Eamonn said he'd phone you shortly, he said that he was fine, but better off staying away . . . some kind of emergency, he said."

"Jesus Christ Almighty," said Frank, with as level a tone as he could manage. Apart from his concern for his son and staff, and his growing suspicion that the abandoned hearse was connected in some way to Vincent Cullen, he had the more imminent problem of having funerals to man.

"Get on to Neligan's," he said, grim-faced. "We're going to have to borrow some men."

THIRTY-FOUR

4:10 p.m.

There were only a few places I could go to hide out. Cullen, who'd have saturated Dublin with his soldiers, had his mind on nothing but my blood and wouldn't stop until he'd spilled every bit of it. I could never go back to Mourne Road again. There'd be somebody there around the clock now. All my mementoes and photographs of Eva I could kiss goodbye, along with my passport and computer, and everything else I owned. I'd already dumped my phone in town—if they had my laptop, they could track me with it—but not before I'd sent its contents to my e-mail and taken down a few numbers. The only thing I could hope to hold on to was my life, and even that was a long shot.

I'd been keeping to alleyways and side streets the whole way across town, expecting a car to roll up beside me at any moment and reef me into the back of it, but I made it to the vacant market space at the back of the Liberties and slipped into the safety of George Perrin's yard. George was a mechanic and crash-repair specialist who'd been a close friend of my father's and the equivalent of an uncle to me since I was a teenager. I don't think I'd ever seen him out of his green overalls, and I knew he felt more at home in his yard in Newmarket than he did anywhere else in the world. He had an Icelandic look about him with a beard like William Shakespeare's and kind, streetwise eyes. I'd pop into George's regularly for a chat, but today I needed something beyond the pleasure of his company and safe house.

As was often the case, I found him lying under a car—a 7 Series Beamer—working on an engine.

"George," I said.

"Good morning," said George, as he always did no matter the time of day. "Who's that? Paddy?"

"How's it going?" I said, as he wheeled himself out from beneath the car on a wooden board.

"Haven't seen you in a while," said George, wiping the grease from his hands with a piece of mutton cloth.

"Listen," I said. "I need a favor."

"What do you need?"

"A car for a few days—mine is out of action."

"Matter what kind?"

"No. As long as it goes."

"There's a '93 Fiesta down there beside the MG. Keys are in it. Take it away," he said.

"And do you mind if I use your phone for a minute?"

He pulled it out of his pocket. "As long as you're not calling Honolulu."

"Thanks, George," I said.

Now that I could unwind a little, my mind turned to Brigid. I punched her number in to George's phone and sat in the Fiesta.

"Hello?" said Brigid.

"It's Paddy."

"Hi. Are you finished with your funerals?" I could tell by her voice she was smiling.

"Yeah," I said. "I'm finished."

"Do you want to come over?"

"I'd love to . . . but I can't."

"Where are you?"

"In town."

"Shall I come in to you?"

"No, that's probably not a good idea," I said, finding us in a cul-de-sac already.

". . . Why, what's going on?" she said, the smile in her voice vanished. There was nothing I could say to her. I couldn't involve her in a bit of it, not even by telling her I was on the run or mixed up with people who wanted to kill me. As much as I'd wanted to, I'd never gone past four veils with her. I was hiding so much. Not just the incident with her mother, but what had happened on James's Street, too, and everything surrounding it. I was torn between wanting to tell her everything and being able to tell her nothing, and I wondered would we ever be able to move past that. Maybe I could tell her about the Cullens in time, but not now and not on the phone.

"Brigid, there's so much I want to tell you, about how I feel about you, as well as everything else, but I can't tell you now. I'm in a bit of a tight corner . . ."

There was silence from the other end that sent my focus searching over the cracks in the windscreen.

"Are you in trouble?" she said, beginning to sound nervous

and concerned. I'd wanted to avoid upsetting her from the outset, but it seemed to be where I was bringing her nonetheless.

"No," I said. "I'm not in trouble at all. I'm just in the middle of negotiating my way out of the funeral business, and it's proving a little trickier than I'd first imagined."

"You're leaving your job?"

"I've already left it. I'm just tying up some loose ends, then I'm out of here."

"I'd no idea you were even thinking about it," she said, with genuine surprise.

"Yeah, it's been brewing for a while, even though it came up faster than I'd expected in the end."

"And what will you do?" I could hear the excitement creeping back into her voice, which only ignited my own. And then, as I became enveloped in the warm glow that happened whenever we were around each other, I let myself forget about the Cullens and the trouble I was in, and indulged us both in our fantasy, even if it was to remain unreachable.

"I was thinking of cracking the art world," I said.

"Really?" said Brigid, getting a little laugh out. "Where? Here?"

"No, I've had enough of this town. Across the water maybe . . ."

"London?"

"Yeah, see what they make of me."

"Well," she said, still laughing. "When am I going to see you so you can tell me more about it?"

"In London," I said.

"In London?" she said, her laughter stopping.

"Yeah, I'm catching a plane tonight."

"Are you serious?"

"Deadly serious. There's a little more to all this than I can tell you now on the phone, but I am leaving the country tonight . . . and I wanted you to know, Brigid, that meeting you has changed everything for me."

"Same," she said simply, making my heart swell.

"When are you heading back yourself?"

"At the weekend."

"Can I phone you?"

"Make sure you do," she said, rescued from any trace of worry.

"Okay, I'll get back into it here and I'll see you in London."

"Okay, see you in London," she said, her voice smiling.

"And I'll bring the wine this time."

"Right."

"Bye," I said, and ended the call. The phone went black, but the glow stayed with me, offering little glimpses of salvation that nearly made a future seem possible. But I wasn't that much of a fool. I knew that death was very close. I'd spent my life around it. The likelihood of escaping Cullen's clutches was slim, I knew that, and deep in my heart I feared that the price on my head would be paid in full and that very soon Paddy Buckley would be nothing more than an engraved name on a breastplate and a blemished memory.

THIRTY-FIVE

5:20 p.m.

Trembling like a snared rabbit, Jack lay trapped in the back of Sean's car in total darkness, his mind boggling at what Vincent and his men might want from Paddy. Jack had read every newspaper article he'd ever come across on the Cullens and had long marveled at their brazen and longstanding hold over Dublin's underbelly. But Paddy didn't fit into their world. The funeral had gone off without a hitch. What could they possibly want him for? If he remained in Scully's boot for a week, he'd never guess that it was Paddy who killed Donal. In fact, the only reason that Jack could conceive of was that Vincent had somehow noticed the Polikoff Special on Donal's suit and was more than a little angry about it.

After what felt like an eternity, he heard a door open somewhere near the car and heavy footsteps get nearer and nearer until they stopped right next to the back bumper. The boot was pressed open, filling the space around Jack with early evening light and the shadow of Matser's big frame. That's when his trembling gave way to shaking. Matser reached in and pulled him onto his feet before frog-marching him across an enclosed courtyard through the back door of a nightclub, not stopping until he'd brought him into a little windowless room where he released his grip.

Jack placed his hand on a small table and turned around to see Matser's fist coming down hard to belt him across the face. He cowered and raised his arms to defend himself but received a continuous pounding of slaps and kicks for his trouble, the only sound, apart from the slaps themselves, being the irregularity of both men's breathing. Matser punctuated the end of it with a final punch to the nose, leaving Jack in a heap on the floor with blood streaming over his mouth and chin.

"Now fucking stay there," said Matser.

Matser straightened his jacket and left the room, leaving the door ajar.

After a few minutes lying as still as he could to try to ease the pain, Jack slowly moved himself into a sitting position by the wall and held his pounding head in his hands. He ached all over; he felt as if he'd been run over by a bus. Which in some ways he had. All he could think about was his wife and son, and whether he'd be killed. And from what he knew about Cullen from the papers, he figured he'd be dead by suppertime.

Be brave, he told himself. *Be brave, be brave, be brave, and stop crying.* He did his very best to stay as silent as he could, knowing full well that whoever was outside the door could hear his blubbering. With considerable effort Jack managed to reduce his weeping to a kind of barely controlled silent whimpering.

And then Vincent walked in, which only brought Jack right back to square one. As he was helped to his feet, he started hyperventilating. Vincent pulled out a chair and sat Jack down, resting his hand reassuringly on his shoulder.

"Shhhh. Stop crying now," he said softly, before leaving the room again only to return moments later with a bowl of steaming hot water and a cloth. He pulled another chair right up next to Jack's and sat down on it. Jack kept his eyes on the table beside them and tried to control his shaking. His face was caked in a mixture of dried and oozing blood, and his nose, which was now broken, had swollen to twice its normal size. He looked like a boxer who'd spent too long in the ring with a fighter who wanted to kill him.

"Shush now," said Vincent, as he gripped Jack's face and tilted his head back, sending his gaze from the table to the ceiling. Fear gripped him again as he grappled with the fact that Vincent Cullen was wiping his face clean, and while trying to level his fitful breathing, Jack expelled a rather large clot of blood through his nose that sprayed all over the table and the sleeve of Vincent's suit. Horrified, Jack looked into Vincent's eyes for the first time.

"I'm sorry . . . I'm sorry."

Vincent stood up and very calmly slipped his jacket off, which he hung behind his chair before sitting back down and dipping the cloth in the water.

"Stop crying," he said, while concentrating on bathing Jack's face. "Now."

Jack nodded his head, and by the combined wills of both men, he'd succeeded in putting an end to his tears within a few minutes.

Vincent moved in close to Jack's ear and whispered, "Tell me about Buckley."

"I don't know where he is," said Jack wearily. "I haven't a clue . . . I don't even know what this is about, I swear, I don't know . . ."

Now that Jack's face was largely clean of blood, Vincent's focus was on Jack's hair, which he went about gently stroking and shaping.

"How long have you known Buckley?" he said.

"Nearly two years," said Jack, doing his best to remain relaxed.

"Two years, right. Do you trust him?"

"Yeah," said Jack hesitantly. "I do."

"Listen to me, Jack. Paddy Buckley killed my brother and then came into my house and sat with me, drank coffee with me, he stayed in the funeral parlor with me during my last moments with my brother as if he was a friend, when what he was doing was turning a knife in my back. Trustworthy? Well, he hasn't put you in the picture, has he? Buckley doesn't give a bollocks about you. And in case you're in any way confused as to where you stand with me, I don't give a bollocks about you, either. Clear?"

"Yeah," said Jack, with as straightened a nerve as he could manage.

"Now, what I want is for you to start talking to me like there's no tomorrow."

Jack's chin was a mass of little quivers as he looked soulfully into Vincent's eyes.

"I will tell you everything I know, but I don't know anything about Paddy knocking down your brother, I swear, nobody tells me anything . . ."

"Come on, Jack, Buckley involves you in all his activities. You think I don't know about you? I know all about you, Jack—how your wife is unhappy working in that school in Finglas, how you struggle to get the money together for your kid's medication. You work with Buckley to look after your family, Jack, I know. Now, your single motivation is to keep thinking about your family. Do you want to see them again, Jack?"

Vincent gently wiped away Jack's tears and moved his fingers affectionately over the curve of his jaw.

"Of course I do," said Jack.

"Right, then start talking to me," said Vincent in a whisper, brushing his lips against Jack's cheek.

"I don't know what to tell you," said Jack, trying his best to pray and answer Vincent's questions at the same time.

"Just tell me the truth, Jack, okay? Now, how much do you make off this betting syndicate?"

"Em . . . my end usually comes to around three hundred a race, sometimes five."

"And how much do you put in?"

"We work off a core amount they've been using for years."

"So you never put any money in."

"No."

"And where is this core amount kept?"

"In the funeral home, in Paddy's locker."

"And that's never touched."

"No, that's the money we work off," Jack repeated.

Jack had stopped crying, and Vincent was sitting back in his chair with his hands on his lap.

"Right," he said. "Right. You see, you do know something, Jack. You needn't have been crying at all."

Jack swallowed hard as he looked back at the floor, utterly unnerved by Vincent's behavior. Vincent sitting so close to him had started it, but being touched by him and whispered to as if he were a woman had crystallized the experience for Jack. It was the strangest and most terrifying encounter of his life.

"Would you like a cup of tea, Jack?"

Jack just shook his head. Vincent stayed there another few minutes, looking at him. He seemed to derive a strange kind of enjoyment from watching him squirm. He got up then, picked up the bowl and cloth slowly and deliberately, and left the room.

Jack sat there, breathing through his mouth, his eyes fixed on Vincent's jacket hanging on the back of the chair. Then Matser came in, escorted him outside, put him in the boot of Sean Scully's car, and drove him up the Dublin Mountains, where he was thrown out and left there, without his phone.

As the taillights of Scully's Chrysler disappeared into a darkening Dublin, Jack took in the tall pine trees surrounding him and felt the cold October air fill his lungs. As he settled his eyes on the blinking lights of Poolbeg Power Station in Ringsend, he noticed his legs and hands were still trembling. His experience with Cullen had left him more shaken than he'd ever been, but it had also given him a renewed and profound appreciation for his simple life, never mind that his nose was broken, his ribs badly bruised, and his head swollen and aching.

THIRTY-SIX

6:45 p.m.

If there was a running motif throughout my brief life, it would
be the close and present nature of death. I'd known it inti-
mately from the start. My mother's when I was four, my father's
when I was thirty-three, and, of course, my wife's and unborn
daughter's when I was forty. And there'd been plenty more along
the way—aunts, uncles, friends, acquaintances, never mind Lucy's
and Donal's and the few thousand other funerals I'd attended. It
seems there are two types of deaths: the ones your heart goes out
to and the ones your heart gets pulverized by. By its very nature,
death gives pause for thought on the essence and brevity of
life, but when it calls close to home and we're submerged, heart
first, into the depths of grief, and the questioning and processing
and ultimate accepting it necessitates, the worldview we held pre-
viously can often be dismissed out of hand while we're rewired for
life without the love we took for granted, or even treasured. There
were times during my grieving when I wanted to go myself, when
I pondered at length the likelihood of being struck down by a

sudden heart attack or the dreaded cancer or by a brain hemorrhage like Eva's to the point where I looked forward to it, even
invited it in. But no matter how dark the days got, no matter how
miserable and lonely and scared I was, taking myself out was
never really an option. That was the Almighty's job.

In terms of exiting the dream, my father's death was probably
the easiest. He'd been driving back from Brittas Bay in his van
along a hedge-lined road when an oncoming car towing a trailer
half a foot proud of the car's width had pulled out to accommodate a pedestrian and clipped the van in the process, sending Shay
sailing through the windscreen, landing thirty yards up the road.
It was an instant death, thankfully, but it robbed the world of the
pleasure of maybe twenty more years of his inimitable and mar-
velous company. And placed me next in line for the reaper.

The last time I saw my father alive was in Perrin's yard, where
he'd been playing chess with George. They'd had a game going for
thirty years, always playing beside the potbelly stove under the
shelter of the garage, where they'd smoke their cigarettes and
drink coffee. It was a Saturday and I'd dropped in a hearse for a
spray job, and there I found him, happy as he always was, leaning
over the board, puffing on his smoke—Major extra size. The way
he looked that day is burned into my memory forever: He wore a
thick black fisherman's cardigan over his brown suede waistcoat
with the navy flat cap I'd bought him in Skibbereen, and when I
remember him smiling from behind the chessboard, it's his play-
ful wisdom I remember etched into every crevice of his face. I
stayed for a cigarette and a chat, never knowing it would be our
last. It was nearing the end of that particular game, which was a
close one, and everyone's focus was on the last few moves.

"God plays chess and the Devil plays poker," he said, while moving in for mate. "God's game is the one: strategy, positioning, control; you can play poker and win, but the Devil will get you in the end." It was the last thing of any note he said to me. I stayed for the rest of my smoke, kissed him on his head, and walked back to Uriel Street. The following Tuesday he was dead.

The places I could go in Dublin now were few, and I had only a handful of hours left to me, so I'd driven to Esker to Eva's and my parents' grave to gather myself for my exit. Sitting on the edge of the sandstone slab while the light faded, I felt closer to death than perhaps I ever had. Closer to Eva and to Shay and to the mother I never really knew. It was perhaps because of my hunted status that I remembered the fox my father used to feed in our back garden at nighttime and how he tamed him over a six-week period. I'd seen him do the same thing with the wild cats in Gallagher's yard, having them literally leap into his arms by the time he'd worked his charms on them.

As a boy, I'd go to bed each night in our house on Arnott Street in Portobello and watch my father from my bedroom window tending to his radishes and carrots and French beans. On a clear night in the spring I turned twelve, I saw a fox stop on top of the seven-foot wall at the end of our garden and look down at my father, who stilled himself and returned the fox's gaze. For five minutes, they stayed like that, the silent intimacy between them a communion only they could understand. The fox moved on then, unhurried, but returned a few nights later to repeat the exchange. And again the next night, and the night after that. Until it became their nightly ritual. After a couple of weeks, Shay brought out a plate of cod's liver and nibbled on it himself during their little meeting. After a few nights of this, he stood up and extended a bit of food in his hand to the fox, whose desire to taste what he'd only been able to smell for three nights trumped his caution, and gingerly bringing his snout down to meet Shay's fingers, he carefully ate the cod's liver out of Shay's hand and continued to lick his lips and whiskers for ten minutes afterwards. For three weeks, this was as close as the fox would let him get. And then one night, after Shay had stopped reaching out to him but had kept the plate of food on the ground beside him, the fox crawled down the wall like a big cat and licked the plate clean and stuck around afterwards to get his chest rubbed. In the end, Shay had succeeded in gaining the fox's trust so completely that the animal would come into the kitchen and eat pieces of cured meat out of his hand. Whatever it was about him, my father had the same effect on nearly every living being.

Though the tide of death may well have been sweeping close and my hunters closer, I didn't want to die yet. I wanted to make it to London. I wanted to see Brigid one more time. I wanted to get away from the never-ending stream of corpses and coffins, and from all the details that constantly reminded me of what I'd lost. To where I could venture into the unknown, reinvent myself, and rise again.

Cemeteries, as junctures of wounds and remembrance, tend to bring up memories of what's been lost, and my greatest loss, of course, was Eva. As I readied myself to leave behind Dublin, the memory of Eva sitting under the Mickey Mouse clock in our kitchen at six on the morning she died stirred inside me. I'd woken to find the space in the bed beside me empty—she was heavily pregnant and her sleep patterns had become erratic—so I ventured downstairs and found her in the kitchen stirring a bowl of black tea. There she sat: white nightie, swollen belly, no makeup—just natural, beautiful, unadulterated. I sat down opposite her and placed my hand over hers and watched her slip a sugar cube onto her tongue and suck it.

"The baby is making me remember funny things," she said to me, a little regretfully.

"What kind of things?"

"The bad things I've done." I massaged her perfectly proportioned hands in mine, and felt her long nails and soft olive skin.

"Come on," I said. "How bad?"

"I was a thief," she said. *"Une voleuse."*

I couldn't help smiling at how adorable she was. "What did you thieve?"

"I was fourteen. *Maman* had got me a job for the summer with a friend of hers who had a cleaning company in Nantes. And I worked with those women for two months. They were older than I was, and they were kind." She took her hand back and slipped her thumbnail between the gap in her teeth while her eyes became glazed with shame. "It was a Friday and everyone had been paid the day before. I was in the locker room on my own and I saw the money sticking out of the bag of one of the women, in her locker. It was locked, but the door was bent at the top, and I knew I'd be able to reach the money. It was, how do you say, a wad?"

"A wad," I said, nodding.

"I didn't need it and I hadn't thought of stealing before I saw it, but it was an impulse inside me so strong, I couldn't resist. I checked that there was no one, and then I stuck my fingers in and took it. It was nearly two thousand francs, a week's wages for the woman who had worked hard for it on her hands and knees."

"Did you get caught?"

"Before the end of the day, I came into the little kitchen for the cleaners, and the eight women were sitting at the table, looking sad, like they knew I had taken it. And the woman who I'd stolen it from, Madeleine, she looked terribly betrayed. I acted like an innocent and asked what had happened. My mother's friend told me, very serious, and they all looked to see my reaction. And I continued my act of innocence, and there were no more questions for me. But everyone knew. I am sure of it."

"What happened in the end?"

"Nothing happened. I finished working there two weeks later, and it faded into my past. But I never forgot it completely. And now today I wish I could say sorry to Madeleine and give her the money back. I feel terrible, Paddy," she said, with tears forming in her eyes. I took her hand in mine and kissed it and told her how admirable her sense of contrition was. Twenty-two years after her crime and her guilt still haunted her. Her remorse stopped her from stealing again and had probably helped shape her beautiful, compassionate character, but any chance she had of making amends to Madeleine went to the grave with her that very same day.

Eva wasn't a subscriber to any scripted faith, but rather listened to her heart, which informed her principles and moral code of love and tenderness and empathy and kindness. So I'd organized her a simple unpolished oak coffin without any handles, and instead of a crucifix, I painted two love hearts with sealing wax, one on the breast of the coffin, the other where her womb would be, and stamped them with my fingerprints. In lieu of a church, I held her service outside under the octagonal roof of the Phoenix Park bandstand in the handsome little hollow she loved so much with its crooked white benches and naked winter trees. The attendance and outpouring of sympathy were enormous—Eva would have held her hands to her face with astonishment—and we all cried together to the music of Damien Rice and the poetry of Séamus Heaney and Patrick Kavanagh and Charles Bukowski. Little did I know then what dreams were still to come.

The night had returned and had brought the rain along with it, giving rise to a mist coming up from the cemetery soil like upward tears from the dead. I kissed the gravestone goodbye and wandered back towards the car, my heart trying to balance the trepidation I felt with the sliver of hope I clung to and the lust for life that my parents had instilled in me.

THIRTY-SEVEN

7:55 p.m.

My dream of Hampstead was a perfect one, full of delightful restaurants and cafés and bookshops and well-educated people with exquisite English accents like Lucy's and sophisticated senses of humor. I'd discover what culture was to Brigid's artist friends over delicious food at intimate dinner parties, and Brigid and I would walk on Hampstead Heath, holding hands, confidants and lovers, neither of us with any family left but only each other to hold. In the morning, I'd wake her with croissants and coffee, and I'd taste every part of her, and we'd spend whole weekends making love. We'd go to Camden Town and Covent Garden and to art galleries, and we'd take trips to Scotland and have weekends away in Oxfordshire, and England would embrace us and our golden silences. I could reach and touch this vision of England. If only I could cheat the Devil and escape quietly.

I parked on Lamb Alley and stepped out of the car into a drizzling and balmy night, and smelled the hops from Guinness's on the breeze, reminding me of the pints I'd had with Brigid only the night before. I smiled while thinking if there ever would be a next time to sink a pint, it would be in Hampstead, a thought that gave me great excitement.

Just before I turned the corner to Uriel Street, I noticed a blue Subaru just like Richie's parked behind a battered yellow skip. I walked over and looked in the window. There was nothing to tell me it was his, and there were plenty of blue Imprezas around the place, but even still, the excitement in my belly was gone and in its place was a bowel-curdling dread. I checked my watch. It was a minute to eight.

I gingerly crossed the road and made my way into An Capall Dubh, which was filled with the usual punters drinking pints, watching greyhound racing on the television.

"Paddy," said Gerry, with a nod while pulling the pints.

"Gerry," I said, and skipped up the stairs to the Gents. I closed the door, turned off the light, and locked myself in the cubicle. I stood up on the toilet and peered out through the little square window into the front office of Gallagher's, which was empty and in darkness. Craning my neck slightly, I could see the parlor door was ajar, and I was barely able to make out the outline of a man standing in profile. Whoever it was had hair. Probably Richie. Then I saw a spark and a flame and Richie's brow lighting up as he sucked on his cigarette, and just beside him for the brief moment the flame was alive, I saw a face full of malice: Vincent's.

I slid down to a seated position on the toilet while my lungs deflated and I grabbed hold of my hair; my dreams of London dead like a flicked match. *Fuck it.*

Christy, who'd never been late in his life, was undoubtedly in there. With Cullen. It was all over. My time was up. But even though it was my time, I couldn't let it be Christy's. His loyalty and first-rate friendship had got him into the ugliest fix in Dublin, and it was all my fault. I could only plead mercy for his life. It was the only card I had.

I shuffled out of the toilet and plodded slowly down the stairs with legs of cement. Vincent wasn't going to let Christy go and I was kidding myself if I thought he might. He'd only give me Christy's life if I had one to bargain with, and mine didn't count—it had to be one he didn't want to kill.

The cheering from the bar at the TV sent my focus to the slow-motion replay of the winning greyhound crossing the line, chasing the hare, and in a sanctified moment of serendipity, the answer presented itself like an ace being slipped to me right from the dealer's hand: the dog.

THIRTY-EIGHT

8:25 p.m.

I took a long pull on my cigarette and pushed the smoke deep into my lungs, thinking of Christy in the parlor taking the hiding of a lifetime. On the seat beside me were three plastic-sealed packets of duck-liver pâté, a bottle of water, and a fresh pack of Carrolls cigarettes. I'd parked on the road outside Vincent's house behind a line of cars, opened the window, and waited. I didn't want to leave Christy in Uriel Street any longer than I had to, but the dog over the wall could well end my time before her master got a chance, so I allowed myself one last smoke before I tried her. This is what my life had come down to: a final cigarette, the dog owned by the most dangerous man in the world, and if I was lucky, Christy's release and my subsequent execution.

The few drops of rain making it in through the window onto the side of my face were a welcome sensation, considering the violent end that was waiting for me. It was cold and refreshing, and coupled with the wind, gave my skin the last semblance of solace it would ever know and reminded me that I was still very much encased in it.

I couldn't face the dog with any trace of fear inside me; she'd smell it like the last time—she'd maybe even see it for all I knew. I had to free myself of it completely. But shaking it was easier said than done.

I stepped out of the car, flicked the butt away, and took a good look at the wall. It was about eight feet high. I could get over it with a running jump, but once on the other side, I'd be with Dechtire, with no room for faltering. It was time for communion.

I padded my pockets to make sure I had everything I needed, and with my adrenaline pumping, I made it over on the first effort and crouched down under a cluster of Scots pines to get my bearings. Save for a couple of windows glowing with a golden light, the place was in darkness, and there was no sign of the dog. There was only one car, and it was parked between me and the house, a silver Subaru, presumably belonging to Vincent's wife. I approached it quietly and tried opening the front passenger door. It was open. Of course it was—who in their right mind would rob a car from Cullen's house? I located the gate zapper and put it in my pocket. I clicked the door shut and retreated to the shelter of a giant oak tree fifty yards from the house, got down on my hunkers, and let out a low whistle.

"Dechtire," I said, no louder than if she'd been right beside me, and settled my focus on the side of the house where I'd seen the kennel on Wednesday morning.

"Dechtire," I said again a few moments later, and made a clicking sound with my tongue. After maybe a minute, she appeared from behind the house and stopped still to look at me across the drive, the light from the window reflecting in her eyes. I'd only ever seen her in Vincent's study and over by the greenhouse. Out here in the shade of night with the elements alive around her, she took on a far more majestic presence. The rain was lashing down on her and there was steam rising from her back and a beautiful stillness emanating from her eyes. I returned her gaze without as much as a blip of fear and felt my father come alive inside me. I could feel my dimples deepening just like his, and though I couldn't see it, it felt as if my right eye twinkled like his used to, and with a few more clicks of the tongue, I coaxed the dog over. Coupled with her stillness was a wariness, which was slowly turning into curiosity. Apart from our unusual introduction on Tuesday morning, she'd seen her master welcome me, give me refreshments and a gift, so off the bat, I was no threat.

Tentatively at first, she walked through the rain to the dry ground under the giant oak and arrived beside me to meet the back of my hand, which I gently stroked against her chest.

"Good girl," I whispered, moving my hand up to her snout where, while rubbing her, I got her to relax even more, her eyes closing with pleasure when I hit an itchy spot. I took the pâté out of my coat pocket and opened it up. With the trust established between us, she was ready for a taste, totally alert now in a sitting position and licking her lips. I put a bit on my fingers and let her lick it off. As careful as she was not to hurt me with her teeth, it was clearly one of the most delicious things she'd ever tasted and she hungrily gobbled down every bit I offered her until she'd licked the packet clean. She let out a satisfied groan then and lay down on her back, opening her legs submissively while I gave her belly a good scratch.

Now that I had her eating out of my hand, I was faced with the difficult bit. I reached into my pocket and pressed the button that opened the gate. Dechtire stood up immediately and looked towards it. I straightened up, took out another packet of pâté, and took a few steps towards the road. The dog stayed where she was, looking at me, aware of every factor at play. She knew she wasn't meant to come with me, but she also knew I meant her no harm. The intelligence Chris O'Donoghue talked about was well evident in the dog's demeanor, but I wasn't hearing Chris's words in my head as I stood there with her in the rain. I was thinking my father's thoughts. It wasn't enough to will the dog to come with me, I had to expect her to come.

"Let's go down to Vincent," I said, and nodded towards the gate. "Come on." I started walking and kept going with my head down till I was out on the road. I turned around to see her standing in the same spot thirty yards away. The wariness was back. I was halfway across a tightrope that was leading to my dream's end and I didn't want to take Christy with me. I wasn't sure what the dog could or couldn't see, what she knew or didn't know, or how bright or exceptional she was, but I needed her to come with me. I closed my eyes and felt my father closer than ever. *Please, get the dog to follow me. Make her come.* I opened my eyes again to see the dog in exactly the same place.

We were at a crossroads, Dechtire and I, but this was the end of the line for me, I knew that. My life was over and I'd just reached the point where I was okay with that. The world of Paddy Buckley was soon to be a lesson learned, and I'd be returned to spirit. With this acceptance came a kind of direct knowing, an exultant feeling of arrival, having traveled a long and laborious journey. And I knew exactly what I had to do before checking out.

I crouched down and stretched my left hand out in front of me and focused on my palm and centered every part of me in it. Nothing else mattered now. I felt my palm pulse and get warmer, and then, with the ease of just intending it, my consciousness rippled down my left arm until my palm became the seat of my subtle self, housing the perceiving part of me. Instead of looking at my palm as I'd started out, I looked back at my face from the seat of my palm. And just like on Monday night in my bed in Mourne Road, I detached. And rose above myself. Independent Channel 24 perceptible only to Dechtire and me.

I looked down at my crouching self with my hand still outstretched and saw myself stand up. Watching myself in the rain, I continued rising until I was ten feet above my head, and I stopped. I looked to where Dechtire was standing, still in the same place, but she was watching me now in my suspended state, floating high above my body. An excitement took hold of her. I tossed the pâté a few inches in the air and caught it. "Come on," I said. "Let's go down to Vincent."

I drifted weightlessly above my body as I started walking towards the car and watched her lick her lips excitedly and briskly walk out the gate after me. I got to the car and opened the passenger door for her. She hopped in and sat down. I got in the other side and started the engine. With us both seated side by side, Dechtire seemed perfectly comfortable dealing with the two parts of me: my material self behind the wheel and the invisible part of me floating just above the dashboard, which was the one she watched with lucid eyes. I opened up the pâté and gave her the lot. She sat down further on the seat and busied herself with eating it while I started the drive back to the yard.

It's a strange feeling, surrendering to death. Fear and resistance drop away. Every facet of life around you seems valid and beautiful and oddly perfect. What once sounded like a cacophony takes on a symphonic quality; the seemingly disparate and disconnected elements of life combine to make up strands of the same fabric, blending together in a perfect euphony. And a limpid calm descends.

The dog sitting beside me would have ripped me to shreds if it wasn't for the unique understanding between us, but we weren't finished with each other just yet. When she'd eaten her food, she sat erect and watched the road till we'd parked around by George Perrin's, a five-minute walk from Gallagher's.

I took the last packet of pâté out of my coat and placed it on the dash. The dog looked at it and then back to me, probably more concerned with getting out of the car, and I could see she was expecting to come with me. I rubbed her snout again, but she didn't go along with it this time. She just stared at me, suspended as I was. I couldn't go in to Vincent without her collar. Getting it, though, was another matter—if she was going to turn on me, that's when she'd do it, even if I was inhabiting the ether beside her.

I closed my eyes and relaxed my body, knowing this would be the last time I ever could, and as I imagined meeting Eva again, I could hear the fleeting echo of her laughter—I searched around me but she wasn't there. I was removed from my skin and senses, yet I could still detect her scent near me, like a subtle harbinger of our imminent reunion. The thought of holding her close to me, feeling her at one with me, made the price of any pain I might be subjected to beyond worth it.

Facing Vincent removed from my body would be the easy way to exit my life; with one foot already in the grave, so to speak. But I had penance to pay. My independent channel had successfully helped usher my passenger to where I needed her to be, but the threshold awaiting me was to be crossed with honor and courage, and in the flesh. I had to face Vincent as a man. With my intention firmly set, I started breathing slowly and deeply into the base of my belly, and I dug my heels into my shoes and the floor. Slowly, I moved away from the windscreen, closer to my body, until I felt myself sitting into my skin, fully encased in it again with my blood rushing through my veins and my scalp tingling around my skull.

While I was still immersed in my final meditation, the dog placed her head down on my lap, stretching herself across the two seats, and let out a tired groan. I stroked her head gently and massaged behind her ears, making her moans more constant and relaxed. This was the communion my father had known with animals all his life. While continuing to stroke her head and neck, I slowly unbuckled her collar, pulled it from around her neck, and put it in my pocket.

"Dechtire," I said softly. She raised her head to look at me. "I'll be back with Vincent. Stay here and I'll bring him back with me." I lowered the window an inch and took the keys from the ignition while she sat back up, her pregnant belly more obvious, elevated on the passenger seat. I opened the pâté and placed it by her front paws, and I pulled the handle on the door.

"Stay here, I won't be long." I got out of the car and closed the door while she continued to sit there, staring at me. Whether she somehow understood what was going on and was helping me in some selfless capacity because of our special connection or she was just a dog who could be manipulated and cajoled, I'll never know. But she'd given me what I needed, nonetheless. She'd trusted me just long enough. Now that I was armed with Dechtire's collar, the likelihood of both Christy's release and mine was far more probable, never mind that we were going to different places.

THIRTY-NINE

9:10 p.m.

I placed my hands on the cold bars of the cast-iron gates and pushed them open, sending a creaking sound vibrating through the wall of the front office. It was time for my purging, to lay down my life and join my beloved Eva. But not before my final charade: poker masquerading as chess. I slipped Dechtire's collar along the inside of my belt, stepped through the open door of the back office, and readied myself for my personal apocalypse.

The place was in darkness and as quiet as a nest of caterpillars. I heard footsteps on carpet and then from the shadowy doorway came Matser, who seemed to drift, his strides were so long.

"Buckley," he said, taking a grip of my shirt and pressing me against the wall to frisk me. The man with the glass eye came in from the corridor, holding a short length of gaffer tape, which he pressed over my mouth. I could tell by the way he was smiling at me he was a sadist, as he seemed to derive great pleasure from silencing me, and then, as if to confirm it, he took a rough hold of my throat with one hand and squeezed my balls tight with the other. Then to compound it, he let go of my balls and kneed them full force. I doubled up and groaned behind the tape, but was pulled up immediately by both men, who took an arm each and paraded me into the pitch-black of the front parlor.

"Lights, Richie," said Vincent, his menace a gliding calm. The lights turned up to a soft glow to reveal Vincent, Sean, and Richie, all standing, glowering at me with malevolent intent, and Christy sitting by the wall with his mouth taped up and his eyes glazed over with the fear of death. He was bloodied and bruised, and his glasses were gone. I could only imagine what kind of darkness they'd been filling his head with. I hadn't counted on being silenced like this, and with my arms immobile, I couldn't reach for the collar.

Vincent held up the black plastic bag with the syndicate money in it and tossed it on the bier. "Back for the money," he said. "A greedy cunt like you couldn't keep away from it." He moved to the armchair at the end of the bier and sat down on it, in no rush to go anywhere.

"You're not as wide as you'd like to think, Buckley. I met one other sham like you in my time. I was fifteen years old and my mother had a stall up on Thomas Street. The number one spot on the street, she had. A little goldmine, it was. She had it for years. And it took a pox like you to turn it sour on her. She was always the first to have her stall set up in the morning, and this particular day was a Saturday. She was there on her own when this hungry pig turns up and breaks her face up, tears her stall apart, and tells her she's finished on the street. She ended up in James's for a month with her heart broke. I caught up with the fucker a week later and tied him down, got stuck into him, and dismembered every part of his poxy body. I talked to him before I killed him, and it turns out it was himself and his mother in it from the start. So I emptied his parts all over her stall in the middle of Thomas Street, right in front of her, and I told her the same thing I told her son: that he was only a lowly cunt. And that's what you are, Buckley. And tonight you get the same treatment, with a slightly different twist. But you'll know what's coming, I'll demonstrate on your boyfriend first."

He got up from the chair and led the way out of the room. I made urgent sounds through the tape, pleading to be heard, but Richie didn't want to hear it. He gripped my lapels roughly and hammered his forehead twice into my face, sending flashes of searing pain into the center of my head and a dizziness I thought would floor me.

"Shut your fucking hole, Buckley," he said, and grabbed hold of Christy with Sean and shoved him along ahead of me. Apart from holding one of my arms, Matser also had a grip of my hair and, along with the glass-eyed man, dragged me into the embalming room behind Christy.

The fluorescent tubes suspended over the two steel tables bounced alive, filling the room with such stark and unappealing light that nobody present would ever be able to erase the night from their memory. I was shoved into a sitting position on a bin by the wall while Christy was pulled onto one of the embalming tables and pushed onto his back. He grunted and squirmed under their force, his left leg trembling so violently it banged the steel repeatedly, but they pulled him and stretched him out until he was rigidly still. Vincent stood by the counter, taking a good look at the instruments laid out before him, which Eamonn had left sparkling clean.

"Open his shirt," said Vincent. Sean ripped it open, sending the buttons dropping to the floor, while Richie struggled to hold Christy down.

"Matser," said Sean. "Give us a hand over here."

Matser left my side to help them, giving the glass-eyed man both my arms to hold. I had to somehow get Vincent's attention without getting head-butted again.

"Want to cut that, Vincent?" said Sean, pointing to Christy's vest. Vincent picked up a scalpel and moved to Christy's side while Matser, Richie, and Sean held him down.

Christy's breathing quickened through flared nostrils while his eyes locked wildly with mine. I sounded the syllables of Vincent's name as urgently as I could, imploring him to look at me, but he didn't. He took a hold of the neck of the vest and cut it down the middle to expose Christy's bare chest and belly.

I tried to get his attention again with my voice and even tried to shake my hip out to expose the collar but got a knee to my right kidney and a thumb dug deep into my neck, which was kept up afterwards. Christy just groaned for mercy, his face a maddened grimace.

Vincent's hand glided over the different instruments until he stopped above the trocar, which he picked up and gripped in his hand and pursed his lips approvingly. He turned to me with a mirthless little smile.

"I've got to get my back into it, is that what you said?"

I pointed my head desperately towards my belt, willing them to look, but all I got was the thumb stuck deeper into my neck.

"Watch now, keep fucking watching," whispered the glass-eyed man, with his mouth pressed to my ear.

Christy's feet writhed around in agonized circles while he expelled fearful fits of breath. I grunted and moaned as loud as I could and shook my pelvis against the force being applied to me.

"Now, a triangle, Buckley, between the sternum, the naval, and just here on the left, is it?" said Vincent, getting the trocar ready to penetrate the skin over Christy's abdomen. Christy's eyes rolled madly, and he writhed and groaned.

I steeled myself with everything I had, violently shaking my whole frame until I'd freed myself enough to be able to reach for the collar and fling it onto the table beside them. Before I could see Vincent's reaction, the glass-eyed man had jumped on me and was pounding my face and head in a frenzy of elbows and fists. I held my hands up to stop him and then saw Vincent pushing him aside and reaching down to pull me up, lifting me by my throat and slamming me down hard on the empty table. I could hardly breathe with the strength of his grip around me.

"What the fuck is this?" he said, holding the collar, and then he crawled up on top of me. Up until now there'd been a controlled stillness to his menace. But seeing the collar changed all that. He'd just let the animal out of its cage.

I grunted from behind the tape. He ripped it off me, picked my head up, and slammed it back down on the steel.

"What have you done?" His voice was guttural.

My heart thumped inside my head.

"I've got the dog . . ."

He gripped the skin of my mouth and cheeks in his hand like he was about to tear it off, and with his free hand, he picked up the trocar like a dagger and buried it in my left shoulder. The pain was excruciating and immediate and spread instantly across my chest and up my neck, restricting my breathing to shallow gasps.

"Call," said Vincent, through clenched teeth, still gripping the trocar. In my peripheral vision, I saw Sean put a phone to his face. The room went silent while he waited, Vincent never once taking his focus off me.

"Angela, it's Sean. Listen to me, check where Dechtire is, will you? . . . Thanks, love."

How many more beats before my heart gave me up? It was drumming through them fast, regardless, getting me closer to Eva all the time. I fought back a momentary urge to smile and thought of Christy, who I had to get out of there before I could drop the body. I couldn't turn my head to look at him with the trocar still in me, but I knew he was all right, at least for the moment. If I could get him out in one piece and unpunctured, I would die willingly.

"Right. No, don't worry . . . bye." Sean ended the call and turned to Vincent. "Nowhere. And the gate's wide open."

Vincent pressed the trocar forward, making me roar, the severity of the pain nearly knocking me out.

"Where is she?" he said, stilling the trocar. I winced to talk.

"You can have her back as soon as you let Christy go."

"Nobody's going fucking anywhere, Buckley. Now whoever's holding the dog, get them on the phone . . . now."

"No," I said, and braced myself for the worst. He moved the trocar back and forth like he was changing gears, sending the pain shooting down my whole trunk and arm and into the pit of my stomach and bowels. This was the purging. This was my agony in the garden. The blood collected on the table behind my shoulder and streamed down to my armpit and left side.

"Get them on the phone right fucking now," said Vincent. He'd stopped moving the trocar and waited along with everyone else in the room for my answer.

"There is no phone, just a straightforward trade: Christy's life for the dog's. I've come here to die—your brother's blood is on my hands—but Christy did nothing. Let him go and you get the dog back tonight."

Vincent pulled me up by the lapels.

"Everything's veneer with you, Buckley. You drive your wife's car while keeping the murder weapon concealed in your fucking garage. You laugh behind my back while playing the caring friend. And now there's no fucking phone. Maybe there's no one holding the dog, either. You drugged her, didn't you? You drugged her and have her in the boot of your car. Tell me the truth, Buckley," he said, squeezing my face in his hand. I could only talk through gasps of breath I was so overwhelmed by the intensity of the pain, and the swelling bruises on my head pulsed relentlessly.

"The dog isn't hurt and will remain that way. She's with a person who's got acres of land and nothing but love for the dog, and you'll never find her. I never made the phone call an option because they're not equipped to talk to you and I wouldn't put them in the position."

"And you organized this tonight, did you?"

"I made it happen tonight, but it occurred to me that it'd be the perfect life for the dog on Wednesday in your garden when I was petting Dechtire." This was my last act, and knowing he could read the truth, I loaded my story with the truth of Christy's right to live, which came straight from my heart. Everything else was just dressing. "If Christy walks, the dog will be delivered to Terenure tonight."

"How will they know Boylan has walked?"

"Webcam, O'Connell Bridge."

"You want me to take your word on all this, do you?"

"You know the truth when it's uttered. I surrender, you've got me, and you get the dog back tonight, unharmed, once Christy has walked."

I don't know if Vincent expected me to tell him the dog's throat was going to be cut or that she'd be drowned, but whatever it was about my answer, he climbed off me and spat on his hands to wipe the blood off while his men waited patiently for his decision. He took a grip of the trocar, which was sticking straight out of me, and pulled it out, leaving me bleeding badly and unable to sit up. Vincent moved across to Christy's side and tapped the stainless steel table with the trocar.

"Get up," he said. Matser and Richie released their grip, and Christy climbed down off the table and faced Vincent, who raised the bloodied trocar to Christy's jugular.

"Now, Boylan," he said. "Deirdre's sixteenth birthday . . ." He let the words hang there for Christy, who just stared at him, horrified that his daughter's name was known by Cullen, never mind mentioned.

"That'll be a nice day for the family," said Vincent softly, the picture of composure again. He stared at Christy a few moments longer. "Be wide now," he said, and moved the trocar down by his side. Christy looked over at me, his mouth sealed, his eyes the saddest I'd ever seen them, and slowly shook his head.

"Get him out of here," said Vincent. Sean pushed Christy out through the door into the selection room, and they were gone.

The glass-eyed man had cut another length of gaffer tape and was in the process of pressing it over my mouth when Vincent raised the trocar.

"Leave it off him. I want to hear him scream," he said, looking at me, deadpan. It was reluctantly taken off me while Matser and Richie each took a hold of my arms and legs respectively, and stretched me out just like they had Christy. My shoulder ached badly, and the temptation to try to access my independent channel was enormous, but I held fast. This was my cross to die on, my rack to purge into; there'd be pain, and plenty of it, but not fear. And waiting on the other side was Eva.

Sean came back in and joined them all in looking down at me. I'd never been faced with such collected contempt in my life; the hatred in Scully's eyes was matched by every other man standing, except Vincent, whose eyes contained something different: smoldering fury, a thirst for vengeance, and a resolution to uphold his code of honor. But not hatred. He slowly unbuttoned my shirt to expose my bare torso and gently ran his hand down my chest and belly. I tried to level my breathing, knowing it would only be moments now till I was joined again with Eva. I closed my eyes and imagined her waiting for me, whispering that everything would be okay, that this was just the slipping of the skin.

"Do his kidneys first," said the glass-eyed man.

"Shut it, Geno," said Sean. I kept my eyes closed and waited for the plunge, knowing the climax of pain would last only minutes; a few minutes of torture and then I'd disconnect like I had in my bedroom on Monday night and with Dechtire in Terenure tonight. The cold steel point of the trocar dragged across my belly and stopped at the point of entry. I stopped breathing and rolled my eyes to the top of my head as I anticipated the agony.

A door closed in the office, shifting everyone's focus in an instant. It sounded like the back office.

"Vincent," Christy called out, walking through the selection room. I opened my eyes to see everyone looking to the door, which was wide open.

"What the fuck!" said Sean, losing his patience.

Christy arrived at the door, looking pale but determined, and directed his attention at Vincent.

"The fuck do you want?" said Vincent.

"I'm not going without Paddy. You can kill me, too, but if you want the dog, you'll have to let the pair of us go."

Sean pulled a gun from the back of his trousers and walked over to Christy and pressed it hard against his head.

"Fuck off out of here, you stupid baldy cunt," said Sean, continuing to press it into Christy's forehead, trying to push him away.

"Shoot me then," said Christy with a shaky voice, standing his ground. "I'm not leaving without Paddy."

Vincent moved slowly away from me over to Christy, the trocar still in his hand.

"Put the gun away, Sean," he said calmly. Sean put the gun back where he'd pulled it from but looked no happier about Christy's presence. I could see Christy's focus was on the trocar, and he looked like he was expecting to be stabbed with it. Every move

Vincent made was controlled and measured, and when he spoke, he spoke slowly and deliberately.

"Christy, it's a brave thing you did coming back in here, but pointless. My will is stronger than yours, so if it means me killing you and finding my dog at a later stage, then so be it. Paddy Buckley dies tonight. You can fuck off now with your life intact, knowing you did what you could to save your so-called friend, but the truth is he doesn't deserve it." Vincent was right next to Christy now and was slowly putting his arm around his neck. Christy looked back at Vincent like a defiant, beaten child. Vincent was holding the trocar in such a way that he could very effectively stab Christy with it at any moment, and his men all looked on like they were expecting him to.

"He doesn't deserve this, Vincent," said Christy, trying to reason with the wrong man. "It was an accident. He didn't even see him."

Vincent squeezed his arm around Christy's neck and pulled him close, lining the trocar up to point into Christy's left eye.

"It wasn't an accident taking the money though, was it?" he said in almost a whisper. Christy's fear diminished.

"Paddy didn't take any money."

"I didn't take the money," I said. Vincent turned around, lowering the trocar but keeping his hold on Christy, and looked right into my eyes.

"You took the twenty grand, Buckley," he said.

"I never took a penny off him," I said. Vincent's eyes became very black as he released his grip on Christy and looked up to Geno, the glass-eyed man, who shook his head and smiled.

"Geno," said Sean, with revelatory darkness.

"Don't you fucking lie to Vincent Cullen!" said Geno, jabbing me hard in the neck.

"Geno," said Vincent. "Look at me." He looked at Vincent with the same smile, but he'd become nervous and shifty. Vincent kept moving closer, the trocar down by his leg now. Sean, Matser, and Richie were all looking at Geno, and I could feel Matser's grip loosening around my arms. Christy was cowering by the wall, focused, too, on Geno.

"Hang on a minute now," said Geno.

"For what?" said Sean.

"Stay where you are, Gene," said Vincent. "Now, just tell me once that you didn't lift the money."

Geno swallowed hard and then, instead of saying anything, he pulled a gun from his belt and pointed it frantically at Vincent, then to Sean, who had his hands raised slightly, and back to Vincent.

"Back up!" he said, looking like he could shoot at any time. Both Matser and Richie had fully released their grip on me, and I stayed there, as still as a stone. Vincent kept moving towards Geno fearlessly.

"Put it down, Gene," he said calmly.

Matser shifted his weight to block Vincent and went to slap the gun away, but Geno squeezed off a shot, getting Matser in the belly, dropping him. The sound was deafening.

"Matser!" said Richie, rushing to his side.

Sean pulled his gun out and pointed it at Geno, but Geno shot first, spinning Sean back to hit the wall. Sean brought his hand to his head to press against the blood above his ear, but he seemed fine.

Vincent kept moving fearlessly towards Geno, who backed towards the selection room door. Sean had his gun raised now and fired a shot into the selection room after Geno. And then both he and Vincent were gone in after him.

Matser groaned, doubled up on the floor. "Get him," he whispered to Richie, who rushed in after the others. There were more shots fired and more shouting.

Christy straightened up and moved quickly to the door out to the yard and silently opened it with his keys. I rolled onto my right side with my ears ringing and slightly deafened from the shots. Christy pulled me up by my right arm, and as gently as he could, helped me down to my feet. Matser's back was to us and he was dealing with his own pain anyway, so we were able to hobble out into the yard unnoticed and make our way down towards the gate. As we passed by the opaque windows of the selection room, we could hear it all. The shots had stopped, and it sounded as if they'd disarmed Geno.

"Let's start with the kidneys, Gene," said Vincent, sounding like an animal again. As we staggered out the gate, Geno's gurgled screams slowly subsided to soundless whimpering.

We made it to Christy's Renault on Clanbrassil Street and sat into it, neither of us having said a word to each other since we'd left the yard. We were stunned just to be alive, and I think we were both still expecting to see Sean or Vincent come storming around the corner at any moment.

"Are you all right?" said Christy.

"I can't really move my left arm, but yeah, I'm okay."

"Let's get the fuck out of here."

"I'm parked around by George's," I said.

I was still getting my head around being alive. I'd resigned myself to death so completely that I hadn't figured on life beyond the embalming room, and by life I mean powered by a beating heart. Yet I was alive, and all because of Christy. Feeling so close to being reunited with Eva had spun me out, too. I'd taken the leap but had landed here, and Eva and I were to remain separated. But I wasn't out of Dublin yet.

We pulled up outside George's beside the Fiesta to see the dog sitting up and looking right at us.

"You've got the dog," said Christy, surprised that Cullen had nailed it.

"Yeah," I said, not so sure what kind of reception I'd get now that I was covered in blood and Cullen's scent.

"What kind of a dog is that?" said Christy.

"A special one," I said, and got out of the car. Even covered in blood, I wasn't carrying a trace of fear, and I was abundantly grateful for the help she'd given me, however unwittingly. I unlocked the door and opened it. The dog jumped out and stood there on the path beside me, looking up like she was my dog. I crouched down as best I could and rubbed her chest with my good hand. She closed her eyes and groaned and made me smile for the first time since I'd been with Brigid.

"You're going to have to find your own way home, Dechtire," I said, fully confident that she was up to the task—if ever I'd met an animal that could take care of itself even on the streets of Dublin, it was Dechtire. I gave her a final scratch on her snout and got in the car.

"Follow me," I said to Christy, and closed the door. I drove up the street with Christy trailing behind me, while the dog stood along the roadside looking after us until we were gone around the corner.

I DIDN'T PARTICULARLY like goodbyes, but parting with Christy after he'd just saved my life felt like a little funeral. A man who owed me nothing, who had willingly come face-to-face with the cruelest death and was ready to give up all that he had and die beside me on the small chance that we'd be freed together, had rendered me speechless and closer to tears than I'd like to admit.

We'd driven to a little strip of shops in Drumcondra on the other side of the city and bought a bottle of vodka from an off-license, which we used to soak my wound. The bleeding had largely stopped, but I'd been cut deep, so I had to keep my arm still to prevent it from opening, which we did by making a sling from strips torn from my ripped and bloodied shirt. For a bandage, I'd bought a Guinness T-shirt and another one to wear under my suit, and we'd bought takeaway coffees, which we sipped in silence in a car park under the neon sign of a Chinese restaurant.

Christy opened his coat and pulled out the money he'd wrapped in newspaper.

"I can't take that, Christy . . ."

"Fuck you, Buckley, you're taking it."

"Christy . . ."

"Take the fucking thing," he said, poking it at me. I took a hold of it, shaking my head.

"You're an awful man." I opened up the paper. It was a few grand. "Christy, it's too much."

"Better in your pocket, Paddy, than under my mattress. Yours to keep."

"I'll never forget it," I said, and lobbed it into my car. "Come here, I've one more favor to ask."

"Shoot."

"Swap coats?"

"Of course," said Christy, slipping his off. Mine was saturated from being out with the dog. We exchanged them, and with nothing more to give each other, we fell silent. It was goodbye time.

"Well," I said. "This is it." Neither of us had properly digested what had happened over the last few days, but we'd undoubtedly remember little moments and beats in startling clarity as the days went by. And added to these moments were the myriad memories we'd shared over the years, which for Christy would be accessed daily when he'd visit the churches and hospitals and nursing homes of Dublin. As for me, I'd yet to make it out alive.

I wanted to hug him warmly, and with one arm, I could only give him half a hug, but I needn't have worried. Christy hugged me tight and ended it with a slap on the back.

"Get out of here," he said. "How are you going to drive with that arm?"

"I'll manage. See you next time," I said, and got into the car. And without another word, I drove away, leaving Christy standing there in my wet coat, waving goodbye.

FORTY

6:05 a.m.

It had been a long night, most of which had been spent horizontal on top of the cabin of an articulated lorry. When Liam Conway had told me on Tuesday that he'd a truck going to the UK on Friday morning, I never imagined I'd be hitching a ride with it. I'd driven up to Louth after leaving Christy and watched two men load up the lorry with coffins and caskets at midnight. And afterwards, when they'd gone back into the warehouse, I dragged myself on top of the driver's cabin and tucked in tight to the fold of the aerodynamic fin, which gave me ample shelter. The warmth came from the money Christy had given me, which I used to line the inside pockets of my coat.

I'd known the Conways a long time and liked them. Liam's father had been making Saturday visits to Gallagher's yard since I was a teenager, and I'd regularly shared cups of tea with him, but to announce my intentions to them tonight was out of the question. The way out was to stow away.

Up until I'd been snared by Cullen in the yard, I'd been

planning on catching the red-eye out of Knock, but now Cullen would have every airport in the land crawling with his men, so my only hope out was by ferry, and even that was unlikely. They'd been three steps ahead of me all along, but they'd more on their hands to deal with now than catching me. Matser was down, they'd Geno's remains to dispose of, and they'd the cops to evade, who would have been called by somebody after all the gunfire.

The hour-long drive down to Dublin Port nearly lulled me to sleep, but knowing I was playing out my last chance of escape had kept me conscious and focused. And now the truck was parked in a line along with a few hundred other vehicles waiting to board the ferry to Holyhead while the early morning light began to filter through the grayness of the clouds. I was floating between two worlds, the old and familiar Dublin behind me and the bastion of hope that was England on the other side of the sea.

The lure of England gave rise to my fantasies of Hampstead, but the urgent knocking on the driver's door below my feet put an end to them.

The driver lowered his window.

"Yeah?"

"Detectives Mangan and McMahon. What are you carrying?" It was the unmistakable sound of Sean Scully's voice, whose confident and determined manner would discourage anyone from asking for identification, although for all I could see he had some.

"Coffins," said the driver.

Sean didn't miss a beat. "Open her up for me there," he said. The driver hopped out.

"What are you looking for?" he said, taking them down towards the back.

"An escaped criminal," said the other man with Scully, Chris O'Donoghue, who'd probably been pulled out of bed in the middle of the night by Cullen. And then they moved out of earshot.

The stress that came alive in me seemed to collect itself in my wound, which had paralyzed me again. If I'd been more mobile, I would have tried hopping down, but with my shoulder as bad as it was, I'd more than likely be caught and dragged away. I'd no choice but to stay put.

Of all Cullen's men, Scully was undoubtedly the most cunning and thorough, and after I eluded him earlier, he'd be more desperate than ever for my blood. And Chris O'Donoghue, who had more egg on his face than any of them, having paved the way in for me, had a lot of atoning to do for endorsing me in the first place. I was backed into a corner, so close to escape I could smell the sea, but that was just the irony of it. My number was up.

I heard the back doors of the truck close and their voices become audible again.

"He wouldn't be under there, would he?" said the driver.

Scully must have been on his back, underneath the body of the truck, checking every possible crevice. I only had moments left. My eyes locked on the entrance to my hiding place. Every sensation now became amplified by the horrible expectation of capture. My feet felt cold in my shoes. My hands clutched handfuls of coat. My head pressed against the fiberglass of the fin. The air was filled with smells of engines and oil and sea and brakes and rubber. The seagulls squawked above me. My heart pumped blood through my arteries and veins. And I held my breath.

And then in an instant, a hand gripped the side of the fin and Chris O'Donoghue's head rose to become level with mine, and our eyes met. And with the composure of a poker ace, he jumped back down.

"Nothing," he said conclusively, and they moved on. In that tiny moment between us, he'd saluted our friendship by delivering my reprieve and astonishing me with his kindness. Instead of seeing a killer, he'd seen an innocent whose dealings with the Cullens were accidental and reactive. I breathed again and tasted the sweetest air I'd ever known. I relaxed on the cabin top, humbled and exalted by a man without whose grace I would have been ravaged and killed, and whose code of clemency had given me my freedom.

Four hours later, I walked out of the rent-a-car office in Holyhead a newborn baby. It was all behind me now: the funerals, Cullen, and my ramshackle existence. I'd been delivered from them all to a new life. And I was at the very beginning of it.

I turned the key in the rented Vauxhall Astra and headed for a place where I'd be offered shelter and understanding. And a lot more besides.

BUCKLEY (Dublin 12), November 8, suddenly in Manchester, Patrick (Paddy), beloved husband of the late
Eva; deeply regretted by his relatives and friends. May
he rest in peace. Funeral and cremation have already
taken place in Manchester. Memorial Mass this coming Monday, December 29, at 10 o'clock at Church of
Our Lady of Good Counsel, Mourne Road. No flowers
by request; donations, if desired, to the Irish Heart
Foundation.

Sean Scully walked out the back door of the house holding a
newspaper and headed for the pen where Vincent was tending the pups. He stopped by the gate with a backward nod of the
head and waited. Vincent had a male pup in his hands, examining
it. Out of the eight, it was the biggest and most relaxed and, judg-
ing by the look in its eyes, the most intelligent. It was beyond any
doubt the alpha male. As Vincent stroked its little snout affectionately, Dechtire lay beside him, utterly at ease with him studying
her pups. It was there in that dark December morning while Sean

stood patiently at the gate that he decided to keep the little dog. And he'd call him Setanta.

"Well?" said Vincent, knowing by Sean's posture that he'd something important to tell him. Sean held out the paper, folded open on the death notices.

"I thought you'd want to see this," he said.

Vincent walked over with the pup still in his arms and took the paper off him. Circled in blue ballpoint was Paddy's death notice. He read it, handed the paper back, and returned his attention to the dog.

"What do you think?" said Sean.

Vincent looked him over. He could see that Sean didn't know what to believe, that when it came to Paddy Buckley, he wasn't about to take anything for granted.

"Fuck him," said Vincent, turning his back on Sean, leaving him to walk away.

"Fuck him is right," said Sean, and retreated to the house, knowing that Buckley wouldn't be discussed again. Whether he was dead or not, that was the end of him as far as his boss was concerned.

Vincent let the pup down to observe its behavior around the others. It was a good-looking dog, with its rusty brown coat, bushy black tail, and eyes that shone like jewels, just like its mother's. The pups were four weeks old now and itching to go beyond the confines of the pen. In another day or two, he'd let Dechtire take them out to the garden, and he'd enjoy the spectacle of their curious exploration.

As they continued to play under the watchful eye of their mother, he turned his focus inward, to Buckley. He knew he wasn't dead, but Paddy had announced himself dead regardless. A decision, no doubt, driven by fear and expedience.

Never before had someone invaded his fold so furtively, and in this regard, Paddy had set a new benchmark and provoked pledges of vengeance from every one of Cullen's men. And when he'd slipped away after Geno had provided the perfect distraction before being disemboweled in Paddy's place, the pledges had become more fervent, particularly from the convalescing Matser. Mowing down Vincent's brother had been by far Paddy's biggest mistake, but sitting with Vincent afterward like an ambulance chaser when he was grieving a brother was what laid down the cherry.

Vincent knew well that Paddy would stay gone now and leave it all behind—the house, the job, the life—but a man like him had only so many places he could go, and Vincent prayed for the day their paths would cross again.

He rested his hand on the pen gate, paused for a moment, and looked around to Dechtire only to find her looking right back at him. She'd arrived back to Terenure at one o'clock that Friday morning from wherever Paddy'd taken her, unharmed and unfazed. He'd wondered more than a few times how Paddy had bewitched her and got the collar off her, and he'd wonder many times again. It was something he knew he'd be curious about forever, unless, of course, he was to catch up with Buckley.

With a glinting eye, he walked away from the pen and moved on with the business of the day.

IT HAD BEEN a funny day for Christy. Paddy's memorial Mass had passed without a hitch, everybody believing, with the exception of himself, Frank, and Eamonn, that Paddy had died of a heart attack in England. Being witness to the gathered grieving had felt peculiar and more than a little wrong, even though he knew it was vital that no one be privy to the fact that Paddy was alive and kicking elsewhere.

Mourne Road church had been packed to capacity, the urn supposedly holding Paddy's ashes taking the spotlight at the top of the center aisle. Christy had been sitting beside Corrine and Jack, who were both demonstrably upset, and in an effort to fit in, he'd held his hand over his face, which had worked, not that he was being paid any undue attention.

And now here he sat at a table in An Capall Dubh, the ashes on the seat beside him, two pints on the table in front of him. As always, there was no more than a handful of old men sitting at the bar. Gerry had pulled a pint for Paddy along with Christy's. "Both on the house," he'd said. "We couldn't have him in here and without a drink."

Coming to the pub was Frank's idea. "It's what you'd do if he *was* dead," he'd said. "Might as well do what people expect." The others in the yard had already gone home, and Frank was on his way out to make arrangements, so it was a solitary affair for Christy, and a nice time to spend remembering his friend, even if these weren't his ashes beside him.

Christy had put Frank in the picture the morning after Paddy had disappeared. Things had gone too awry to leave him in the dark, from the unexplained vanishing of his staff to the bloodstain on the carpet in the selection room and the bullet holes in the walls. Christy had gone back into the office after leaving Paddy and cleaned up the place as much as he could. They'd left their mark. The syndicate money had been taken from the front parlor, there were cigarettes stubbed out on the carpet, but the biggest mess to clean was in the embalming room where they must have eviscerated Geno. His body was gone, but the blood that was all over the tables and floor took Christy hours to clean up.

Christy had stayed the night and was there to greet Frank when he came in at seven o'clock. The more he learned, the less angry he'd become, and it wasn't long before he was fully abreast of the situation and utterly forgiving of Paddy. In light of the new information, Paddy's behavior throughout the week made perfect sense to him, and he was eager to help as he could, even if it was just to facilitate and endorse the bogus funeral.

While Christy sat daydreaming, swirling the end of his pint around in his glass, he became aware of a presence beside him and looked up to see Sean Scully pulling up a stool and sitting down uncomfortably close to him.

"Jesus," said Christy, placing his pint down. "What do you want?"

"Here to pay my respects," said Sean, reaching for the urn.

Before he could get near it, Christy snatched the urn away and moved to get up, but Sean had him pinned to the wall in an instant, twisting his collar around until his face was dangerously red. Every head in the bar turned to watch the awkward tussle.

"Drop the box," said Sean through gritted teeth, but Christy held fast to it.

"Fuck off," he said.

Sean's knee jolted heavily into Christy's groin, doubling him over with a low moan.

"Drop the fucking thing," he said. Christy let the urn drop to the seat beside him and Sean released his grip, sending Christy sliding to a sitting position. Before he could sit down himself, he turned to the bar to see Gerry coming around with his sleeves rolled up.

"Out!" said Gerry. "Get out!"

"Just a minute now, Gerry. Paddy Buckley killed Donal and this bald prick was in on it, so get back behind the bar and mind your business."

Gerry stopped just short of Sean.

"Paddy Buckley didn't kill anyone and that's a certainty. Now get fucking out of here!"

Sean turned to Christy.

"Tell him he did it," he said, but Christy just sat there, shaking his head.

"Tell him!" said Sean, but Christy stayed mute, prompting Sean to step in close and belt him hard in the mouth, splitting his lip and knocking his glasses off.

That was enough for Gerry, who grabbed Sean by the shoulders to drag him outside. But Sean was bigger, stronger, and angrier. He shrugged Gerry off before dropping him to the floor with a single punch to the chin. The old lads just sat there with their eyes wide. Satisfied that Gerry was staying down, Sean took a seat in front of Christy and pulled the urn close.

"Now, let's see what we have in here," he said, lifting the lid off. Christy stayed put this time and observed, swishing his blood between his teeth. Sean scooped up a handful of ashes and examined them closely for a moment before letting them fall back inside. Minor disappointment registered on his face before he snorted back the contents of his nasal passages, creating an ample ball of phlegm in the back of his throat, and then while looking at Christy, he spat into the ashes before putting the lid back on. Then he rose to his feet, winked at Christy, and walked out of the bar.

On the outside, Christy looked like a beaten man, and he was a bit shaken, but on the inside, it was a different story. He felt triumphant. Cullen and Co. had been outdone and he'd been at the wheel of it. The plan had worked. The lengths they'd gone to had been worth it; the bogus funeral had fooled them. He felt an urge to laugh rise inside him but stifled it immediately.

The other patrons helped Gerry to his feet and Christy to a hankie to nurse his bloodied lip, which was already starting to swell. He pressed the hankie to the wound and relaxed into his seat while Gerry walked back behind the bar.

"This one's on the house, lads," he said, regaining his composure, and went about getting everyone a drink.

One of the old men stayed with Christy.

"Where was he going, accusing Paddy of killing Cullen?" said the old lad, with his despairing amber eyes and deeply wrinkled head. "And spitting in his ashes? It's a bleeding disgrace that crowd is."

"Don't mind them," said Christy. "They're lashing out in all directions."

"That's just plain wrong," said the old lad, and he walked back to the bar, leaving Christy alone with the ashes, his swollen lip the safety catch on a smile he'd otherwise find impossible to contain.

The ashes in the urn were the real thing all right, but collected from twelve different urns, made up by skimming little portions off the top of each one. As nasty a full stop as it had been, Sean spitting in the ashes like that was still the end, and for Paddy's sake, the desired one.

He wanted to call by Paddy's house to sit down and tell him about how perfect it had been. The two of them would laugh so joyously. But Paddy wasn't there.

As a fresh pint was placed in front of him, Christy swallowed down the little knot of excitement, realizing he'd have to keep it to himself. There was no one he could share it with. Not even Frank would appreciate it properly. And this made him feel lonely.

It was going to take time to get used to Paddy being gone. He'd been there too long and had been loved too much to be forgotten overnight. But while the others would continue to think of him as dead, Christy would think of him standing by the barrier at the track in some sunny place, eyeing up the horses at the starting gates, and it gave him comfort.

Behind the bar, Gerry raised a pint of stout and looked down to Christy.

"To Paddy," he said, prompting everyone to raise their drinks.

"To Paddy," said everyone together, and at last, Christy could smile.

SURROUNDED BY white-chopped ocean and slate-colored mountains, Brigid's lonely figure marched wearily along the shore, her hair tossed behind her in the wind. Her father was born in Mayo so she'd come down to Louisburgh to feel that bit closer to him. Of all the counties in Ireland, Mayo was her favorite even though she seldom made it down anymore. But here today, with the mist being whipped from the waves beside her, she vowed to come back every December, in remembrance.

The days since Dublin hadn't been easy on her. Losing both her parents had dealt quite a blow, regardless of how romantic their tandem passing may have seemed to her. While Paddy had been there tentatively wooing her, the punch of her loss had been dissipated by the promise of love, but now that it was just herself and the sandpipers sharing their beach walk, her only solace was the wind that wiped her tears away.

When Paddy hadn't rung her the week following the funeral, she'd called Gallagher's for a contact number only to be told that he'd died of heart failure in Manchester, having gone there to visit a friend. Whatever hope she'd held for a fruitful and emotionally secure future with him was crushed by that single sentence, and it was then, as she gripped the phone in her Hampstead home, that her heart shattered inside her.

She'd known Paddy for all of four days, but crammed into those few days was a chemical charge of such magnitude that her feelings for him had amplified and her heart had fully bloomed. To have it punctured so violently had robbed her equanimity and compounded her grief.

She was alone again. And if she was to be alone, then she'd go somewhere she could honor the order. West.

She'd set her studio up in a little cottage just up from White Strand, and she'd stay there for the foreseeable future, painting, walking, grieving, and being alone. She was lucky she could pour her pain into her pictures and make them all the richer for it.

However dark they'd turn out, they wouldn't be bereft of hope. The hope would be evident in its different guises of sorrow and grieving, processing and moving on.

She knew she'd get over Paddy, just as she'd get over her parents' deaths, but she also knew she'd never forget him or the way he made her feel, or those kind eyes that seemed to know more than they should. Whatever it was about the way he looked at her, she missed it terribly. He'd be in her heart now, forever, like a perpetually burning candle, which she'd occasionally cup her hands around to feel the glow of their fleeting brush with love.

The tide was going out now, leaving pools deep and wide for her to negotiate her way around, and the light was fading. With her hands rooted deep in her pockets, she turned herself towards the cottage and her thoughts to a painting of a man in a dark suit and bowler hat, with a gentle heart and a burgeoning affection bubbling beneath his funereal veneer.

THE VIEW FROM the open doorway is a perfect one. Endless acres of green fields peppered with poplars and giant oak trees, lending shelter to the horses and cows that graze there under the morning sun. The French countryside has always appeased my soul, particularly in Nantes, where I now stand, cradling a whiskey in my hand, and breathing in the moistness of the dewy air.

Patrice and Blandine, Eva's parents, are behind me at the kitchen table doing their post-breakfast ritual: he puffing his pipe, she gathering the plates. The whiskey is Patrice's idea, to warm us for our morning walk. It reminds me of the days I used to go fishing with my father on Lough Mask, casting our flies back and forth, waiting for a rise. Whenever my attention would wane and turn from the fly on the water, Shay would say, "Any minute now," which always brought me back to the fly. And when the weather was harsher than usual, we'd pass Shay's hip flask between us, the taste of Bushmills never failing to give my mouth the touch of a smile.

Patrice knows his whiskey, and for the occasion, he's pulled out a bottle of Midleton Very Rare, which he rubbed reverently while displacing it from its spot beside the Pernod in the cupboard. I know that my coming here has meant the world to them. It's the first time they've seen me since the funeral. They knew I'd crumbled under the loss of their daughter, and while dealing with their own grief, they'd worried deeply about mine. To have me turn up on their doorstep during the run-up to Christmas, unannounced, has gladdened their hearts and opened their wells of kindness.

For me, it's the ultimate safe house. And one where I can now breathe in deeply the memories and smells of all things Eva without cutting myself on the blades of my grief. I'm stronger now than I've ever been, and with a bit of distance from those last days of October, I decided to come home. To Eva.

Since Chris O'Donoghue let me off the hook at the ferry terminal, I haven't looked back. With the help of Kershaw, I'd put paid to all my problems: my shoulder, Cullen, and beautiful Brigid Wright.

I miss Dublin, there's no doubt about it. I miss the gray skies, the quick wit, the daily chance encounters, and Gallagher's yard. And I miss the funerals. But even if I could go back, I wouldn't. Dublin will remain a dirty shirt to me now. I'm finished with it, and it's finished with me, too. There's nothing there for me anymore.

Standing by the fair fields of France now, considering Lucy

Wright while her distant laughter echoes in my mind, I think if ever I met someone who was in charge of her life it was Lucy. And wouldn't someone who knew what to do know when to go? Could she have stopped taking her warfarin tablets on purpose and then, when serendipity smiled, abandoned herself to the act of love with me as recklessly as she did, knowing her heart wouldn't be up to the task, to follow her husband elsewhere so their love could continue? Having learned what I know about her from Brigid and Shay Mac Giolla, it seems well within the scope of her character and a fitting end to a class act.

I've come to call my last days in Dublin my crazy days, for never before have I skirted so close to being killed or to permanently breaking someone's heart. Through my own wishes, I brought about my exit from the dark womb I'd been living in, and in the throes of labor, I grabbed at anything within reach to mollify the pain of being expelled. The greatest casualty, of course, was Brigid and our impossible love.

Our love was doomed the moment my lips touched Lucy's and I'd known it all along. Any notions I harbored of spending a life with Brigid were simply reflections of her own desires, which, coming from a base of purity and truth, were diametrically opposed to my own. While Cullen had been unnerving me throughout the week, the stolen moments I shared with Brigid were the perfect antidote to my fear. It kept me level. There was no denying the caliber of our attraction, and under more normal circumstances, it could possibly have run a successful course of love. The circumstances, however, were far from normal, and the further I drove from Holyhead, the clearer my thinking became, and it wasn't long before I fully appreciated its futile nature.

There was also the more pressing matter of Vincent Cullen to deal with. I didn't fancy a life on the run. Much better to put an end to it all and sleep easy. So, with the tools and powers of two funeral companies at my disposal, I puppeteered the play of my own demise. Kershaw went one better than merely facilitating my funeral and awarded me the princely sum of twenty thousand pounds for sticking my neck out in the first place.

I put the twenty grand down, ante post, along with every other penny I had, on a horse called Liberty Girl, running down the Curragh at fifty-to-one and afterwards deposited a hundred grand of my winnings into Christy's bank account. I never doubted Vincent's word on the horse, but I couldn't help smiling at the irony of it, either: the man responsible for making me being the very man bent on my undoing.

Patrice and I have taken to walking the surrounding fields in the mornings, sharing our stories and memories. And I'm in no rush away. Blandine has been helping me with my French in the afternoons, and the evenings I've been spending eating out, getting to know the area and the people.

There are still times I find myself thinking of Brigid, like when I fleetingly catch her scent when out walking, and the pictures of her I keep in my head linger and walk with me. But they pass, and my thoughts drift away from Brigid to where I am now, the world of Eva. And I like it here, now that my heart has healed.

Patrice gets to his feet behind me and puts his coat on.

"Ready, Paddy?" he says.

"Ready," I say. And I am.

ACKNOWLEDGMENTS

The keys given and graces shown to me by friends and family throughout this book's journey have been plentiful and greatly appreciated. Very special thanks to my parents for their ceaseless love and support; to my father, Conor, who opened my heart to the treasures and joys of what a great story can be; to my mother, Anya, for always believing; and to my brothers, Angus, Zeb, and Paddy, and my sisters, Samantha and Alyanya, for being my co-conspirators.

I'm eternally grateful to Professor O'Donoghue of Roscrea for lighting the fire; to Jonathan Philbin Bowman and Eoghan Harris for fanning the flames; to Kieran Ring for suggesting I write the novel in the first place; to Paddy Brady for being as wide as a kite and for being such a great inspiration; and to Lorcan Walshe and Mannix Flynn for paving the way.

A special word of thanks to Adam Hyland for his invaluable reports. Massive gratitude and big love to Mića Bikicki for doing the first edit, and for his ingenious understanding of story. Thank you, David Bateman, for being a reader like no other. Thank you to my in-laws, Bill and Jill Barham, for the shelter and love in Melbourne. And thank you, Niel Vaughan and Miin Chan, for the esoteric advice.

Heartfelt thanks to Julia Lord, and to my amazing agent, Ginger Curwen, for believing as she does, and for bringing Paddy Buckley to the Promised Land. I'm deeply indebted to the team at Riverhead, who have been an absolute delight to deal with. In particular, I'd like to thank my editor, Jake Morrissey, whose wizardry will never be forgotten; and special thanks to assistant editor Alexandra Cardia, eagle-eyed copy editor David Hough, and designer Grace Han for making such a beautiful jacket.

And finally, to Holli, my love and story consultant, and to my richest treasures, Lughnasa, Finnegan, and Coco, who all made the telling of this story possible.